S0-ADM-457

THE FLAME
(IL FUOCO)

BY

GABRIELE D'ANNUNZIO

TRANSLATED BY DORA KNOWLTON RANOUS

INTRODUCTION

Gabriele D'Annunzio, poet, novelist, and dramatist, was born in 1864, on the yacht Irene near Pescara in the Abruzzi, his mother being the Duchess Maria Galesse of Rome. His education was begun in the College of Prato, in Tuscany, and finished in the University of Rome. His mind early showed signs of extraordinary power and brilliant versatility; he studied art and produced very creditable work while a mere lad, and at the age of sixteen he published his first poem, Primo Vere, which attracted flattering attention and caused him to be hailed as an infant prodigy. In 1880 he went to Rome and became a contributor to the Cronaca Bizantina, a magazine of art and literature. He remained in Rome three years, producing in that time Terra vergine ("Virgin Soil"), Canto novo ("New Song"), and Intermezzo di rime ("Intervals of Rhyme"), all of which were received with admiration and amazement, and with not a little criticism for their unconventional boldness of expression.

D'Annunzio left Rome in 1884 and returned to his native hills, where he wrote Il libro delle vergine ("The Book of the Virgins") in 1884; San Pantaleone (1886), and Isottèo Guttadauro. Then, abandoning his revolutionary and realistic though splendid and intoxicating poetry for prose, the young genius next surprised his public with a novel, Giovanni Episcopo, followed by Il Piacere ("The Child of Pleasure"), in 1889. The former is a strong yet repelling story of crude brutalism, told by a victim of relentless fate; the latter is a kind of poem in prose, in which there is something above mere facility of literary touch; he shows the power of the master poet or painter to see the world at a glance, and with a dextrous hand to draw for eyes less keen that world in all its changeful aspects.

His next important novel, Il trionfo della morte ("The Triumph of Death") was produced in 1896. This brought upon him a storm of mingled applause and criticism—admiration for its marvelous beauty of literary expression, condemnation of the realistic study of a degenerate whose sins lead him to suicide. But, with a proud defiance of criticism, with eyes fixed only on his art, he dared after this achievement to write the self-revelatory novel that is known as his masterpiece—Il fuoco ("The Flame"). In this great novel, which may fairly be called unique, we recognize the personification of a renascence of Latin genius. Under the thinnest veil of disguise, the author presents his own figure and that of one of the world's greatest tragic actresses, revealing the most intimate details of their well known friendship. On this picture of the most romantic of love-affairs, in Venice, the most romantic of cities, he has lavished his finest strokes of genius, writing of feminine nature with rare truth and skill, and an exquisite intuition as to the workings of a woman's mind and the throbbings of her heart.

Besides his poems and novels, D'Annunzio has written several plays, the best known being La Gioconda ("Joy"), La Gloria ("Glory"), La morta città ("The City of the Dead"), and Francesca da Rimini. He is unquestionably the greatest Italian writer of to-day, and few works of Italian fiction appear that do not show something of his influence. A European critic of keen discernment says: "Read his works, all ye men and women for whom life has no secrets and truth has no terror."

D. K. R.

BOOK I
THE EPIPHANY OF THE FLAME

TO TIME AND TO HOPE

Without hope, it is impossible to find
the unhoped-for.

—HERACLITUS OF EPHESUS.

He who sings to the god a song of
hope shall see his wish accomplished.

—ÆSCHYLUS OF ELEUSIS.

Time is the father of miracles.

2

—HARIRI DI BASRA.

CHAPTER I
THE BELLS OF SAN MARCO
"Stelio, does not your heart quail a little, for the first time?" inquired La Foscarina, with a fleeting smile, as she touched the hand of the taciturn friend seated beside her. "I see that you are pale and thoughtful. Yet this is a beautiful evening for the triumph of a great poet."

With an all-comprehensive glance, she looked around at all the beauty of this last twilight of September. In the dark wells of her eyes were reflected the circles of light made by the oar as it flashed in the water, which was illuminated by the glittering angels that shone from afar on the campaniles of San Marco and San Giorgio Maggiore.

"As always," she went on, in her sweetest tones, "as always, everything is in your favor. On such an evening as this, what mortal could shut out from his mind the dreams that you may choose to evoke by the magic of your words? Do you not feel already that the multitude is well disposed to receive your revelation?"

Thus, delicately, she flattered her friend; thus she pleased herself by exalting him with continual praise.

"It is impossible to imagine a more magnificent and unique festival than this, to persuade so disdainful a poet as you to come forth from his ivory tower. For you was reserved this rare joy; to communicate for the first time with the people in a sovereign place like the Hall of the Greater Council, from the platform where once the Doge harangued the assembled patricians, with the Paradiso of Tintoretto for a background, and overhead the Gloria of Veronese."

Stelio Effrena looked long and searchingly into her eyes.

"Do you wish to intoxicate me?" he said, with a sudden laugh. "Your words remind me of the soothing cup offered to a man on his way to the scaffold. Ah, well, my friend, it is true: I own that my heart quails a little."

The sound of applause rose from the Traghetto di San Gregorio, echoed through the Grand Canal, reverberating among the porphyry and serpentine discs ornamenting the ancient mansion of the Dario, which now leaned over slightly, like a decrepit courtesan loaded with her jewels.

The royal barge passed.

"There is the one person among your audience whom etiquette demands that you shall crown with some of your flowers of oratory," pursued the charming flatterer, alluding to the Queen. "I believe that, in one of your earlier books, you

3

own to a taste and respect for ceremonials. One of your most extraordinary flights of fancy is that description of a day of Charles the Second, King of Spain."

When the royal barge passed the gondola, the man and the woman saluted it. The Queen, recognizing the poet, the author of Persephone, and the distinguished tragic actress, turned to gaze at them with a movement of instinctive curiosity. She was blonde and rosy, and her face was lighted by her ever-ready smile, as she looked out from the cloud of creamy Buranesi laces clinging around her shoulders. Beside her sat Andriana Duodo, the patroness of Burano, where, on that industrious little island, she cultivated flax, and raised the most marvelous old-fashioned flowers.

"Does it not seem to you that the smiles of those two women are so similar as to be twin-like?" said La Foscarina, gazing at the silvery ripples in the wake of the barge, wherein the double light seemed to prolong its self.

"The Countess has a magnificent and ingenuous soul—one of those rare Venetian spirits that preserve their warmth, as their ancient paintings retain their vivid color," said Stelio, earnestly, as if in gratitude. "I have an absolute devotion for her sensitive hands. They fairly quiver with pleasure when they touch rare lace or rich velvet, lingering over the texture with a grace that seems almost shy of betraying such voluptuous joy in mere touch. One day, when I had accompanied her to the gallery of the Academia, she stopped before the Massacre des Innocents by the first Bonifazio. You recollect, of course, the green robe of the prostrate woman that one of Herod's soldiers is about to kill—a thing impossible to forget! She paused long before it, seeming fairly to radiate from her own person the perfect joy that filled her senses; then she said to me, 'Let us leave this place now, Effrena! Take me away, but I must leave my eyes on that robe—I cannot look at anything more!' Ah, do not smile at her, dear friend! She was perfectly simple and sincere in saying that: she really did leave her spiritual vision behind her on that bit of canvas which Art, with a touch of color, has made the center of an infinitely pleasurable mystery. Besides, it was really a blind woman that I accompanied there, but I was suddenly seized with reverence for the privileged soul for whom the magic of color had power to abolish for the moment all memory of commonplace life, and to cut off all other worldly communication. What should you call such a state of mind? A filling of life's goblet to the brim, it seems to me. It is exactly what I should like to do to-night, if I were not discouraged."

A new clamor, louder and more prolonged, rose between the two guardian columns of granite, as the royal barge approached the bank of the Piazzetta, now black with the waiting throng. During the slight pause that followed, the movement of the crowd shifted, like the changing of eddies in a current, and all the galleries of the Palace of the Doges were filled with a confused buzzing, like the mysterious murmur within a sea-shell. Suddenly the buzz rose to a shout, rending the clear air and finally dying away in the gathering twilight. The multitude seemed to realize the divinity of that poetic hour, amid those incomparable surroundings; and perhaps, in its acclaim to youthful royalty and beauty, it expressed a vague longing to forget its prosaic existence, and to revel in the gift of eternal poetry with which its storied walls and waters were endowed.

4

"Do you know, Perdita," Stelio suddenly exclaimed, "of any other place in the world that possesses, like Venice, at certain times, the power to stimulate all the forces of human life by the exaltation of all desires to a feverish intensity? Do you know of any more irresistible temptress?"

She whom he called Perdita did not reply; she bent her head as if from desire to concentrate her thoughts; but through all her being she felt the indefinable thrill always felt at the sound of the voice of her friend when it revealed the vehemence and passionate soul toward which this woman was drawn by a mingling of love and terror that had no limit.

"Peace! Oblivion! Do you find them down there, at the end of that deserted canal, when you go home exhausted and fevered after inhaling the commingled breath of the crowd that you are able to rouse to wild enthusiasm by a single gesture? As for myself, when I float on these dead waters, I feel my vital powers increase with bewildering rapidity; at certain times my brain seems on fire, as if I were in delirium."

"The flame and the power are within yourself, Stelio," said La Foscarina almost humbly, without raising her eyes.

He was silent, absorbed. Poetic imagery and impetuous music took form within his brain, as if by virtue of some magic fecundation; and his spirit reveled in the unexpected delight of that flood of inspiration.

It was still that hour which, in one of his books, he had called "Titian's hour," because all things glowed with a rich golden light, like the nude figures of that great painter, appearing almost to illumine the sky rather than to receive light from it.

"Perdita," said the poet, who, at the sight of so many things multiplying their beauties around him, was conscious of a kind of intellectual ecstasy, "does it not seem to you that we are following the funeral train of the dead Summer? There she lies in her funereal barge, robed in golden draperies, like a Doge's wife, like a Loredana, a Morosina, or a Soranza of the golden age; and her cortège conducts her toward the Isle of Murano, where some lord of the flames will place her in a coffin of opaline crystal, so that, submerged in the waters of the lagoon, she can, at least, through her transparent eyelids, behold the supple movement of the seaweed, and thus fancy herself enwrapped in the undulating tresses of her own hair, while waiting for the sun of resurrection to dawn."

A spontaneous smile spread over La Foscarina's face, born in her eyes, which glowed as if they really had beheld the vision of the beautiful dead.

"Do you know, Perdita," resumed Stelio, after a moment's pause, during which both gazed at a file of small boats filled with fruit, floating upon the water like great baskets, "do you know anything about a particularly pretty detail in the chronicles of

5

the Doges? The Doge's wife, to meet the expenses of her robes of ceremony, enjoyed a certain percentage of the tax on fruit. Does not this seem delightfully appropriate? The fruits of these isles clothed her in gold and crowned her with pearls! Pomona paying tribute to Arachne! an allegory that Paolo Veronese might well have painted on the dome of the Vestiario. When I conjure up the figure of the noble lady, tall and erect in her high, jeweled buskins, it pleases me to think that something fresh and rustic is connected with the rich folds of her heavy brocade: the tribute of the fruits. What a savor this seems to add to her magnificence! Only fancy, my friend, that these figs and grapes of the new-come Autumn are the price of the golden robe that covers the dead Summer."

"What delightful fancies, Stelio!" said La Foscarina, whose face became young again when she smiled, as a child to whom one shows a picture-book. "Who was it that once called you the Image-maker?"

"Ah—images!" said the poet, his fancy warming. "In Venice, just as one feels everything to a musical rhythm, so he thinks of everything in poetic imagery. They come to us from everywhere, innumerable, diverse, more real and living to our minds than the persons we elbow in these narrow streets. In studying them, we can lose ourselves in the depths of their haunting eyes, and divine, by the curve of their lips, what they would say to us. Some art tyrannical as imperious mistresses, and hold us long beneath the yoke of their power. Others are enfolded in a veil, like timid virgins, or are tightly swaddled, like infants; and only he that knows how to rend their veils can lead them to the perfect life. This morning, when I awakened, my soul was filled with images; it was like a beautiful tree with its branches laden with chrysalides."

He paused, with a laugh.

"If they come forth from their prison to-night," he added, "I am saved; if they do not, I am lost!"

"Lost?" said La Foscarina, gazing earnestly at him, with eyes so full of confidence that his heart went out to her in gratitude. "No, Stelio, you will not lose yourself. You are always sure of yourself; you bear your own destiny in your hands. I think your mother never could have felt any apprehension on your account, even in the most serious circumstances. Is not that true? Pride is the only thing that makes your heart falter."

"Ah, sweet friend, how I love you—how I thank you for saying that!" said the poet frankly, taking her hand. "You continually foster my pride and encourage me to believe that I have already acquired those virtues to which I never cease to aspire. Sometimes you seem to have the power of conferring I know not what divine quality on the things that are born in my soul, and of making them appear adorable in my own eyes. Sometimes, too, you fill me with the awe-struck wonder of the sculptor who, having in the evening borne to the sacred temple the marble gods still warm from his hands—I might say still clinging to the fingers that moulded them— the next day beholds them standing on their pedestals, surrounded by clouds of

6

incense, and seeming to exhale divinity from every pore of the insensate matter from which he fashioned them with his perishable hands. And so, each time that Fortune grants me the favor of being near you, I realize that you are necessary to my life, although, during our long separations, I can live without you, and you without me, despite the fact that both of us well know what splendors would be born of the perfect union of our lives. Thus, knowing the full value of that which you give me, and, still more, of that which you could give me, I think of you as lost to me; and, by that name which it pleases my fancy to call you, I try to express at the same time this consciousness and this regret."

He interrupted himself, because he felt a quiver of the hand he clasped in his own.

"When I call you 'Perdita,'" he resumed softly, after a pause, "I fancy that you can see my desire approaching you, with a deadly blade deep in its palpitating side. Even should it reach you, the chill of death has already touched its audacious hand."

The woman experienced an oft-felt suffering as she listened to the poetic words that flowed from her friend's lips with a spontaneity that proved them sincere. Again she felt an agitation and a terror that she knew not how to define. She felt that she was slipping out of her own life, and was transported into a kind of fictitious life, intense and hallucinating, where even to breathe was difficult. Drawn into that atmosphere, as fiery as the glow surrounding a lighted forge, she felt that she should be capable of passing through any transfigurations that it might please the master of her spirit to work in her to satisfy his continual craving for poetry and beauty. She comprehended that, in his idealistic mind, her own image resembled that of the dead Summer, wrapped in its opalescent cerements. She felt a childish desire to gaze into the poet's eyes as in a mirror, to contemplate the likeness of her real self.

That which rendered her melancholy most painful, was the recognition of a vague resemblance between this agitation and the anxiety that always possessed her when she sank her own personality in that of some sublime creation of dramatic art. Was not this man drawing her, in fact, into a similar region of higher but artificial life; and, that she might figure there without remembrance of her everyday self, did he not seek to cover her with a splendid disguise? But, while she was unable to maintain so great a degree of intensity except by a painful effort, she knew that he dwelt within that state of exaltation with perfect ease, as if in his natural atmosphere, ceaselessly enjoying a marvelous world of fancy, which he could renew or change at his own pleasure.

He had come to realize in himself the intimate union of art and of life, thus finding, in the depths of his own soul, a source of perpetual harmony. He had become able to maintain within himself, without lapse, the mysterious psychological condition that engenders works of beauty, and thus, at a single stroke, to crystallize into ideal types the fleeting figures of his varied existence. It was to celebrate this conquest over his own mental powers that he put the following words into the mouth of one of his heroes: "I witnessed within myself the continual genesis of a

7

higher life, wherein all appearances metamorphosed themselves as if reflected in a magic mirror." Endowed with an extraordinary linguistic facility, he could instantly translate into words the most complicated workings of his mind, with a precision so exact and vivid that sometimes, as soon as expressed, they seemed not to be his own, having been rendered objective by the isolating power of style. His clear and penetrating voice, which, so to speak, seemed to define each word as distinctly as if it were a note of music, enhanced still more this peculiar quality of his speech, so that those who heard him speak for the first time experienced an ambiguous feeling—a mingling of admiration and aversion, because he revealed his own personality in a manner so strongly marked that it seemed to denote an intention to demonstrate the existence of a profound and impassable difference between himself and his listeners. But as his sensibility equaled his intelligence, it was easy for those that knew him well and liked him to absorb, through his crystalline speech, the glow of his vehement and passionate soul. These knew how illimitable was his power to feel and to dream, and from what fiery source sprang the beautiful images into which he converted the substance of his inner life.

She whom he called Perdita knew it well; and, as a pious soul awaits from God some supernatural help that shall work out its salvation, so she seemed to be waiting for him to put her into the state of grace necessary to enable her to elevate and maintain herself in those fiery regions toward which a mad desire to be consumed impelled her, despairing as she was at the thought of her vanished youth, and the fear of finding herself left alone at last in a desert of ashes.

"It is you now, Stelio," she said, with the slight smile she used to hide her sadness, "who wish to intoxicate me." She gently drew her hand from his. Then, to break the spell, she pointed to a loaded barge that was slowly approaching them, and said:

"Look! Look at your pomegranates!"

But her voice shook a little.

Then, in the dreamy twilight, on the water as silvery-green as the leaves of the willow, they watched the passing boat overflowing with that emblematic fruit which suggests things rich and hidden: caskets of red leather, surmounted by the crown of a royal donor; some closed, others half-open, revealing their close-packed gems.

In a low tone, the tragic actress repeated the words addressed by Hades to Persephone in the sacred drama, at the moment when the daughter of Demeter tastes the fatal pomegranate:

Quando tu coglierai il colchico in fiore su'l molle
Prato terrestre, presso la madre dal cerulo peplo.

"Ah, Perdita! how well you know how to throw a shadow into your voice!" interrupted the poet, feeling the harmony of the twilight that seemed to throw a mystic vagueness over the syllables of his lines. "How well you know how to

8

become nocturnal, even before the evening is upon us! Do you recall the scene where Persephone is on the point of throwing herself into Erebus, to the wailing of the chorus of the Oceanides? Her face is like yours when a shadow passes over it. Her crowned head leans backward, as she stands rigidly erect in her saffron-colored peplum; and the very spirit of the night seems flowing into her bloodless flesh, deepening under her chin, in the hollows of her eyes and around her nostrils, giving her face the look of a tragic mask. It is your mask, Perdita! While I was composing my Mystery, the remembrance of you aided me in evoking her divine person. That little saffron-velvet ribbon you so often wear around your neck gave me the note for Persephone's peplum. And one evening at your house, when I was about to take leave of you at the threshold of a room where the lamps were not yet lighted—an agitated evening of last autumn, you remember?—you succeeded, with a single movement, in bringing to full light in my being the creature that had lain long there undeveloped; and then, without dreaming that you had brought about that sudden birth, you shut yourself again within the solitary obscurity of your own Erebus. Ah, I was certain that I could hear you sob, yet a torrent of uncontrollable joy ran through my veins. I never have spoken to you of this before, have I? I ought to have consecrated my work to you, as to an ideal Lucina."

She shrank under the eyes of the master of her spirit; she suffered because of that mask which he admired on her face, and because of that strange joy that she was aware was continually up-springing within him, like a perpetually playing fountain. She felt oppressed by her own personality; troubled because of her too-expressive face, the muscles of which possessed a strange power of mimicry; pained to think of that involuntary art which governed the significance of her gestures, and of that expressive shadow which sometimes on the stage, during a moment of anxious silence, she knew how to throw over her face like a veil of grief—that shadow which now threatened to remain among the lines traced by time on the face that was no longer young. She suffered cruelly by the hand she adored—that hand so delicate and noble which, even with a gift or a caress, had power to hurt her.

"Do you not believe, Perdita," Stelio continued after another pause, "in the occult beneficence of signs? I do not mean astral science or horoscopic signs. I mean that, like those that believe themselves under the influence of one planet or another, we can create an ideal correspondence between our own soul and some terrestrial object, in such a way that this object, becoming impregnated, little by little, with the essence of ourselves, and being magnified by our illusion, finally becomes for us the representative sign of our unknown destiny, and takes on an aspect of mystery when it appears to us in certain crises of our life. This is the secret whereby we may restore to our withering hearts something of their pristine freshness. I know by experience the beneficial effect we may derive from intense communion with some earthly object. From time to time it is necessary for our natures to become like a hamadryad, in order to feel within us the circulation of new energy drawn from the source of life. Of course you understand that I am thinking of your words just now, when the boat passed. You expressed the same idea when you said 'Look at your pomegranates!' For you, and for everyone that loves me, the pomegranate never can be anything but mine. For you and for them, the idea of my personality is indissolubly linked to that fruit which I have chosen for an emblem,

9

and which I have charged with significant ideals, more numerous than its seeds. Had I lived in the times when men excavated the Grecian marbles and found under the soil the still damp roots of ancient fables, no painter could have represented me on his canvas without putting in my hand the Punic apple. To sever from my person that symbol would have seemed to the ingenuous artist like the amputation of a living member, for, to his pagan imagination, the fruit would have seemed to grow to my hand as to its natural branch. In short, he would not have conceived me in any different way than he thought of Hyacinthus or Narcissus or Ciparissus, all three of whom would appear to him as youths symbolized by a plant. But, even in our day, a few lively and warm imaginations exist that comprehend all the meaning and enjoy all the savor of my invention.

"You, yourself, Perdita, do you not delight in cultivating in your garden a pomegranate, the beautiful 'Effrenian' tree, that you may every summer watch me blossom and bring forth fruit? In one of your letters, flying to me like a winged messenger, you described to me the graceful ceremony of decorating the tree with garlands the day you received the first copy of Persephone. So, for you, and for those that love me, I have in reality renewed an ancient myth when, in fancy, I have assimilated myself with a form of eternal Nature. And when I am dead (and may Nature grant that I am able to manifest my whole self in my work before I die!), my disciples will honor me under a symbol of that tree; and in the sharp outline of the leaf, in the flame of the flower, and in the hidden treasure of the ripe fruit, they will recognize certain qualities of my art. By that leaf, by that flower and fruit, as if by a posthumous teaching of the master, their minds will be formed to a similar sharpness, flame-like intensity, and treasured richness.

"You will see now, Perdita, what is the real beneficence of symbols. By affinity, I am led to develop myself in accord with the magnificent genius of the plant which it pleases me to fancy as the symbol of my aspirations toward a full, rich life. This arboreous image of myself suffices to assure me that my powers should follow nature in order to attain naturally the end for which they were created. 'Nature has disposed me thus' is the epigraph of Leonardo da Vinci, which I placed on the title-page of my first book; and the pomegranate, as it continually blossoms and bears its fruit, repeats to me that simple phrase over and over again. We obey only the laws written in our own substance, and by reason of this we shall remain intact in the midst of dissolution, in the unity and plenitude that make our joy. No discord exists between my art and my life."

He spoke with perfect freedom, as if the mind of the listening woman were a chalice into which he poured his thoughts till it was full to the brim. An intellectual felicity filled him, blended with a vague consciousness of the mysterious action whereby his mind was preparing itself for the effort it was soon to make. From time to time, as if by a lightning flash, his mental vision beheld, as he bent toward his beloved friend and listened to the beat of the oar in the silence of the great estuary, the crowd, with its thousand faces, gathering in the vast hall; and he felt a rapid throbbing of his heart.

10

"It is a very singular thing, Perdita," said he, gazing at the pale distance of the waters, "to observe how readily chance aids our imagination in ascribing an element of mystery to the conjunction of certain appearances with the aim we have fancied. I do not understand the reason why the poets of to-day are so indignant at the vulgarity of the present, and complain that they were born either too late or too early. I am convinced that to-day, as always, every man of intelligence has power to create for himself his own beautiful fable of life. We should study the confused whirl of life with the same lively imagination that Leonardo encouraged in his disciples when he advised them to study the stains on the wall, the ashes on the hearth, the clouds, even mud, and similar objects, in order to find there 'wonderful inventions' and 'infinite things.' In the same way, he declared, one can find in the sound of bells every name and every word that can be imagined. That great master knew well that chance—as the sponge of Apelles had already shown—is always the friend of the ingenious artist. For example, I never cease to be astonished at the ease and grace with which chance favors the harmonious development of my inventions. Do you not believe that the dark god Hades forced his bride to eat the seven seeds of the pomegranate in order to furnish me with the subject of a masterpiece?"

He interrupted himself with one of the bursts of boyish laughter that revealed so clearly the persistence of natural joyousness in the depths of his heart.

"See, Perdita," he continued, still laughing, "whether I am not right. Early in October last year I was invited to Burano by Donna Andriana Duodo. We passed the morning in her flax-fields, and in the afternoon we went to visit Torcello. At that time I was beginning to saturate myself with the mythical story of Persephone, and already my poem had begun to take shape in my brain, and it seemed to me that I was floating on the waters of the Styx, and that I should arrive at the abode of the Manes. Never had I experienced a purer and sweeter understanding of death, and this feeling seemed to render me so ethereal that I fancied I could tread the field of asphodel without leaving there the least trace of my footsteps. The air was damp, warm, the sky was gray; the canals wound between the banks covered with half-faded verdure. (You know Torcello only by sunlight, perhaps.) But all this time some one was talking, arguing, and declaiming in Charon's boat. The sound of praise roused me from my reverie. Francesco di Lizo was speaking of me, regretting that such an artist, so magnificently sensual—I quote his own words—should be obliged to live apart from the obtuse and hostile throng, and to celebrate the feast of sound, color, and form in the solitary palace of his dream. He abandoned himself to a lyric impulse, recalling the joyous and splendid life of the Venetian painters, the popular favor that swept them, like a whirlwind, up to the heights of the glory, beauty, strength and joy which they multiplied around them in producing countless images on walls and domes.

"Then Donna Andriana said: 'Well, I promise solemnly that Stelio Effrena shall have his triumphal feast in Venice.' The Dogaressa had spoken! At that moment I beheld, on the low, mossy bank, a pomegranate laden with fruit, which, like the hallucination of a vision, broke the infinite squalor of that place. Donna Orsetta Contarini, who was sitting beside me, uttered a cry of delight, and held out her hands, as impatient as her lips. Nothing pleases me so much as a frank, strong

11

expression of desire. 'I adore pomegranates!' she cried, and she seemed fairly to be tasting its fine, sharp flavor. She was as childish as her name is archaic. Her cry moved me; but Andrea Contarini appeared severely to disapprove of his wife's vivacity. He seemed to me like a Hades that has little faith in the mnemonic virtue of the seven seeds as applied to legitimate marriage. But the boatmen, too, were stirred with sympathy, and rowed toward the shore, approaching it so close that I was able to jump out first, and I began at once to despoil the tree, my brother. It was another case, albeit from the lips of a pagan of the words of the Last Supper: 'Take, eat, this is my body, which is given for you. Do this in remembrance of me.' How does this seem to you, Perdita? Do not think that I am inventing this story. I assure you it is true."

La Foscarina allowed herself to be fascinated by the free and elegant fancy whereby he exercised the quickness of his wit and his facility of expression. In his words was something intoxicating, variable, and vigorous, which suggested to her mind the double and diverse image of water and of fire.

"Now," he continued, "Donna Andriana has kept her promise. Guided by that hereditary taste for magnificence which she shows so plainly, she has prepared a truly ducal feast in the Palace of the Doges, in imitation of those that were held there toward the end of the sixteenth century. She conceived the idea of rescuing from oblivion the Ariadne of Benedetto Marcello, and of making her sigh in the same place where Tintoretto painted the daughter of Minos receiving the crown of stars from Aphrodite. Don't you recognize in the beauty of this idea the woman who wished to leave her dear eyes behind her on that ineffable green robe? Remember, too, that this musicale in the Hall of the Greater Council has a historic precedent. In fifteen hundred seventy-three, in this same Hall, was performed a mythological composition by Cornelio Frangipani, with music by Claudio Merulo, in honor of his most Christian Majesty Henry Third. Own, Perdita, that my erudition astonishes you. Ah, if you only knew all that I have learned on that subject! I will read you my lecture on it, some day when you deserve a severe punishment!"

"What! Are you not to read it to-night at the festival?" inquired La Foscarina in surprise, fearing that, with his well known heedlessness of engagements, Effrena had resolved to disappoint the expectant public.

He understood her anxiety, and chose to amuse himself with it.

"This evening," he replied, with tranquil assurance, "I shall take a sherbet in your garden, and delight my eyes with the sight of the pomegranate, with its jewels gleaming in the starlight."

"Ah, Stelio! What do you mean?" she cried, half rising.

In her words and movement was so keen a regret, and at the same time so strange an evocation of the expectant gathering, that his mind was troubled. The image of the formidable monster with innumerable human faces amid the gold and somber purple of the vast hall reappeared before his mental vision; in fancy he felt

12

its fixed regard and hot breath. He realized also the peril he had resolved to face in trusting only to the inspiration of the moment, and felt a horror of a possible sudden mental obscurity, an unexpected confusion of his thought.

"Reassure yourself," he said. "I was only jesting. I will go ad bestias, and I will go unarmed. Did you not see the sign reappear just now? Do you believe, after the miracle of Torcello, that it reappeared in vain? It has come to warn me again that the only attitude that suits me is the one to which Nature disposes me. Now, you well know, my friend, that I do not know how to speak of anything but myself. And so, from the throne of the Doges, I must speak to my listeners only of my own soul, under the veil of some seductive allegory, with the charm of flowing musical cadences. I purpose to do this extemporaneously, if the fiery spirit of Tintoretto will only inspire me, from the heights of his Paradise, with sufficient ardor and audacity. The risk tempts me. But into what a strange error I was about to fall, Perdita! When the Dogaressa announced the feast to me, and begged me to do the honors, I undertook to compose a dignified discourse, a really ceremonious effort in prose, ample and solemn as one of those great robes of state behind glass in the Correr Museum; not without making in the exordium a profound genuflexion to the Queen; nor omitting to weave an impressive garland for the head of the most serene Andriana Duodo! And for several days it has given me a curious pleasure to dwell in spiritual communion with a Venetian patrician of the sixteenth century, a master of letters like Cardinal Bembo, a member of the Academy Uracini or Adorni, a frequent visitor to the gardens of Murano and the hills of Asolo. Certain it is that I felt a marked resemblance between the turn of my periods and the massive gold frames that surround the paintings on the ceiling of the Hall of Council. But, alas! yesterday morning, when I arrived here, and, in passing along the Grand Canal, when I wished to steep my weariness in the damp, transparent shade where the marble still exhales the spirit of the night, I had a sudden impression that my papers were worth much less than the dead seaweed tossed by the tide, and they seemed as strange to me as the Trionfi of Celio Magno and the Favole Marittime of Anton Maria Consalvi, quoted and commented on in them by me. What should I do, then?"

He threw around him an all-sweeping glance, as if exploring the waters and the sky in search of an invisible presence, or a newly arrived phantom. A yellowish light spread toward the solitary shores, which stood out in sharp lines like the dark veins in agate. Behind him, toward the Salute, the sky was scattered with light rosy and violet ribbon-like clouds, giving it the appearance of a glaucous sea, peopled with Medusas. From the gardens near the water descended the odor of foliage saturated with light and heat—an odor so heavy one might almost see it float on the waves like aromatic oil.

"Do you feel the Autumn, Perdita?" Stelio asked his dreamy friend, in a penetrating voice.

Again she had a vision of the dead Summer, enclosed within opalescent glass and sunk among the masses of seaweed.

13

"Yes, I feel it—within myself!" she replied, with a melancholy smile.

"Did you not see it last night, when it descended upon the city? Where were you last night, at sunset?"

"In a garden of the Giudecca."

"I was here, on the Riva. When human eyes have contemplated such a spectacle of joy and beauty, does it not seem to you that the eyelids should close and seal themselves forever? I should like to speak to-night, Perdita, of these hidden, secret matters. I should like to celebrate within myself the nuptials of Venice and Autumn, in almost the same tonality that Tintoretto used when he painted the nuptials of Ariadne and Bacchus for the hall of the Anticollegio—azure, purple and gold. Last night an old germ of poetry suddenly blossomed in my soul. I recalled a fragment of a forgotten poem that I wrote when I began to write in nona rima, one September in my early youth, when I had come by sea to Venice for the first time. The title of the poem was simply 'The Allegory of Autumn,' and the god was no longer represented as crowned with vine-leaves, but with jewels, like one of Paolo Veronese's princes, his being aglow with passion, about to approach the Anadyomenean City, with her arms of marble and her thousand green girdles. But the idea had not at that time reached the right degree of intensity to be admitted to the realm of Art, and instinctively I gave up the effort to manifest it in its entirety. But, in an active mind, as in a fertile soil, no seed is lost; and now this idea returns to me at an opportune moment and urgently demands expression. What a just and mysterious fatality governs the mental world! It was necessary that I should respect that first germ in order to feel its multiplied virtues develop in me to-day. That Vinci, who looked deep into all things profound, certainly meant something of this kind in his fable of the grain of millet that says to the ant: 'If you will be kind enough to let me satisfy my desire to be born again, I will render myself to you again a hundredfold.' Admire the touch of grace in those fingers capable of breaking iron! Ah, he is always the incomparable master! How can I forget him for a time, that I may give myself to the Venetians?"

The playful irony with which he had been speaking was suddenly extinguished in his last words, and again he seemed plunged in his own thoughts.

"It is already late; the hour approaches; we must return," he said presently, rousing himself as if from a troubled dream, for he had seen reappear that formidable monster with the thousand human faces filling the depth and width of the great hall. "I must go back to the hotel in time to dress."

Then, with a return of his boyish vanity, he thought of the eyes of the unknown women who would see him that evening for the first time.

"To the Hotel Danieli," La Foscarina said to the boatman.

While the dentellated iron of the prow swung around on the water, with a slow, animal-like movement, each felt a sadness different but equally painful at

14

leaving behind them the infinite silence of the estuary, already overcome by da and death, and being compelled to return toward the magnificent and tempting whose canals, like the veins of a full-blooded woman, began to burn with the fev of night.

They were quiet for some time, absorbed by their interior agitation, which shook each heart to it depths. And all things around them exalted the power of life in the man who wished to attract to himself the universe in order not to die, and in the woman, who would have thrown her oppressed soul to the flames in order to die pure.

Both started at the unexpected sound of the salute at the lowering of the flag on board a man-of-war anchored before the gardens. At the summit of the black mass they saw the tricolored flag slide down the staff and fold itself up, like a heroic dream that suddenly vanishes. For a moment the silence seemed deeper, and the gondola glided into darker shadows, grazing the side of the armed colossus.

"Do you know that Donatella Arvale who is to sing in Ariadne?" said Stelio suddenly.

"She is the daughter of the great sculptor, Lorenzo Arvale," La Foscarina replied, after an instant of hesitation. "I have no dearer friend than she—and in fact she is my guest at present. You will meet her at my house this evening, after the festival."

"Donna Andriana spoke to me of her last night as a prodigy. She said that the idea of resurrecting Ariadne had come to her on hearing Donatella Arvale sing divinely the air: Come mai puoi—Vedermi piangere? We shall have some divine music at your house, Perdita. Oh, how I long to hear it! Below there, in my solitude, for months and months, I hear only the music of the sea, which is too terrible, and my own music, which is too tumultuous."

The bells of San Marco gave the signal for the Angelus, and their powerful notes spread in great waves of sound over the water, vibrating among the masts of the vessels, and creeping out upon the infinite reach of the lagoon. From San Giorgio Maggiore, San Giorgio dei Greci, San Giorgio degli Schiavoni, San Giovanni in Bragora, and San Moisé, from the Salute, the Redentore, and beyond, over the entire domain of the Evangelista, to the distant towers of the Madonna dell' Orto, San Giobbe and Sant' Andrea, tongues of bronze responded, mingling in one great chorus, seeming to extend over the silent stones and waters a single immense and invisible dome of metal, the vibration of which might almost reach the first sparkling stars. Those sacred voices seemed to lend to the City of Silence an ideal and infinite grandeur.

"Can you still pray?" said Stelio in a softened voice, looking at the woman who, with eyes downcast, and hands clasped on her knees, seemed absorbed in a silent orison.

15

She did not reply; she only pressed her lips together more closely.

The minds of both were confused by the strange, the new image, and the new name, that had risen between them. Perturbation and passion seized them again, drew them near each other with such force that they dared not look into each other's eyes, for fear of what might be read there.

"Shall I see you again this evening, after the festival?" said La Foscarina, with a slight unsteadiness in her voice. "Are you free?"

She was eager now to hold him, to make him her prisoner, as if she feared he would escape her, as if she had hoped to find this night some magic philter that would bind him to her forever. And, though she comprehended now that the gift of all she had to give had become necessary, she realized only too clearly, nevertheless, even through the intoxication that bewildered her, the poverty of the gift so long withheld. And a mournful modesty, a mingling of terror and pride, contracted her slender frame.

"I am free—and I am yours!" the young man answered in a half whisper, without raising his eyes to hers. "You know that nothing is worth to me what you can give."

His heart, too, was stirred to its depths, with the two aims before his ambition toward which, this night, all his energy bent, like a powerful bow: the city and the woman, both tempting and mysterious, weary with having lived too much, and oppressed with too many loves; both were too much magnified by his imagination, and both were destined to disappoint his hopes.

In the moment that followed, a violent wave of mingled regret and desire swept over him. The pride and intoxication of his hard, persistent labor; his boundless ambition, which had been curbed within a sphere too narrow for it; his intolerance of mediocrity, his demand for the privileges of princes; his superb and empurpled dreams; his insatiable need of preëminence, glory, pleasure—surged in his soul with a confusing tumult, dazzling and suffocating him. And the craving of his sadness inclined him to win the final love of this solitary, nomadic woman, the very folds of whose garments seemed to suggest the frenzy of the far-off multitudes, whom she had so often thrilled and shaken with her art, by a cry of passion, a sob of grief, or a death-like silence. An irresistible impulse drew him toward this woman, in whom he fancied he saw the traces of all emotions and experiences, toward that being, no longer young, who had known so many caresses, yet was unknown by him.

"Is it a promise?" he murmured, bowing his head lower to conceal his agitation. "Ah! at last!"

She made no reply, but fixed on him a gaze of almost mad intensity, which he did not see.

16

They relapsed into silence again, while the reverberation of the bells passing overhead was so penetrating that they felt it in the roots of the hair, as from a quiver of their own flesh.

"Good-by," said La Foscarina, as they were landing. "When we leave the hall, let us meet in the courtyard, near the second well, the nearest to the Molo."

"Good-by," he answered. "Take some place where I may see you, among the crowd, when I speak my first word."

A confused clamor arose from San Marco, above the sound of the bells, spread over the Piazzetta, and died away toward the Fortuna.

"May all light be on your brow, Stelio!" said La Foscarina, holding out her burning hands to him passionately.

CHAPTER II
THE FACE OF TRUTH

When he entered the court by the south door, Stelio Effrena, seeing the black and white throng that swarmed up the Giants' Stairway, in the ruddy light of the torches fixed in the iron candelabra, felt a sudden sensation of repugnance, and paused at the entrance. He noted the contrast between this paltry crowd and the noble architecture which, magnified by the unusual nocturnal illumination, expressed, by their varied harmoniousness, the strength and the beauty of a day that was past.

"Oh, how miserable!" he exclaimed, turning to the friends that accompanied him. "In the Hall of the Greater Council, from the throne of the Doges, how is it possible to find metaphors that will move a thousand starched shirt-bosoms? Let us go back; let us inhale the odor of the real crowd, the true crowd. The Queen has not yet left the royal palace. We have time enough."

"Until the moment that I see you on the platform, I shall not feel sure that you will really speak," said Francesco de Lizo, laughing.

"I believe that Stelio would prefer the balcony to the platform," said Piero Martello, wishing to flatter the master's taste for sedition, and his factious spirit, which he himself affected, in imitation. "He would like to harangue, between the two red columns, the mutinous people who threatened to set fire to the new Procuratie and the old Libreria."

"Yes, certainly," said Stelio, "if the harangue had power to prevent or to precipitate an irreparable act. I hold that we use the written word to create a pure form of beauty, which, even in an uncut book, is enclosed and shut in, as in a tabernacle that may be entered only by election, with the same premeditated will used in the breaking of a seal. But the spoken word, it seems to me, when it is addressed directly to a multitude, should have only action for its aim. On this

17

condition alone can a proud spirit, without lessening itself in dignity, communicate with the masses by means of voice and gesture. Otherwise, his effort becomes merely histrionic. And so I repent bitterly of having accepted this function of an ornamental orator, who must not speak unless he speaks agreeably. Consider, I ask you, how humiliating for me is the honor that they think to do me, and consider also the uselessness of my speech. All these people, strangers here, have left their mediocre occupations, or their favorite amusements, to come and listen to me with the same vain and stupid curiosity that would lead them to listen to some new virtuoso. For the women that will listen to me, the art with which I have tied my cravat will be much more appreciated than the art with which I shall round my periods. And, after all, the only effect of my speech will be a clapping of hands, deadened by gloves, or a brief, discreet murmur, to which I shall reply with a gracious inclination of the head. Does it seem to you that I am about to attain the summit of my ambition?"

"You are wrong," said Francesco de Lizo. "You should congratulate yourself for this happy occasion, which will allow you, for several hours, to impress the rhythm of art on the life of a forgetful city, and to make us dream of the splendors that might embellish our existence by a renewed union of Art with Life. If the man that built the Teatro di Festa were there, he would praise you for that harmony which he predicted. But the most wonderful thing about this affair is the fact that, notwithstanding your absence, and your ignorance of the project, the festival seems to have been prepared under the direct inspiration of your genius. This is the best proof that it is possible to restore and diffuse taste, even in the midst of the barbaric present. Your influence to-day is more powerful than you think. The lady who has desired to honor you—she that you call the Dogeressa—at every new idea that came to her, asked herself: 'Would it please Effrena?' If you only knew how many young and eager spirits put to themselves to-day the same question, when they consider the aspects of their inner life!"

"And for whom should you speak, if not for them?" said Daniele Glauro, the fervent and sterile ascetic of Beauty, with that melodious voice which seemed to reflect the frank and inextinguishable ardor of the soul beloved by the master as one of the most faithful. "If, when you stand upon the platform, you will look about you, you will easily recognize the expression in their eyes. There are many of them, and some have come a long distance; they await your words with an eagerness that you perhaps do not understand. They are those who have imbibed the spirit of your poetry, who have breathed the fiery ether of your dream, and felt the grip of your chimera; those to whom you have announced the transfiguration of the world by the miracle of a new art. The number that you have attracted as an apostle of hope and of joy is very great. They have heard that you are to speak in Venice, in the Ducal Palace—one of the most splendid and glorious places on earth. They will be able to see you and listen to you for the first time, surrounded by the magnificence that seems to them an appropriate frame to your personality. The old Palace of the Doges, which has so long been wrapped in nocturnal darkness, is suddenly illuminated and aroused this night for you, and, to their minds, it is you alone that have had the power to rekindle these long-extinguished torches. Do you understand now the eagerness of their expectation? Does it not seem to you that to them only

18

you ought to speak? The condition you impose on the man that harangues a multitude may be fulfilled. You can awaken an emotion in their breasts that shall turn them forever toward the Ideal. For how many of them, Stelio, you might make this Venetian night an experience never to be forgotten!"

Stelio laid his hand on the prematurely bent shoulders of the mystic doctor, and, smiling, repeated Petrarch's words: "Non ego loquar omnibus, sed tibi, sed mihi, et his."

He saw within himself the radiant eyes of his unknown disciples, and heard within his soul, in clear tones, the sound of his own exordium.

"Nevertheless," he replied gayly, addressing Piero Martello, "it would be amusing to conjure up a tempest on this sea."

They were standing under the arch, near a column, in contact with the noisy, unanimous crowd, which gathered in the Piazzetta, stretched out toward the Zecca, was swallowed up near the Procuratie, barred the Torre dell'Orologio, occupied every space like a wave without form, and communicated its living warmth to the marble columns and the walls, against which it surged in its violent movement. From time to time, a louder cry arose from the distance, at the farther end of the Piazza, swelling higher and stronger until it burst out near them like a clap of thunder, then diminishing until it died away in a murmur.

"I should like to-night to find myself for the first time with a woman I loved, on a floating couch, over there, beyond the gardens, toward the Lido," said the romantic poet, Paris Eglano, a blond, beardless youth, whose handsome mouth, with its full red lips, contrasted with the almost angelic delicacy of his other features. "Within an hour, Venice will present to some Nero-like lover, hidden in a gondola, the spectacle of a city set on fire by its own delirium."

Stelio smiled, noting to what extent his intimates had become imbued with his own spiritual essence, and how deep the seal of his own style had stamped itself on their minds. Suddenly the image of La Foscarina flashed across his mental vision: La Foscarina, poisoned by too much art, remembering too many amatory experiences, with the stamp of maturity and of corruption on her eloquent mouth, the aridity of the vein fever that burned in those hands that pressed out the juices of deceitful fruits, and the marks of a hundred masks on that face which had simulated the fury of all mortal passions. Thus she appeared to his ardent thought of her, and his heart throbbed faster as he pictured her emerging soon from the multitude, as from some element that enslaved her, and thought that from her glance he should draw the necessary inspiration.

"Come, let us go," said he resolutely to his friends. "It is the hour."

The cannon announced that the Queen had left the royal palace. A prolonged quiver ran through the living human mass, like that which precedes a storm at sea.

19

From the bank of San Giorgio Maggiore, a rocket rushed up with a long hiss, rising in the air like a fiery stem and bursting into a mass of pink splendor at the top; then it curved, grew fainter, and dissolved in trembling sparks, extinguished finally with a slight crackling in the water. And the joyous clamor that greeted the beautiful Queen, repeating her name—the name of the starry, white flower and of the pearl—evoked in Stelio's imagination the pomp of the ancient Promissione, the triumphal procession of the Arts escorting the new Dogaressa to the palace; the wave of joy on which Morosina Grimani mounted to her throne, shimmering with gold, while all the Arts bowed before her, laden with gifts as if they bore horns of plenty.

"Certainly," said Francesco de Lizo, "if the Queen loves your books, she will wear all her pearls this evening. You will have before you a veritable labyrinth of jewels—all the hereditary gems of the Venetian patricians."

"Look toward the foot of the stairway, Stelio," said Daniele Glauro. "A group of devotees is waiting for you to pass that way."

Stelio stopped at the well indicated by La Foscarina. He leaned over the bronze edge, his knees touching the little carved caryatides, and saw in the dark water the reflection of the stars. For the moment his soul isolated itself, shut out the surrounding sounds, and withdrew into the shadowy disc, from which rose a slight dampness betokening the presence of water. His excited desire felt a need to attain even greater intoxication than this night promised him, and he felt that in the farthest depths of his being lay a secret soul, which, like this dark, watery mirror, remained immovable, strange, and intangible.

"What do you see there?" inquired Piero Martello, also leaning over the rim, worn in places by the ropes of centuries.

"The face of Truth!" the master answered.

In the apartments contiguous to the Hall of the Greater Council, once occupied by the Doge, but now by the pagan statues that were seized as booty in ancient wars, Stelio awaited the summons from the master of the ceremonies to mount to the platform. He was quite calm, and smiled on the friends that spoke to him, but their words reached his ear between pauses, like interrupted sounds borne from afar by the wind. From time to time, with an abrupt, involuntary movement, he drew near to one of the statues, and ran his hand nervously over it, as if seeking some weak spot, that he might break it; or he bent curiously over some rare medal, as if to read on it some indecipherable sign. But his eyes saw nothing of all this; they were turned within, where the multiplied power of his will evoked the silent forms that his voice would presently transform into the perfection of verbal music. His whole being contracted itself in an effort to raise to the highest degree of intensity the representation of the extraordinary feelings that possessed him. Since he could speak only of himself, and of his own universe, at least he would unite in one ideal figure the sovereign qualities of his art, and show to his disciples by his genius for imagery what an invincible force hastened him through this life. Once more he intended to show them that, in order to obtain the victory over men and

20

circumstances, there is no other way than to persevere in exalting oneself and to magnify one's own dream of beauty or of power.

He bent over a medallion by Pisanello, feeling at his temples the ardent, rapid pulsation of his thought.

"See, Stelio," said Daniele Glauro to him, with that pious reverence which veiled his voice whenever he spoke of his religion, "see how the mysterious affinities of Art work upon you, and how an infallible instinct leads you, amid so many forms, and at the very moment when your thought is about to reveal itself, toward the example of the most perfect expression, the highest model of style. At the very instant of coining your own idea, you are led to study one of Pisanello's medallions; you are attracted by the impression of one of the greatest stylists that ever have lived in the world, the most frankly Hellenic soul of the whole Renaissance. And suddenly your forehead is illumined by a ray of light."

The pure bronze bore the effigy of a young man with beautiful, waving hair, an imperial profile and Apollo-like neck, and the head was so perfect a type of elegance and vigor that the imagination could not picture him in life except as free from all decadence and eternally unchangeable, as the artist had presented him in this circle of bronze.—Dux equitum præstans Malatesta Novellus Cesenæ dominus. Opus Pisani pictoris.—And beside it was another medallion by the same artist, bearing the effigy of a virgin, with narrow chest, a swan-like throat, and hair drawn back in the shape of a heavy bag; the forehead, high and receding, seemed already to promise the aureole of the blessed, and she was like a vase of purity sealed forever, hard, precise, and limpid as a diamond, an adamantine pyx where the spirit, consecrated like the Host, rested as a sacrifice.—Cicilia Virgo, filia Johannis Francesco primi Marchionis Mantuae.

"Here comes La Foscarina, with Donatella Arvale," announced Francesco de Lizo, who had been watching the crowd that climbed the Censors' Stairway and pressed into the vast hall.

Again Stelio Effrena felt a wave of agitation sweep over him. The murmur of the throng seemed to come from afar and mingle in his ears with the throbbing of his arteries, and in this murmur he fancied he heard once more the last words of Perdita.

CHAPTER III
THE NUPTIALS OF AUTUMN AND VENICE
The murmur swelled louder, diminished, then ceased, as Stelio, with firm, light movement, ascended the marble steps of the platform. As he turned toward the audience, his dazzled eyes rested upon the formidable monster with a thousand human faces, amid the gold and somber purple of the immense hall.

A sudden thrill of pride gave him complete self-control. He bowed to the Queen and to Donna Andriano Duodo, who smiled upon him with the same twin

21

smiles he had seen from the gliding gondola on the Grand Canal. He threw a keen glance toward the scintillating first rows, seeking La Foscarina, then looked toward the farther end of the hall, where only a dark zone, dotted with white spots, could be distinguished. The silent, attentive multitude seemed to him like an enormous, many-eyed chimera, its breast covered with glittering scales, extending its black bulk under the arches of the rich, heavy ceiling that hung over it like a suspended treasure.

Dazzling was that chimeric breast, where sparkled necklaces that must once have flashed their fires under the same ceiling on the night of a coronation banquet. The tiara and the necklaces of the Queen—the rows of pearls, like grains of light, somehow suggesting the miraculous image of a smile just about to appear—the dark emeralds of Andriano Duodo, taken long ago from the handle of a scimitar; the rubies of Giustiniana Memo, set in the semblance of carnations by the inimitable craftsmanship of Vettor Camelio; the sapphires of Lucrezia Priuli, taken from the shoes in which the Most Serene Zilia had walked to her throne on the day of her triumph; the beryls of Orsetta Contarini, delicately set in dull gold by the art of Silvestro Grifo; the turquoises of Zenobia Corner, bathed in a strange pallor by the mysterious malady that, in a single night, changed them as they lay on the warm breast of the Princess de Lusignan, among the delights of Asolo—all the rich jewels that had illumined the nights of the Anadyomenean city glowed with renewed fire on the breast of the chimera, from which rose a moist odor of feminine breaths and many perfumes. The rest of that strangely marked and shapeless body extended to the rear of the hall, in a sort of long tail, passing between the two gigantic spheres, which recalled to the memory of the "Image-maker" the two bronze spheres that the monster with the bandaged eyes presses with his paws in Giambellino's allegory. And this vast animal life, devoid of all thought for the time before him who alone at that moment must think, endowed with the inert fascination of enigmatic idols, covered with its own silence as with a shield capable of receiving and resisting any shock, awaited the first thrill of his dominating word.

Stelio Effrena measured this silence, upon which his first syllable must fall. While his voice was rising to his lips, an effort of will summoning it and fortifying it against instinctive hesitation, he perceived La Foscarina standing near the railing that encircled the celestial sphere. The pale face of the tragic actress rose from her bare neck, and the purity of her white shoulders was just above the orbit of the zodiacal figures. Stelio admired the art of this apparition. With his own eyes fixed upon those distant, adoring ones, he began to speak slowly, as if the rhythm of the oars still lingered in his ears.

"One afternoon, not long ago, while I was returning from the gardens along the warm bank of the Schiavoni, where the souls of poets sometimes believe they see I know not what magic golden bridge spanning a sea of light and silence toward a dream of infinite beauty, I thought—or rather, I witnessed with my thoughts, as at some intimate spectacle—of the nuptial alliance, under those skies, of Autumn and Venice.

22

"Everywhere was disseminated a spirit of life, arising from passionate expectation and restrained ardor, which made me marvel at its vehemence, but which seemed not altogether new to me; I had already seen it in some shadowy zones, under the almost death-like immobility of Summer; and sometimes I had felt it vibrating, like a mysterious pulse, in the strange feverish odor of the water. Thus, I thought, it is true, then, that this pure city of Art aspires to a supreme state of beauty which for her returns annually, as the flowers return to the forest. She tends to reveal herself in full harmony, as if always she bore within her bosom, powerful and conscious, the same desire of perfection from which she sprang and was formed throughout the ages, like some divine creature. Under the motionless fire of Summer, she seemed to palpitate no more, to breathe no more, but to lie dead in her green waters. My feeling did not deceive me, however, when I fancied I saw her secretly inspired by a spirit of life sufficient to renew the most sublime of the ancient miracles.

"That is what I thought, and what I saw. But how can I convey to you that listen to me any idea of that vision of joy and beauty? No sunrise, no sunset, could equal the glory of that hour of light on the water and the marble. The unexpected apparition of the beloved woman in a forest in springtime could not be as intoxicating as this sudden revelation by daylight of the heroic and voluptuous city, which carries in its marble embrace the richest dream of a Latin soul."

The voice of the orator, clear, penetrating, almost icy at the beginning, was suddenly warmed by the invisible sparks kindled within him by the effort of improvisation, yet governed by the extreme nicety of his ear. While his words flowed without hesitation, and the rhythmic line of his periods set forth their beauty with the clearness of a figure drawn at one stroke by a bold hand, his auditors were conscious of the excessive tension of his mind, and it captivated them as one of those terrifying feats at the circus, where all the herculean energies of the athlete show the test by his quivering tendons and swelling arteries. They felt the reality, the living warmth of the thought thus expressed, and their pleasure was the greater because unexpected, for most of his auditors had anticipated from this indefatigable searcher after perfection the studied reading of a laboriously composed discourse. His devotees observed with emotion this audacious test, as if they saw before them, unveiled, the secret labor that had brought forth the forms that had given them so much joy. And this first wave of emotion, spreading by contagion, indefinitely multiplied and becoming unanimous, returned to him who caused it, and seemed almost to overcome him.

This was the expected danger. Under the pressure of a wave so strong, the speaker faltered. For a few seconds a thick cloud darkened his brain; the light of his mind was extinguished, as a torch before an irresistible wind; his eyes grew dim, as if he were about to faint. But he felt how mortifying would be the shame of defeat if he yielded to this seizure; and in that darkness, by a sort of effort of brute force, or like the striking of steel on flint, his will rose in triumph over the instinctive weakness. With glance and gesture, he directed the eyes of the assemblage to the great masterpiece in the ceiling of that hall, spreading there in a kind of sun-like radiance.

23

"I am certain," he exclaimed, "that Venice appeared thus to Paolo Veronese, when he sought within himself for an image of the Queen triumphant."

He explained the reason why the great master, after throwing upon his canvas a profusion of gold, jewels, silks, purple, ermine, and all imaginable richness, at last could represent the glorious face only in the nimbus of a shadow.

"We ought to exalt Veronese for that shadowy veil alone! Representing by a human face the Queen of Cities, he yet knew how to express its essential spirit, whose symbol was an inextinguishable flame seen through a watery veil. And one I know well, who, having plunged his soul in this sublime element, has withdrawn it enriched with a new power, and consequently has lived a fuller and more ardent spiritual life."

This one he knew well—was it not himself? In the assertion of his own personality he found again all his courage, and felt that henceforth he was master of his thoughts and words, freed from danger, capable of drawing within the charmed circle of his dream the enormous, many-eyed chimera, with the glittering breast— the ephemeral and versatile monster from whose side emerged its offspring, the Tragic Muse, her head rising above the constellations.

Obedient to his movement, the innumerable faces turned toward the Apotheosis, their awakened eyes contemplating with wonder this marvel, as if they beheld it for the first time, or under a new aspect. The naked back of the woman with the golden helmet shone under the cloud with an effect of muscular life so perfect that it looked as attractive as palpable flesh. And, from this nudity, more realistic than all the rest, victorious over Time, which had darkened around it heroic images of sieges and battles, seemed to emanate a powerful enchantment, the sweetness of which was augmented by the breath of the autumn night coming through the open windows; while, from above, the princesses of a former day, leaning over the balustrades between two columns, inclined their illumined faces and opulent breasts toward their worldly sisters below.

Under the new spell of enchantment, the poet threw off his winged words, harmonious as lyric strophes. He described the Queen City palpitating with ardor within her thousand green girdles, extending her marble arms toward the wild Autumn, whose humid breath reached her, balmy with the delicious death of the fields and islands, making her sigh like a bride awaiting her hour of joy. By the magic of his words, Venice seemed to be possessed of marvelous hands, with which she wove for herself the inimitable tissue of allegory that covered her.

"And since, in all the world, poetry alone is truth, he that knows how to contemplate it, and to draw it into his own soul by the virtue of his thought, will be very near to mastering the secret of victory over life."

In pronouncing these last words, Stelio sought the eyes of Daniele Glauro, and saw that they sparkled with happiness beneath that large, meditative brow, which

24

seemed swollen by the weight of an unborn world. The mystic doctor was there, near the platform, with several of those unknown disciples that he had described to the master as eager and anxious, full of faith and expectation, impatient to break the chain of their daily servitude, and to know the free intoxication of joy and sadness. Stelio noted that they were grouped, like a nucleus of compressed force, against the great red bookcases, wherein lay buried innumerable volumes of useless and forgotten lore. He marked their eager and attentive faces, their long hair, their lips, half parted with child-like absorption, or closed tightly in a kind of violent sensitiveness, their bright eyes, to which the breath of his words carried lights and shadows, as a changeful breeze stirs a parterre of delicate flowers. He felt that in his own hand he held all their souls blended into one spirit, which he could at will agitate, crush, tear, or burn, as if it were a filmy scarf.

While his mind expanded and relaxed, in its continued effort, he still retained a strange power of exterior investigation, a faculty of material observation which became the clearer and more penetrating with the warmth and quickening of his eloquence.

Suddenly he saw with his mental vision the picture he wished to present, and his verbal expression of it was after the manner of the master painters that had reigned in that place, with the luxuriance of Veronese, and the fire of Tintoretto.

"All the vitalities and all the transfigurations of the ancient stones, where Time has accumulated so many mysteries, and where glory has set her emblems; all the alternations of marvelously easy creations and destructions were reflected in the water; the effulgence of a jubilant light glittered between the crosses of cupolas inflated by prayer, and the slender saline crystals hanging under the arch of the bridges. Like a sentinel on a rampart uttering his shrill cry to him that listens for the signal, so the golden angel from the summit of the highest tower at last flashed out the announcement.

"And He appeared! The Bridegroom appeared, seated in his fiery chariot, which he turned toward the Queen of Cities, and in his youthful, superhuman countenance was a strange fascination springing from an animal-like cruelty and delicacy contrasting with the deep eyes, full of all knowledge. His blood rioted through his veins, from the tips of his fingers to his nimble feet; mysterious, occult things veiled his being, concealing joy as the grape in bloom conceals the vine; and all the tawny gold and purple that surrounded him were like the vestment of his senses.

"With what passion, throbbing under her thousand emerald girdles, and the richness of her jewels, the Queen of Cities gave herself to the magnificent god!"

Swept up in this rushing flight of words, the soul of the multitude seemed to reach the sentiment of Beauty, as if it were a summit never before attained. The pulse of the people and the voice of the poet seemed to give back to those ancient walls their former life, and to reawaken in that cold museum its original spirit: a

25

flood of powerful ideas, concrete, and organized in the most durable substance to attest the nobility of a great race.

The splendor of divine youth descended upon the women, as it might have descended in a sumptuous alcove, for each felt within herself the breathlessness of expectation and the joy of yielding, like that of the Queen of Cities. They smiled with vague languor as if wearied by the strain upon their emotions; their cool, polished shoulders rose from their corollas of jewels.

Stelio looked down upon the sparkling breast of the great, many-eyed chimera, on which rose and fell many fluttering feather fans, like tiny wings; and over his spirit passed an intoxicating glow that disquieted him. The vibration of his nerves, acting upon those of his auditors and thus reacting upon himself, unsettled him so much as almost to unbalance him. For an instant he felt that he was oscillating above the crowd, like a concave and sonorous body, the resonances of which were engendered by an indistinct yet infallible will.

He was surprised at the unknown power that dwelt within him, abolishing his own personal limits and conferring the fulness of a chorus on his single voice.

This, then, was the mysterious truce which the revelation of Beauty could grant to the daily existence of wearied man; this was the mysterious will that could possess the poet at the moment when he replied to the souls of his followers who questioned him as to the value of life and tried to raise themselves, if only once, to the height of the eternal Ideal. He was only the messenger through whom Beauty offered to those men, assembled in this place consecrated by centuries of human glory, the divine gift of oblivion. He was only the translator into rhythmic speech of the visible language whereby, in this same place, the noble craftsmen of a former day had expressed the prayers and aspirations of the race. And for one hour, at least, those men would contemplate the world with different eyes; they would think and dream with different souls.

In fancy, he passed beyond the walls that enclosed the palpitating throng in a kind of heroic cycle, a circle of red triremes, fortified towers, and triumphal theories. The place now seemed too narrow for the exaltation of his new feeling; and once more he was drawn toward the real people, the immense, unanimous crowd he had seen outside the palace, who had sent upward in the starry night a clamor that, like blood or wine, intoxicated them as they uttered it.

And not alone to this multitude did his thoughts turn; his fancy beheld an infinity of multitudes, massed together in theaters, dominated by an idea of truth and of beauty, pale and intent before the great arch of the stage, which should open before them some marvelous transfiguration of life, or frenzied by the sudden splendor radiating from an immortal phrase. And the dream of a higher Art, as it surged up again in his thought showed him mankind once more reverencing poets, as those who alone can interrupt at intervals its daily anguish, quench its thirst, and dispense oblivion. He even judged too slight the test he was now undergoing; he felt himself capable of creating gigantic fictions. The still formless work that he

26

nourished in his soul shook him with a thrill of life as he looked again at the tragedienne, standing above the sphere of constellations—the Muse with the transcendent voice, who seemed to carry the frenzy of far-off throngs, now silenced, in the classic folds of her robes.

Almost overcome by the incredible intensity of emotion that had possessed him during the brief pause, he began to speak again in a lower tone. He spoke of the growth of art between the youth of Giorgione and the old age of Tintoretto, and described it as golden, purple, rich and expressive as the pomp of the earth irradiated by the glow of sunset.

"When I consider the impetuous creators of such marvelous beauty, my mind recalls an image from a fragment of Pindar's: 'When the centaurs became acquainted with the virtues of wine, sweet as honey and a conqueror of men, they banished milk from their tables and hastened to quaff their wine from silver horns.' No one in the world better knew than they how to taste the wine of life. They drew from it a kind of lucid intoxication that multiplied their powers and communicated to their eloquence a fertilizing energy. And in their greatest creations, the violent throbbing of their pulses seems to have persisted throughout the ages, like the veritable rhythm of Venetian art.

"Ah, how pure and poetic is the slumber of the Virgin Ursula on her immaculate bed! The most religious silence reigns in that chamber, where the pious lips of the sleeper seem to form themselves into the act of uttering prayer. Through the doors and the windows steals the timid light of dawn, illumining the syllables inscribed on her pillow: INFANTIA is the simple word that spreads around that virginal head, like the fresh aurora of the morning: INFANTIA. She sleeps, the maiden already betrothed to the pagan prince and destined to martyrdom. So chaste, so ingenuous, so fervent, is she not the image of Art such as the precursors saw it, with the sincerity of their child-like eyes? INFANTIA! The word evokes around that couch all those forgotten ones: Lorenzo Veneziano, Simone da Cusighe, Catarino, Jacobello, Maestro Paolo, Giambono, Semitecolo, Antonio, Andrea, Quirizio da Murano, and all the laborious family by whom color—which later was the rival of fire—was prepared in the burning island of furnaces. But would not they themselves have uttered a cry of admiration if they had seen the drops of blood that sprang from the maiden's heart when it was pierced by the arrow of the beautiful pagan archer? A current so red from a virgin nourished on white milk! This victory was a sort of festival: to it the archers brought their finest bows, their richest garments, their most elegant air. The golden-haired barbarian, aiming his arrows at the martyr, with a movement so proud and graceful, does he not resemble an adolescent and wingless Eros? That gracious slayer of innocence (or perhaps his brother), after laying aside his bow, will abandon himself to the enchantment of music to dream a dream of infinite pleasure.

"It was indeed Giorgione that poured into him a new soul, and kindled it with an implacable longing. The music that charms him is not the melody that last night the lutes diffused among the curving arches, over radiant thrones, or diminishing in

27

the silence of distances in the visions of the third Bellini. Under the touch of religious hands, it still rises from the harpsichord; but the world it awakens is full of a joy and a sadness wherein sin hides its head.

"He that has looked at the Concerto with the eyes of wisdom has comprehended an extraordinary and irrevocable moment of the Venetian soul. By means of a harmony of color—whose power of expression is as boundless as the mystery of sounds—the artist reveals the first agitation of an eager spirit to whom life has suddenly appeared under the aspect of a rich inheritance.

"The monk, seated at his harpsichord, and his older companion, do not resemble those monks that Vettor Carpaccio represented as flying before the wild beast tamed by Jerome, in San Giorgio degli Schiavoni. Their essence is nobler and stronger; they breathe an atmosphere higher and richer, propitious to the birth of a great joy, a great sadness, or a superb dream. What notes do those beautiful, sensitive hands draw from the keys on which they linger? Magic notes, no doubt, since they have power to work in the musician a transfiguration so great. He is half-way through his mortal existence, already far from his youth and near his decline, yet only now life reveals itself to him, rich with all good things, like a forest full of ripe, red fruit, the velvety freshness of which his always busy hands never before have known. As his senses still slumber, he has not yet fallen under the domination of a single seductive image, but he suffers a sort of confused anguish wherein regret overcomes desire, while in the web of harmonies that he seeks, the vision of his past—but only as it might have been and was not—weaves itself like the tissue of a chimera.

"His companion divines this inner agitation, for he is already at the threshold of old age; calm, sweet, and serious, he touches the shoulder of the passionate player with a pacifying movement. But there, emerging from the warm shadows like the embodiment of youthful ardor itself, is the young man with hat beplumed and flowing locks, the glowing flower of adolescence which Giorgione created under the influence of a reflection from that Hellenic myth whence arose the ideal form of Hermaphrodite. He is there, present, yet a stranger, separated from the others, like a being that cares only for his own welfare. The music exalts his inexpressible dream, and seems to multiply indefinitely his capacity to enjoy. He knows himself master of that life which escapes the other two, and the harmonies sought by the musician seem to him only the prelude to his own feast. His glance is sidewise and intent, turned toward a certain point, as if he would attract to himself something that charms him; his closed lips are ready with a kiss as yet ungiven; his brow is so spacious that the thickest garland would not encumber it; but if I think of his hands, I fancy them crushing the laurel leaves to perfume his fingers."

The hands of the Inspirer illustrated the gesture of the covetous youth, as if they were really pressing out the essence of the aromatic leaf; and his voice lent to the image an illusion so strong that the young men felt that here at last was one who could express their cherished and secret thoughts and dreams, and give voice to their unspeakable, continuous, and ceaseless longings. They occupied the free space at the back of the seated audience, making a living border for that compact mass;

28

and, as the edges of a flag that waves in the breeze have a stronger flutter, these youthful hearts beat faster than those of older men at the warm breath of the poet's words.

Stelio recognized them, distinguishing them by their singularity of attitude, the intensity of emotion revealed by their compressed lips and the glow of ardor in their cheeks. On the face of one, turned toward the open balcony, he read the enchantment of the autumn night, and the delicious breeze coming from the lagoon. The glance of another indicated, by a ray of love, some woman, seated near by, looking as if she were lost in tender recollections, her face white, her red lips slightly parted, like the entrance to a hive moist with honey.

His eyes continually returned to the promised woman, who looked as she stood there like the living support of a starry sphere. He was grateful to her for her choice of this manner of appearing to him when, for the first time, he gave himself to the people. He no longer regarded her as merely the passing fancy of a single night, a woman ripened by long experience, but the marvelous instrument of a new art, the interpreter of the greatest poetry, she that should incarnate in her changeful personality his future fictions of beauty, she whose unforgettable voice should carry to mankind the long-expected word. He now felt attached to her, not by a promise of love, but by a promise of glory; and the formless work that he still cherished in his breast again leaped within him.

"You that listen to me," he continued, "do you not see some analogy between these three symbols of Giorgione's and the three generations, all living at the same time, that illumined the dawn of a new century? Venice, the City Triumphant, reveals herself to their eyes like a great, a superabundant banquet, where all the riches accumulated throughout centuries of war and commerce are to be set out without stint. What richer fountain of pleasure could there be to initiate life in insatiable desire? It is a time of agitation, almost of distraction, which, because of its fulness, is worth an hour of heroic violence. Alluring voices and laughter seem to float from the hills of Asolo where, surrounded by all delights, reigns the daughter of San Marco, Domina Aceli, who found in a myrtle grove of Cyprus the cincture of Aphrodite. Now approaches the youth with the white plumes; he comes to the banquet, followed by his uncurbed escort, and all desires kindle and burn like torches quickened by the wind. And this was the beginning of that divine Autumn of Art toward which men will always turn with deep emotion as long as the human soul strives to transcend the narrowness of its common existence in order to live a life more fervent or to die a nobler death.

"I see Giorgione imminent on the marvelous sphere, but I do not recognize his mortal person; I seek him in the mystery of the fiery cloud that envelops him. He appears to us more myth-like than human. The destiny of no poet on earth is comparable to his. All concerning his life is unknown; some even go so far as to deny his existence. His name is inscribed on no work, and many refuse to attribute any work to him with absolute certainty. But the whole of Venetian art was illumined by his revelation; it was from him that the great Titian received the secret of infusing glowing blood into the veins of the beings he created. In fact, that which

29

Giorgione represents in Art is the Epiphany of the Flame. He deserves to be called 'the Flame-Bearer,' like Prometheus.

"When I consider the rapidity with which this sacred gift has passed from one artist to another, glowing with increasing splendor from color to color, I think of one of those lampadeforie, or festivals, in which the Greeks tried to perpetuate the memory of the Titan son of Japetus. On the day of the festival, a group of young Athenian horsemen would set off at a gallop, riding from Ceramicus to Colonos, their chief waving a torch that had been lighted at the altar of a temple. If the torch was extinguished by the swiftness of the course, the bearer handed it to a companion, who re-lighted it as he rode; and this one gave it to a third; the third to a fourth, and so on, always galloping, until the last bearer laid it, still alight, on the altar of the Titan. This image, with all it suggests of fiery vehemence, represents to my fancy the feast of the master-colorists of Venice. Each of them, even to the least illustrious, held in his hand the sacred gift, if only for an instant. Some of them, like that first Bonifacio, whom we should glorify, gathered with incombustible fingers the inmost flower of the flame."

His fingers made a movement in the air as if to pluck the ideal flower. His eyes turned again toward the celestial sphere, as if he wished to offer the fiery gift to her who guarded the divine zodiacal beasts. "To you, Perdita!" But the woman was smiling at some one at a distance.

Following the thread of her smile, Stelio's eyes were led to an unknown woman, who suddenly seemed to stand out illumined against a shadowy background.

Was not that the creature of music whose name had resounded against the iron sides of the ship that evening, in the silence and the shadow?

She seemed to Stelio to be almost an interior image, suddenly engendered in that part of his soul where the brief sensation he had felt while passing through the shadow of the vessel had remained like an isolated and indistinct point. For a second she was beautiful—as beautiful as were his yet unexpressed thoughts.

"The city to which such creators have given a soul so powerful," he continued, floating himself on the rising wave, "is considered to-day, by the greater number, only as a vast inert reliquary, or as a refuge of peace and oblivion.

"In truth, I know of no other place in the world—unless it be Rome—where a bold and ambitious spirit can better foster the active virtue of his intellect, and all the energies of his being toward the supreme heights, than on these quiet waters. I know of no marsh capable of provoking in human pulses a fever more violent that that which at times steals up to us from the shadows of a silent canal. Nor do those men who, at noontide in the midsummer heat, lie among the ripe grain, feel in their veins a more fiery wave of blood than that which suffuses our eyes when we lean too intently over these waters, to see whether, perchance, we may descry in their depths some old sword or ancient diadem.

30

"Do not all gracious spirits come hither, as to a place of sweet refuge—those that hide some secret pain, those that have accomplished some final renunciation, those that have become weak through some morbid affection, and those that seek silence only to hear the soft step of advancing Death? Perhaps in their fading eyes Venice appears like a clement city of death, embraced by the waters of oblivion. But their presence is no more important than the wandering weeds that float at the foot of the steps of the marble palaces. They only increase the odor of sickly things, that strange, feverish odor on which at times, toward evening, after a laborious day, we nourish the fulness of our own feelings.

"But the ambiguous city does not always indulge the illusions of those that look to her as a giver of peace. I know one who, in the midst of sweet repose on her breast, started up as terror-struck as if when lying beside his loved one, with her hand resting on his weary eyelids, he had heard serpents hissing in her hair!

"Ah, if I only knew how to tell you of that prodigious life which palpitates beneath her great necklaces and her thousand green girdles! Not a day passes that she does not absorb more and more of our souls: sometimes she gives them back to us fresh and intact, restored to their original newness, whereon to-morrow's events will be imprinted with indelible clearness; again, she gives them back to us infinitely subtle and voracious, like a flame that destroys all that it touches, so that, at evening, among the cinders and the ashes, we may light upon some wonderful sublimate. Each day she urges us to the act that is the very genesis of our species: the unceasing effort to surpass ourselves. She shows us the possibility of transforming pain into the most efficacious stimulating energy; she teaches us that pleasure is the most ? certain means of knowledge given to us by Nature, and that the man who has suffered much is less wise than he that has enjoyed much."

At these audacious words, a slight murmur of disapproval passed over the auditorium; the Queen shook her head ever so little, in token of denial; several ladies, in a rapid exchange of glances, seemed to signify to one another a sentiment of graceful horror. But these signs were overbalanced by the acclamation of youthful approval that rose from all sides toward him that taught with a boldness so frank the art of rising to the superior forms of life by the virtue of joy.

Stelio smiled as he recognized his own, and so numerous; he smiled to recognize the efficacy of his teaching, which already, in more than one spirit, had dissipated the clouds of inert sadness, shown it the cowardice of weak tears, and infused it with a lasting disdain for feeble complaint and soft compassion. He rejoiced at having been able to proclaim once more the principle of his doctrine, emanating naturally from the soul of the art he glorified. And those that had retired to a hermit's cell, there to adore a sad phantom that lived only in the dim mirror of their own eyes; those that had created themselves kings of palaces without windows, where, from time immemorial, they had awaited a Visitation; those that had sought to unearth among ruins the image of Beauty, but who had found only a worn sphinx, which had tormented them with its endless enigmas; those that stood every evening at their thresholds to greet the mysterious Stranger bearing gifts under his

31

mantle, and who, with pale cheeks, laid their ears against the ground to catch the first sound of the Stranger's approach; those whose souls were sterilized by resigned mourning or devoured by desperate pride; those that were hardened by useless obstinacy, or deprived of sleep by hope continually disappointed—all these spirits he wished now to summon that they might recognize their ailment under the splendor of that ancient yet ever-new soul.

"In truth," said he, in a tone full of exultation, "if the whole population, abandoning their homes, should emigrate, attracted to-day toward other shores as formerly their heroic youth were tempted by the arch of the Bosphorus, in the time of the Doge Pietro Ziani, and the voice of prayer should no more strike against the sonorous gold of the concave mosaics, nor the sound of the oar perpetuate with its rhythmic stroke the meditation of the silent stones, Venice would still remain a City of Life. The ideal creatures protected by its silence live in the whole past and for the whole future. In them we shall always discover new concordances with the edifice of the universe, unforeseen meetings with the idea born only yesterday, clear announcements of that which is with us only a presentiment as yet, open answers to that which as yet we have not dared to ask.

"These ideal creatures are simple, but they are full of innumerable meanings; they are ingenuous, yet are clothed in strange attire. Should we contemplate them for an indefinite time, they never would cease to pour dissimilar truths into our minds. Should we visit them every day, every day they would appear to us under a new aspect, as do the sea, the rivers, the fields, the woods, the rocks. At times the things they say to us do not really reach our intellects, but reveal themselves to us in a sort of confused happiness, which causes our own substance to dilate and quiver to its inmost depths. Some bright day they will point out to us the path to the distant forest, wherein Beauty has awaited us from time immemorial, buried in her mystic hair.

"Whence came to them their immeasurable power?

"From the pure unconsciousness of the artificers that created them.

"Those profound men ignored the immensity of the things they wished to express. Penetrating with a million roots into the soil of life, not like single trees, but like vast forests, they absorbed infinite elements, which they transfused and condensed into ideal species, whose essences nevertheless remained unknown to them, as the flavor of the apple is unknown to the branch that bears it. They were the mysterious means chosen by Nature in her effort to represent in an integral form those types in which she has not yet succeeded. Because of this, continuing the work of the Divine Mother, their minds, as Leonardo says, have become transformed into 'a likeness of the Divine Mind.' And because creative force rushed to their fingers incessantly, like sap to the buds of trees, they created with joy."

All the desire of the determined artist, panting and struggling to obtain this Olympian gift, all his envy of those gigantic creators of Beauty, all his insatiable thirst for happiness and glory, were revealed in the tone in which he pronounced these last words. Once more the soul of the multitude was under the magic of the poet's spell, strained and vibrating like a single cord composed of a thousand strands, the resonance of which could be incalculably prolonged. That resonance awakened within the multitude the sense of a truth that had lain dormant, but which the poet's words now revealed for the first time.

In the sonority of the deep silence, the solitary voice reached its climax.

"To create with joy! It is the attribute of Divinity! It is impossible to imagine at the summit of the spirit an act more triumphal. Even the words that signify it possess something of the splendor of sunrise.

"And these artists created by a medium that is in itself a joyous mystery: by color, which is the ornament of the world; by color, which seems the effort of matter to become light.

"And the newly awakened musical sense they had for color was such that their creations transcend the narrow limits of figured symbols, and assume the high revealing power of an infinite harmony.

"Never have the words of Vinci, on whom Truth flashed one day with her thousand secrets, appeared so true as when we stand before the great symphonic canvases of the masters: 'Music cannot be called anything but the sister of Painting.' They are not alone silent poetry, but also silent music. The most subtle seekers of rare symbols, and those most desirous to impress the sign of an internal universe on the purity of a meditative brow, seem to us almost sterile compared with these great unconscious musicians.

"When we behold Bonifacio, in the parable of Dives, intoning with a note of fire the most powerful harmony of color in which the essence of a proud and voluptuous nature ever has revealed itself, we do not ask questions about the blond youth, listening to the music and seated between the two magnificent courtesans, whose faces glow like lamps of purest amber; but, passing beneath the material symbol, we abandon ourselves to the power of evocation of those chords, wherein our spirits seem to-day to find a presentiment of I know not what evening, heavy with beautiful destiny and autumnal gold, in a harbor as quiet as a basin of perfumed oil where a galley palpitating with oriflammes shall enter with a strange silence, like a butterfly of twilight darting into the chalice of some great flower.

"Shall we not, with our mortal eyes, really see it, some glorious evening, approaching the Palace of the Doges? Does it not appear to us from a prophetic horizon in the Allegory of Autumn which Tintoretto offers us, like a superior, concrete image of our dream of yesterday?

"Seated on the shore, like a deity, Venice receives the ring from the young, vine-wreathed god who descends into the water, while Beauty floats in the air with a starry diadem to crown the marvelous alliance!

33

"Behold yon distant ship! It seems to bring a message from the gods. Behold the symbolic Woman! Her body is capable of bearing the germs of a world!"

A whirlwind of applause broke out, dominated by the clamor of the young men, who hailed him who had kindled before their anxious eyes a hope so glowing, who had professed a faith so strong in the occult genius of the race, in the lofty virtue of the ideals handed down by their fathers, in the sovereign dignity of their spirit, the indestructible power of beauty, in all the great things held as naught by modern barbarity. The disciples extended their arms toward the master with an effusion of gratitude, an impulse of love, for he had illumined their souls as with a torch. In each lived again Giorgione's creation: the youth with the beautiful white plumes, who advanced toward the rich mass of spoils; and each fancied as multiplied to infinity his own power to enjoy all things. Their cry expressed so plainly their perturbation of spirit, that the master felt an inward tremor and the inrush of a wave of sadness as he thought of the ashes of this sudden fire, and of the cruel wakening of the morrow. Against what sharp obstacles must be broken this terrible desire to live, this violent will of each to shape the wings of Victory to his own destiny, and to bend all the energies of his nature toward the sublime end!

But that night favored youthful delirium. All the dreams of domination, of pleasure and of glory, that Venice has first cradled, then stifled, in her marble arms, seemed to rise anew from the foundations of the palace, to enter from the open balconies, palpitating like a people revivified under the arch of that rich and heavy ceiling, which was like a suspended treasure. The strength which, on the ceiling and the walls, seemed to swell the muscles of the gods, the kings, and the heroes, the beauty which, in the nudity of the goddesses, the queens, and the courtesans, ran like visible music—all that human strength and beauty, transfigured by centuries of art, harmonized itself in a single figure, which these intoxicated ones fancied they beheld, real and breathing, erected before them by the new poet.

They vented their intoxicated enthusiasm in that great cry which they sent up to him who had offered to their thirsty lips a cup of his own wine. Henceforth, all would be able to see the inextinguishable flame through its watery veil. Some one among them already imagined himself crumpling laurel leaves to perfume his hands; and another resolved to seek at the bottom of a silent canal for the old sword and the ancient diadem.

CHAPTER IV
THE SPIRIT OF MELODY
Alone with the statues in one of the rooms of the neighboring museum, Stelio Effrena rested for a moment, shrinking from any other contact, feeling the need of gathering his strength and quieting his nerves, to free himself from the unusual vibration through which it seemed to him all the essence of his spirit had been dissipated and scattered over the composite soul of the throng. Of his recent words, no trace remained in his memory, and of recent images he perceived no vestige. The only phrase that lingered in his mind was that "inmost flower of the flame," which he had conjured up in speaking of the glory of the first Bonifacio, and which he had

34

plucked with his own incombustible fingers to offer to his promised love. He remembered how, at the precise instant of this spontaneous offering, the woman had turned away her head, and how, instead of a glance from her dreamy eyes, he had encountered the indicating smile. Then the intoxicating cloud that had been just on the point of melting away, seemed to condense itself anew in his brain, in the vague form of the creature of music; and he fancied that she held in her hand the flower of flame, as, in a dominating attitude, she emerged above his inward agitation as from the trembling waves of a summer sea.

As if to celebrate that image, from the Hall of the Greater Council came the first notes of the symphony of Benedetto Marcello, the fugue-like movement of which revealed at once its grand style. A sonorous idea, clear and strong as a living person, developed itself in the powerful measure; and in that melody Stelio recognized the virtue of the same principle around which, as around a thyrsus, he had twined the garlands of his poesy.

Then the name that had already resounded against the sides of the vessel, in the silence and the shadow, that name which, in the great wave of sound from the evening bells, had been lost like a sibylline leaf, seemed to his fancy to propose its syllables to the orchestra as a new theme to be interpreted by the musicians' bows. The violins, viols, and violoncellos sang it in turn; the sudden blasts of the heroic trumpets exalted it; and at last a whole quartette, in one great, thrilling chord, flung it toward that heaven of joy where later would sparkle the starry crown offered to Ariadne by the golden Aphrodite.

In the pause that followed, Stelio experienced a singular agitation, almost like a religious ecstasy, before that annunciation. He realized what it was worth to him, in that inestimable lyric moment, to find himself alone amid this group of white and motionless statues. A shred of the same mystery which, under the quarter of the ship, had seemed to float lightly across his senses like a misty veil, again waved before his eyes in that deserted hall, which was so near to the human throng. It was like the silence of the sea-shell, lying on the shore beside the stormy ocean. He again felt a conviction, such as he had already experienced in certain extraordinary hours of his journey, of the presence of his fate, which was about to give to his spirit a new impulse, perhaps to quicken within him a marvelous act of will. And, as he remembered the thousands of obscure destinies hanging over the heads of that crowd, which had been so stirred by his images of an ideal life, he congratulated himself on being able to adore alone the propitious demon that came to visit him secretly, to offer to him a veiled gift, in the name of an unknown mistress.

He thrilled at the burst of human voices that saluted with triumphal acclamation the unvanquished god.

Viva il forte, viva il grande!

The vast hall resounded like a great timbrel, and the reverberation penetrated through the Censors' Stairway, the Golden Stairway, the corridors and the vestibules

35

to the furthermost parts of the palace, like a thunder of joy echoing in the serene night.

Viva il forte, viva il grande!
Vincitor dell' Indie dome!

It seemed indeed that the chorus was saluting the apparition of the magnificent god invoked by the poet on the City Beautiful. It seemed that in those vocal notes the folds of his purple draperies quivered like flames in a crystal tube. The living image hung suspended over the assemblage, which nourished it with its own dream.

Viva il forte, viva il grande!

In the impetuous fugue movement, the bass, the contraltos, the sopranos repeated the frenzied acclamation to the Immortal of the thousand names and the thousand crowns, "born on an ineffable bed, like to a young man in his first youth."

The old Dionysian intoxication seemed born again, diffusing itself through that divine chorus. The fulness and freshness of life in the smile of Zeus, who freed men's souls from sadness, expressed itself in a luminous outburst of joy. The torches of the Bacchantes blazed and crackled in the sound. As in an Orphic hymn, the brightness of conflagration illumined that youthful brow, surmounted by azure hair. "When the splendor of fire invaded the whole earth, he alone checked the whirlwinds of flame." As in the Homeric hymn, there palpitated the sterile bosom of the sea, expressing in regular cadences the measured stroke of the oars that propelled the stout vessel toward unknown lands. The Flower-bearer, the Fructifier, the visible Remedy for mortal man, the sacred Flower, The Friend of Pleasure, Dionysius, the liberator, suddenly appeared before mankind on the wings of song, crowning for them that nocturnal hour with happiness, placing before them once more the cup overflowing with all the good things of life.

The song increased in power; all the voices blended in the rush of melody. The hymn celebrated the tamer of tigers, of panthers, lions and lynxes. A cry seemed to rise from Mænads with heads turned backward, flying locks and floating robes, who struck their cymbals and shook their castanets: Evoé!

But now suddenly surged above these heroic measures a broad, pastoral rhythm, invoking the Theban Bacchus, of the pure brow and gentle thoughts:

Quel che all'olmo la vite in stretto nodo
Pronuba accoppia, e i pampini feconda ...

Only two voices, in a succession of sixths, now sang the flowery nuptials, the leafy marriage, the flexible bonds. Before the eyes of the multitude again passed that image already created by the poet of the barque laden with clusters, like a vat filled with grapes to be made into wine. And again the song seemed to recall the miracle witnessed by the prudent pilot Medeia: "And behold! a sweet and fragrant wine ran

36

over the swift, black boat.... And behold! a vine climbed to the top of the sail, and from it hung innumerable clusters of grapes. And a dark ivy twined about the mast, and it was covered with flowers, and beautiful fruits amid their foliage grew thereon, and garlands were wound about the rowlocks."

The spirit of the fugue then passed into the orchestra, and mounted in exquisitely light roulades, while the voices struck on the orchestral web with simultaneous percussion. And, like a thyrsus waving over the Bacchic troop, a single voice floated out in the nuptial melody, with the laughing joy and grace of the pastoral marriage:

Viva dell'olmo,
E della vite
L'almo fecondo
Sostenitor!

The voices seemed to evoke the image of erect and graceful Tiades, gently waving their thyrsi in the mists of divine intoxication, dressed in long saffron-hued robes, their faces lighted up, ardent as those women of Veronese, who leaned over their aerial balconies to listen to the song.

But the heroic acclamation once more sprang up with final vehemence. The face of the conquering god reappeared amid torches frantically waved aloft. Then, in unison, in a supreme burst of joy, voices and orchestra thundered together at the many-eyed chimera under the suspended treasure of that dome circled by red triremes, armed towers, and triumphal bands:

Viva dell'Indie,
Viva de' mari,
Viva de' mostri
Il domator.

Stelio Effrena had gone as far as the threshold; through the throng that made way before him he penetrated into the hall and halted near the platform occupied by the orchestra and the singers. His restless eyes sought La Foscarina near the celestial sphere, but did not find her. The head of the Tragic Muse no longer rose above the constellations. Where was she? To what place has she withdrawn? Could she see him, although he could not see her? A confused anxiety agitated him, and the remembrance of the early evening on the water returned to him indistinctly, accompanied by the words of her recent promise. Glancing up at the open balconies, he thought that perhaps she had stepped outside to breathe the fresh night air, and that, perhaps, leaning against the balustrade she felt passing over her cool throat the wave of music, which would seem as sweet to her as the delight of a kiss from beloved lips.

But his impatience to hear the divine voice dominated all other impatience, abolished all other desire. He observed that again a profound silence reigned throughout the hall, as at the instant when he had opened his lips to speak his first

37

word. And, as at that instant, the versatile and ephemeral monster, with a thousand human faces, seemed to extend itself and yawn to receive a new soul.

Some one near Stelio whispered the name of Donatella Arvale. He turned his eyes toward the platform, past the row of violoncellos, which formed a brown hedge. The singer remained invisible, hidden in the delicate, quivering forest of bows, whence would arise the mournful harmony that must accompany the Lament of Ariadne.

Amid a sympathetic silence rose a prelude of violins. Then the viols and violoncellos added a sigh more profound to that imploring plaint. Was not this— after the Phrygian flute and the castanets, after the instruments of orgies, which trouble the reason and provoke delirium—was not this the august Doric lyre, grave and sweet, the harmonious support of song? Thus was the Drama born from the boisterous Dithyramb. The great metamorphosis of the Dionysian rite, the frenzy of the sacred festival before the creative inspiration of the tragic poet, were figured in that musical alternance. The fiery breath of the Thracian god gave life to a sublime form of Art. The crown and the tripod, the prize of the poet's victory, had displaced the lascivious goat and the Attic basket of figs. Æschylus, keeper of a vineyard, had been visited by the god, who had infused into him his spirit of flame. On the bank of the Acropolis, near the sanctuary of Dionysius, a marble theater had risen, capable of containing the chosen people.

Thus suddenly opened in the mind of the Master the pathways of centuries, extending through the distance of primitive mysteries. That form of Art, toward which now tended the effort of his genius, attracted by the obscure aspirations of human multitudes, appeared to him in the sanctity of its origins. The divine sadness of Ariadne, up-springing like a melodious cry from the furious Thiaros, made leap once more within him the work he nourished in his soul, unformed yet alive. With a glance, again he sought the Muse of the revealing voice against the sphere of constellations, but he did not see her, and turned once more to the forest of instruments, whence rose the imploring plaint.

Then, amid the slender bows, that rose and fell upon the strings with alternating movement, appeared the singer, erect as a stem; and, like a stem, she seemed to balance herself an instant on the softened harmony. The youthfulness of her agile and robust body shone resplendent through the texture of her robes, as a flame is seen through the thinness of polished ivory. Rising and falling around her white form, the bows seemed to draw their melody from the secret music that dwelt within her. When her lips opened in an enchanting curve, Stelio recognized the strength and purity of the voice before the singer had uttered one modulation, as if she were a crystal statue wherein he could behold the unspringing of a jet of living water.

Come mai puoi
Vedermi piangere?
The melody of a by-gone love and long-dead sorrow flowed from those lips with an expression so pure and strong that suddenly, within the soul of the

multitude, it was changed into a mysterious happiness. Was that strain indeed the divine plaint of the daughter of Minos, as she held out her arms in vain to the fair Stranger on the deserted shore of Naxos? The fable vanished; the illusion of the moment was abolished. The eternal love and eternal sorrow of gods and of men were exhaled in that perfect voice. The futile regret for each lost joy, the recollection of each fugitive blessing, the supreme prayer flying toward every sail on the sea, toward every sun hiding itself among the mountains, the implacable desire and the promise of death—all these things passed into the great, solitary song, transformed by the power of Art into sublime essences which the soul could receive without suffering. The words were dissolved in tone, losing their significance, changed into notes of love and sadness, indefinitely illuminating. Like a circle that is closed, and yet dilates continually in accordance with the rhythm of universal life, the melody encircled the composite soul which dilated with it in immeasurable joy. Through the open balconies, in the perfect calm of the autumn night, the enchantment spread over the peaceful waters and mounted to the watchful stars, higher than the motionless masts of the ships, higher than the sacred towers, inhabited by the now silent bronze bells. During the interludes the singer drooped her youthful head and stood motionless as a white statue among the forest of instruments, where the long bows rose and fell in alternate movement, perhaps unconscious of that world which in a few brief moments her song had transfigured.

CHAPTER V
THE EPIPHANY OF THE FLAME
Descending to the courtyard hastily, in order to escape importunate curiosity, Stelio took refuge in a shadowy corner, to watch, among the crowd coming down the Giants' Stairway, for the appearance of the two women, the actress and the singer, who were to meet him near the well.

Every instant his expectation became more anxious, while around him rose the tumultuous cry that extended to the outer walls of the palace and lost itself among the clouds, now lighted with a glare as of a conflagration. An almost terrible joy seemed to spread over the Anadyomenean City, as if a vehement breath had suddenly dilated all breasts, filling the veins of all men with a superabundance of life. The repetition of the Bacchic Chorus celebrating the crown of stars, placed by Aphrodite on the forgetful head of Ariadne, had drawn a cry from the throng on the Molo beneath the open balconies. When, at the final elevation, the word Viva! rang out from the chorus of Mænads, Satyrs, and Egipans, the chorus of the populace had responded to it like a formidable echo from the harbor of San Marco. And in this moment of Dionysian delirium it seemed as if the people remembered the forests of old that were burned on sacred nights, and had given a signal for the conflagration that must light up the beauty of Venice in final, dazzling splendor.

The dream of Paris Eglano—the spectacle of marvelous flames offered to love on a floating couch—flashed before Stelio's vision. The persistent image of Donatella Arvale lingered in his thought: a supple, youthful figure, strong and shapely, rising erect amid the sonorous forest of bows, which seemed to draw their notes from the hidden music within herself. And, seized with a strange distress,

39

through which passed something like the shadow of horror, he saw the image of the other woman: poisoned by art, worn with experience, with the taste of maturity and worldly corruptness on those eloquent lips, a feverish dryness in those hands, which had pressed the juice from deceitful fruits, and with the marks of a thousand masks on the face that had simulated the fury of all mortal passions. To-night, at last, after a long period of waiting and of hope, he was to receive the gift of that heart, no longer young, which had been claimed by others before him, but which he never yet had called his own. How his heart had throbbed in the early evening as he sat beside that silent woman, floating toward the City Beautiful over the waters that seemed to bear them on with the terrifying smoothness of mysterious machinery. Ah, why did she come now to meet him in company with the other temptress? Why did she place beside her despair and worldly wisdom the pure splendor of innocent youth?

He started suddenly as he perceived in the throng at the top of the marble staircase, by the light of the smoking torches, the form of La Foscarina pressed so closely against that of Donatella Arvale that the robes of both blended into one mass of whiteness. He followed them with his eyes until they reached the lowest stair, anxious as if at each step they had approached the edge of an abyss. The unknown during these hours had already led in the heart of the poet a life so intense that on seeing her approach him he experienced the emotion that would have seized him before a breathing incarnation of one of the ideal creatures born of his art.

She descended slowly on the human wave. Behind her, the Palace of the Doges, filled with streams of lights and confused sounds, made one think of those fairy-tale awakenings which suddenly, in the depths of the forest, transfigure inaccessible castles where for centuries the hair on royal heads had grown longer and longer during a protracted sleep. The two guardian Giants shone red in the blaze of the torches; the cuspid of the Golden Gate sparkled with tiny lights. And still the clamor rose and swelled above the groups of marbles, loud as the moaning of the stormy sea against the walls of Malamocco.

In this tumult, Effrena saw advancing toward him the two temptresses, escaping from the crowd as if from the clasp of a monster. And his fancy pictured extraordinary assimilations, which should be realized with the ease of dreams and the solemnity of liturgic ceremonies. He said to himself that Perdita was leading this magnificent prey to him, that he might discover some rarely beautiful secret, that some great work of love might be accomplished, in which she desired to be his fellow artisan. He told himself that this very night she would say to him most marvelous words. Across his spirit passed once again the indefinable melancholy he had felt when he leaned over the bronze rim to contemplate the reflection of the stars in that dark mirror; he waited in expectation of some event that should stir that secret soul in the furthermost depths of his being, where it lay motionless, strange, intangible. By the whirling of his thoughts, he comprehended that he was again plunged into that delirium which the glamor of the lagoon had given him at twilight. Then, emerging from the shadowy corner, he went forward to meet the two women with an intoxicating presentiment.

40

"Oh, Effrena!" said La Foscarina, as she reached the well, "I had given up all hope of finding you here. We are very late, are we not? But we were caught in the crowd and could not escape."

Then, turning toward her companion with a smile, she said:

"Donatella, this is the Master of the Flame."

Without speaking, but with a slight smile, Donatella Arvale responded to the low bow of the young man.

"We must find our gondola," said La Foscarina. "It is waiting for us at the Ponte della Paglia. Will you come with us, Effrena? We must profit by the opportunity. The crowd is rushing toward the Piazzetta. The Queen will leave by the Porta della Carta."

A long, unanimous cry saluted the appearance of the fair Queen in her pearls, as she stood at the head of the stairs, where long ago, in the presence of the populace, the Doge received the ducal ensign. Again the name of the white starry flower and the pearl arose from the crowd and was echoed among the marbles. Flashes of joy sparkled against the dark sky, a thousand fiery doves flew from the pinnacles of San Marco, like messengers of Fire.

"The Epiphany of the Flame!" cried La Foscarina, as she reached the Molo and gazed upon the marvelous spectacle.

Donatella Arvale and Stelio Effrena stood side by side, astonished; then they looked into each other's eyes, bewildered. And their faces, illumined by the reflections, shone as if they were leaning over a furnace or a glowing crater.

All the innumerable appearances of the volatile and multi-colored Fire spread over the firmament, crept over the waters, curled around the masts of the ships, enwreathed the cupolas and the towers, adorned the friezes, draped the statuary, bejeweled the capitals, enriched every line and transfigured every aspect of the sacred and profane architectures around that profound and mysterious watery mirror, which multiplied these marvels. The astonished eye could no longer distinguish between the contour and the quality of the elements, but it was charmed by a moving vision wherein all forms lived a lucid, fluid life, suspended in vibrating ether, so that the slender prows curving over the waves and the myriad of golden doves against the dark sky seemed to rival one another in the glory of swift motion, and together to reach the summit of immaterial beauty. That which in the twilight had seemed a silvery palace of Neptune, built in imitation of a rare shell, at this hour had become a new temple, erected by the nimble genii of the Fire. It seemed like one of those labyrinthian constructions of our dreams, prodigiously enlarged, that rise on andirons, at the hundred gates of which stand the two-faced augurs who make ambiguous gestures to the watching maiden; or like one of those fairy-like red palaces, at the thousand windows of which appear the faces of salamander princesses, who smile amorously upon the dreaming poet.

41

Rosy as a setting moon, the sphere of the Fortuna, borne on the shoulders of the Atlantides, radiated on the triple loggia, its rays engendering a cycle of satellites. From the Riva, from San Giorgio, from the Giudecca, with a continual crackling, clusters of fiery stems rose toward the clouds, and there blossomed into sparkling roses, lilies, and palms, a flowery paradise, forming an aerial garden that continually faded and bloomed again with yet stranger and richer blossoms. It was like a rapid succession of springs and autumns in the empyrean. An immense sparkling shower of leaves and petals fell from the celestial dissolutions, enveloping all things in its golden shimmer.

From a distance, through gaps in the glittering rain, a flotilla gay with flags could be seen approaching over the waters of the lagoon: a fairy-like fleet such as might float through the dream of a sybarite sleeping his last sleep on a bed steeped in deadly perfumes. Like those, perhaps, their ropes were made from the twisted hair of slaves captured in conquered cities, and still redolent of fragrant oils; like those, perhaps, their hulls were laden with myrrh, spikenard, benzoin, cinnamon, aromatic herbs; with sandal-wood, cedar, terebinth, and all oderiferous woods in rich profusion. The indescribable colors of the flags suggested perfumes and spices. Of blue-green peacock shades, saffron, violet, and indistinct hues, those flaming flags seemed to spring from some burning interior and to have been colored by some unknown process.

"The Epiphany of the Flame!" repeated La Foscarina. "What an unforeseen commentary on your poem, Effrena! The City of Life responds by a miracle to your act of adoration. She burns, through her watery veil. Are you not satisfied? Look! Millions of golden pomegranates are hanging everywhere!"

The actress was smiling, her face illumined by the magic fire. She was suddenly possessed by that singular gayety of hers which Stelio knew well, and which, because of its effect of incongruity with her usual pose, suggested to him the image of a dark, closed house where violent hands had suddenly opened on rusty hinges all the doors and windows.

"We must praise Ariadne," he replied, "for having uttered, in all this harmony, the most sublime note."

Stelio said those flattering words only to induce the fair singer to speak, only through a desire to know the timbre of that voice when it descended from the heights of song. But his praise was lost in the reiterated clamor of the crowd, which overflowed on the Molo, making a longer stay impossible. From the bank, Stelio assisted the two friends into their gondola; then he sat down on a stool at their knees, and the long, dentellated prow sparkled, like all else, in the magic fire.

"To the Rio Marin, by the Grand Canal," La Foscarina ordered the gondolier. "Do you know, Effrena, we are to have at supper some of your best friends: Francesco de Lizo, Daniele Glauro, Prince Hoditz, Antimo della Bella, Fabio Molza, Baldassare Stampa"—

42

"Then it will be a banquet?"

"But not, alas! like that of Cana."

"And will not Lady Myrta, with her Veronese greyhounds, be there?"

"Rest assured that we shall have Lady Myrta. Did you not see her in the hall? She sat in the first row, lost in admiration of you."

Because they had looked into each other's eyes as they spoke, a sudden emotion seized them. The remembrance of that full twilight hour on the water that rippled beneath their oar filled their hearts with a wave of troubled blood; and each was surprised by a swift return of the same agitation felt when leaving the silent estuary already in the power of shadow and death. Their lips refused to utter vain, light words; their souls refused to make the effort to incline themselves through prudence toward the passing trivialities of the superficial life, which now seemed worthless to both; and their spirits became absorbed in the contemplation of the strange fancies that rose from their inmost thoughts in a garb of indescribable richness, like the heaped-up treasures the streams of light seemed to reveal in the depths of the nocturnal waters.

And, because of that very silence, they felt the presence of the singer weigh heavily upon them, as in the moment when her name had first been spoken between them; and little by little the oppression became intolerable. Although Stelio was seated close to her, she appeared no less distant than when she rose above the forest of instruments; she was as absent and unconscious as she had been when her voice soared high in song. She had not yet spoken.

Simply to hear her speak, and almost timidly, Stelio said:

"Shall you remain some time longer in Venice?"

He had pondered on the first words he should say to her, but was dissatisfied with whatever rose to his lips, for all phrases seemed too vivid, insidious, full of ambiguous significance, capable of infinite changes and transformations, like the unknown seed from which may spring a thousand roots. And it seemed to him that Perdita could not hear one of those phrases without feeling that a shadow darkened her love.

After he had spoken those simple, conventional words, he reflected that even that question might suggest an infinity of hope and eagerness.

"I must leave Venice to-morrow," Donatella replied. "I ought not to be here even now."

Her voice, so clear and powerful in the heights of song, was low and sober, as if suffused with a slight opacity, suggesting the image of the most precious metal

43

wrapped in the most delicate velvet. Her brief reply indicated that there was a place of suffering to which she must return, where she must undergo some familiar torture. Like iron tempered with tears, a strong though sorrowful will shone through the veil of her youthful beauty.

"To-morrow!" Stelio exclaimed, not seeking to hide his sincere regret. "Have you heard, Signora?"

"I know," the actress replied, gently taking Donatella's hand. "I am filled with regret to see her go. But she cannot remain away longer from her father. Perhaps you do not yet know"—

"What?" asked Stelio quickly. "Is he ill? Is it true, then, that Lorenzo Arvale is ill?"

"No, he is only fatigued," said La Foscarina, touching her forehead with a gesture perhaps involuntary but which revealed to Stelio the horrible menace hanging over the genius of the artist who had seemed as fertile and indefatigable as one of the old masters—a Della Robbia or a Verrocchio.

"He is only fatigued," repeated La Foscarina. "He needs repose and quiet. And his daughter's singing is very soothing to him. Do you not believe, also, Effrena, in the healing power of music?"

"Certainly," Stelio replied, "Ariadne possesses a divine gift whereby her power transcends all limits."

The name of Ariadne came spontaneously to his lips to indicate the singer as she appeared to his fancy, for it seemed to him impossible to pronounce the young girl's real name preceded by the ordinary appellation imposed by social usage. In his eyes she was perfect and singular, free from the little ties of custom, living her own sequestered life, like a work of art on which style had set its inviolable seal. He thought of her as isolated like those figures that stand out with clear contour, far from common life, lost in mystic reverie; and already, before that impenetrable character, he felt a sort of passionate impatience, somewhat similar to that of a curious man before something hermetically sealed that tempts him.

"Ariadne had for the soothing of her griefs the gift of forgetfulness," said Donatella, "and that I do not possess."

A bitterness perhaps involuntary infused these words, in which Stelio fancied he detected the indication of an aspiration toward a life less oppressed by useless suffering. He guessed at her revolt against a certain form of domestic slavery, the horror of her self-imposed sacrifice, her vehement desire to rise toward joy, and her inborn aptitude for being drawn like a beautiful bow by a strong hand that would know how to use it for some high conquest. He divined that she had no longer any hope of her father's recovery, and that she was saddened at the thought that henceforth she could only be the guardian of a darkened hearth, of ashes without a

44

spark. The image of the great artist rose in his mind, not as he was, since Stelio never had known him personally, but such as he had fancied the sculptor after studying his ideas of beauty expressed in imperishable bronze and marble. His mind fixed itself on that image with a sensation of terror more icy than that which the most appalling aspects of death could have inspired. And all his strength, all his pride and his ardor seemed to resound within him like weapons shaken by a menacing hand, sending a quiver through every fiber of his heart.

Presently La Foscarina lifted the funereal black curtain, which suddenly, amid the splendors of the festival, had seemed to change the gondola into a coffin.

"Look!" she said, pointing out to Stelio the balcony of Desdemona's palace: "See the beautiful Nineta receiving the homage of the Serenade, as she sits between her pet monkey and her little dog."

"Ah, the beautiful Nineta!" said Stelio, rousing himself from his wild thoughts, and saluting the smiling occupant of the balcony, a little woman who was listening to the music, her face illumined from two silver candelabra, from the branches of which hung wreaths of the last roses of the year. "I have not yet seen her this time. She is the gentlest and most graceful animal I know. How fortunate was our dear Howitz to discover her behind the lid of an old harpsichord when he was rummaging in that curiosity shop at San Samuele! Two pieces of good fortune in one day: the lovely Nineta and a harpsichord lid painted by Pordenone. Since that day, the harmony of his life has been complete. How I should like to have you penetrate to his nest! You would find there a perfect example of that which I spoke of this evening, at twilight. There is a man who, by obeying his native taste for simplicity, has arranged for himself with minute art his own little love-story, in which he lives as happily as did his Moravian ancestor in the Arcady of Rosswald. Ah! I know a thousand exquisite things about him!"

A large gondola, decorated with many-colored lanterns, and laden with singers and musicians, had stopped beneath the balcony of Desdemona's house. The old song of brief youth and fleeting beauty rose sweetly toward the little woman who listened with her child-like smile, sitting between the monkey and the lapdog, making a group like one of Pietro Longhi's prints.

Do beni vu gharè
Beleza e zoventù;
Co i va no i torna più,
Nina mia cara....
"Does it not seem to you, Effrena, that these surroundings express the true soul of Venice, and that the other picture, which you presented to the multitude, is only your own fancy?" said La Foscarina, nodding her head slightly in time with the rhythm of the sweet song that spread through the Grand Canal and was reechoed from afar by singers in other gondolas.

"No," Stelio replied, "this does not at all represent the true soul of Venice. In each one of us, fluttering like a butterfly over the surface of our deeper nature, is a

45

lighter soul, an animula, a little playful sprite that often dominates us for the moment, and leads us toward simple and mediocre pleasures, toward puerile pastimes and frivolous music. This animula vagula exists even in the gravest and most violent natures, like the clown attached to the person of Othello; and sometimes it misleads our better judgment. That which you hear now, in the songs and the melodies of the guitars, is the animula, or lighter spirit, of Venice; but her real soul is discovered only in silence, and most terribly, be assured, in full summer, at noonday, like the soul of the great god Pan. Out in the harbor of San Marco, I thought that you felt its mystic vibration during those moments of the great conflagration. You are forgetting Giorgione for Rosalba!"

Around the large gondola beneath the balcony had gathered other gondolas bearing languid women who leaned out to listen to the music in attitudes of graceful abandon, as if in fancy they felt themselves sinking into invisible arms. And around this romantic group the reflections of the lanterns in the water quivered like a flowering of rare and luminous water-lilies.

Se lassarè passar
La bela e fresca età,
Un zorno i ve dirà
Vechia maura,
E bramarè, ma invan,
Quel che ghavevi in man
Co avè lassà scampar
La congiontura.

It was, in truth, the song of the last roses that entwined the candelabra. It called up in Perdita's mind the funeral cortège of the dead Summer, the opalescent veil in which Stelio had wrapped the sweet body in its golden robe. Through the glass, sealed by the Master of Fire, she could see her own image at the bottom of the lagoon, lying on a field of seaweed. A sudden chill stole over her; once more she felt horror and disgust of her own body, no longer young. And, remembering her recent promise, thinking that perhaps this very night the beloved one would claim its fulfilment, she shuddered with a sort of sorrowful modesty, a mingling of fear and pride. Her experience and despairing eyes ran over the young girl beside her, studying her, penetrating her, realizing her occult but certain power, her intact freshness, pure health, and that indefinable virtue of love that emanates like an aroma from chaste maidens when they have arrived at the perfection of their bloom. She felt that some secret current of affinity existed between this fair creature and the poet; she could almost divine the words he addressed to her in the silence of his heart. A bitter pang seized her, so intolerable that, with an involuntary movement, her fingers clutched convulsively the black rope of the arm-rest beside her, so that the little metal griffin that held it creaked audibly.

This movement did not escape Stelio's anxious vigilance. He understood her agitation, and for a moment he experienced the same pang, but it was mingled with impatience and almost with anger, for her anguish, like a cry of destruction, interrupted the fiction of transcendent life that he had been constructing within himself in order to conciliate the contrast, to conquer this new force that offered

46

itself to him like a bow to be drawn, yet at the same time not to lose the savor of that ripe maturity which life had impregnated with all its essences, and the benefit of that devotion and that passionate faith which sharpened his intelligence and fed his pride.

"Ah, Perdita!" he said to himself, "From the ferment of your human loves, why has not a love more than human sprung. Ah, why have I finally vanquished you by my pleading, although I know it is too late? and why do you allow me to read in your eyes the certainty of your yielding, amid a flood of doubts which, nevertheless, never again will have power to reëstablish the abolished interdiction. Each of us knows full well that that interdiction conferred the highest dignity upon our long communion, yet we have not known how to preserve its rule, and at the last hour we yield blindly to an imperious internal call. Yet, a short time ago, when your noble head dominated the belt of constellations, I no longer saw in you an earthly love, but the illuminating, revelatory Muse of my poetry; and all my heart went out to you in gratitude, not for the promise of a fleeting happiness, but for the promise of glory. Do you not understand—you, who understand everything? By a marvelous inspiration, such as always comes to you, have you not turned my inclination, by the ray of your smile, toward a resplendent youthfulness which you have chosen and reserved for me? When you descended the stairway together, and approached me, had you not the appearance of one that bears a gift or an unexpected message? Not wholly unexpected, perhaps, Perdita! For I have anticipated from your infinite wisdom some extraordinary action toward me."

"How happy the beautiful Nineta is, with her monkey and her little dog!" sighed the actress, looking back at the light songsters and the smiling woman on the balcony.

La zoventù xe un fior
Che apena nato el mor,
E un zorno gnanca mi
No sarò quela.
Donatella Arvale and Stelio also looked back, while the light barque, without sinking, bore over the water and past the music the three faces of a heavy destiny.

E vegna quel che vol,
Lassè che voga!
Suddenly, in front of the red palace of the Foscari, at the curve of the canal, they saw the state vessel of the Doge of Venice so brightly illumined that it looked like a burning tower. New streaks of fire flashed against the sky. Other flaming doves flew up from the deck, rose above the terraces, sank among the statues, hissed as they fell into the water, multiplied themselves in thousands of sparks, and floated along in smoke. Along the parapets, from the decks, the poop, the prow, in a simultaneous explosion, a thousand fountains of fire opened, dilated, blended, illuminating with an intense, fiery radiance each side of the canal as far as San Vitale and the Rialto. Then the vessel of the Doge glided out of sight, transformed into a purple thunder-cloud.

47

"Go through San Polo!" called La Foscarina to the gondolier, bending her head as under a storm, and shutting out the roar with her palms over her ears.

Again Donatella Arvale and Stelio Effreno looked at each other with dazzled eyes. Again their faces, lighted by the glare, glowed as if they were leaning over a furnace or a burning crater.

The gondola turned into the canal of San Polo, gliding along through the darkness. A cold shadow seemed suddenly to fall over the spirits of the three silent occupants. Under the arch of the bridge, the hollow echo of the dipping oar struck upon their souls, and the hilarity of the festival sounded infinitely far-away. All the houses were dark; the campanile rose silent and solitary toward the stars; the Campiello del Remer and the Campiello del Pistor were deserted, and the grass breathed there in untrodden peace; the trees, bending over the low walls of the little gardens, seemed to feel their leaves dying on the branches pointing to the serene sky.

CHAPTER VI
THE POET'S DREAM
"So, for a few hours at least, the rhythm of Art and the pulse of Life have again throbbed in unison in Venice," said Daniele Glauro, raising from the table an exquisite chalice, to which only the Sacred Host was wanting. "Allow me to express, for myself and also for the many that are absent, the gratitude and fervor that blend in one single image of beauty the three persons to whom we owe this miracle: the mistress of the feast, the daughter of Lorenzo Arvale, and the poet of Persephone."

"And why the mistress of the feast, Glauro?" asked La Foscarina, smiling in graceful surprise. "I, like you, have not given joy, but have received it. Donatella and the Master of the Flame: they alone merit the crown; and to them alone the glory must be given."

"But, a short time ago, in the Hall of the Greater Council," said the mystic doctor, "your silent presence beside the celestial sphere was not less eloquent than the words of Stelio, nor less musical than the song of Ariadne. Once again you have divinely carved your own statue in silence, and it will live in our memories blended with the music and the words."

Stelio shuddered as he recalled to mind the ephemeral flexible monster from the side of which had emerged the Tragic Muse above the sphere of constellations.

"That is true, very true," said Francesco de Lizo. "I, too, had the same thought. As we looked at you, we all realized that you were the soul of that ideal world which each of us forms for himself, according to his own aspirations and thoughts when listening to the mystic word, the song, the symphony."

48

"And each of us," said Fabio Molza, "felt that in your presence, dominating the throng, before the poet, dwelt a great and rare significance."

"One might almost have said that you alone were about to assist at the mysterious birth of a new idea," said Antimo della Bella. "Everything around us seemed awakening itself to produce it—that idea which must soon be revealed to us, as a reward for the profound faith with which we have awaited it."

The Animator, with another trembling of the heart, felt the work that he cherished within him leap once more, formless yet, but already living; and his whole soul, as if impelled by a lyric breath, suddenly felt drawn toward the fertile and enlightening power that emanated from the Dionysian woman to whom these fervent spirits addressed their praise.

Suddenly she had become very beautiful: a nocturnal creature, fashioned by dreams and passion on a golden anvil, living embodiment of immortal fate and eternal enigmas. She might remain motionless and silent, but her famous accents and her memorable gestures seemed to live around her, vibrating indefinitely, as melodies seem to hover over the cords accustomed to sound them, as rhymes seem to breathe from the poet's closed book, wherein love and sorrow seek comfort and intoxication. The heroic fidelity of Antigone, the oracular fury of Cassandra, the devouring fever of Phædre, the cruelty of Medea, the sacrifice of Iphigenia, Myrrha before her father, Polyxenes and Alceste before the face of death, Cleopatra, fitful as the wind and the fires of the world, Lady Macbeth, the dreamy murderess with the little hands; and those great, fair lilies empearled with dew and tears—Imogen, Juliet, Miranda, Rosalind, Jessica, and Perdita—the tenderest, most terrible, and most magnificent souls dwelt within her, inhabited her body, shone from her eyes, breathed through her lips, which knew both honey and poison, the jeweled chalice and the cup of wormwood. Thus, through unlimited space, and endless, the outlines of human life and substance appeared to perpetuate themselves; and from the simple movement of a muscle, a sign, a start, a quiver of the eyelids, a slight change of color, an almost imperceptible inclination of the head, a fugitive play of light and shade, a lightning-like virtue of expression radiating from that frail and slender body, infinite worlds of imperishable beauty were continually generated.

The genii of the places consecrated by poetry hovered around her, and encircled her with changing visions: the dusty plain of Thebes, the arid Argolide, the parched myrtles of Trezene, the sacred olives of Colonus, the triumphant Cydnus, the pale country of Dunsinane, Prospero's cavern, the Forest of Arden, land dampened with blood, toiled upon with pain, transfigured by a dream or illumined by an inextinguishable smile, seemed to appear, to recede, then to vanish behind her head. And a vision of countries still more remote—regions of mists, northern lands, and, far across the ocean, the immense continent where she had appeared like an unknown force amid astonished multitudes, bearer of the mystic word and the flame of genius—vanished behind her head: the throngs, the mountains, rivers and gulfs, the impure cities, the ancient, enfeebled, savage race, the strong people aspiring to dominate the world, the new nation that wrests from Nature her most secret energies to make them serve an all-powerful work in erecting edifices of iron and of

49

crystal; the bastard colonies that ferment and grow corrupt on virgin soil; all the barbarous crowds she had visited as the messenger of Latin genius; all the ignorant masses to whom she had spoken the sublime language of Dante; all the human herds from which had mounted toward her, on a wave of confused anxieties and desires, the aspiration to Beauty.

She stood there, a creature of perishable flesh, subject to the sad laws of time, but an illimitable mass of reality and poetry weighed upon her, surged around her, palpitated with the rhythm of her breath. And not upon the stage alone had she uttered her cries and suppressed her sobs: this had entered into her daily life. She had loved, fought and suffered violently, in her soul and in her body. What loves? What combats? What pangs? From what abysses of melancholy had she drawn the exaltations of her tragic force? At what springs of bitterness had she watered her free genius? She had certainly witnessed the crudest misery, the darkest ruin; she had known heroic effort, pity, horror, and the threshold of death. All her thirst had burned in the delirium of Phædre, and in the submissiveness of Imogen had trembled all her tenderness. Thus Life and Art, the irrevocable Past and the eternal Present, had made her profound, many-souled, and mysterious, had magnified her ambiguous destiny beyond human limits, and rendered her equal to great temples and natural forests.

Nevertheless, she stood there, a living, breathing woman, under the gaze of the poets, each of whom saw her, and yet in her many others.

"Ah! I will embrace you as in some mad revelry; I will clasp you, shake you; from your ripe experience, I will draw all the divine and abnormal secrets that weigh upon you—the things you have already done, and those on which you still meditate in the mysterious depths of your soul," sang the lyric demon in the ear of the poet, who recognized in the mystery of this woman the surviving power of primitive myth, the renewed initiation of the god that had concentrated in one single ferment all the energies of Nature, and, by a variety of rhythms, had raised, in an enthusiastic worship of himself, the senses and the spirit of man to the highest summits of joy and of pain.

"I have done well, I have done wisely, to wait!" said Stelio to himself. "The passing of years, the tumult of dreams, the agitation of struggle and the swiftness of triumph, the experience of many loves, the enchantment of poets, the acclamations of the people; the marvels of earth, the patience and the fury, the steps in the mud, the blind flight, all evil, all good, that which I know and do not know, that which you know, as well as that which you are ignorant of—all this had to be to prepare the fulness of this night, which belongs to me!"

He felt himself suffocate and turn pale. A wild impulse seized him by the throat, and would not relax its hold. His heart swelled with the same keen emotion that had possessed both in the twilight, as they floated over the water.

And, as the exaggerated radiance of the city and the event had suddenly disappeared, the glory of this woman of the night reappeared to his mind still more

50

closely blended with the city of the wonderful necklaces and the thousand emerald girdles. In the city and in the woman, the poet now saw a power of expression that he never had seen before: each glowed in the Autumn night; the same feverish fire that coursed through the canals ran also in her veins.

The stars sparkled, the trees waved their branches behind Perdita's head, back of which were the shadows of a garden. Through the open balconies the sweet air of heaven entered the room; shook the flames of the candelabra and the chalices of flowers; swept through the doorways, making the draperies wave to and fro, animating that old house of the Capello, wherein the last great daughter of San Marco whom the people had covered with gold and glory had gathered relics of republican magnificence. Galleon lamps, Turkish targets, bronze helmets, leathern quivers, and velvet scabbards ornamented the apartments inhabited by the last descendant of that marvelous Cesare Darbes who maintained the Art of Comedy against the Goldonian reform, and changed the agony of the Most Serene Republic into a burst of laughter.

"I only ask that I may be the humble servitor of that idea," was La Foscarina's reply to Antimo della Bella's words. Her voice trembled a little, her eyes had met Stelio's gaze.

"You alone could make it triumphant," said Francesco de Lizo. "The soul of the people is yours forever."

"The drama can only be a rite or a message," declared Glauro sententiously. "Acting should again become as solemn as a religious ceremony, since it embraces the two constituent elements of all worship: the living person, in whom, on the stage as before an altar, the word of the revealer is made incarnate, before a multitude as silent as if in a temple"—

"Bayreuth!" interrupted Prince Hoditz.

"No; the Janiculum!" exclaimed Stelio, suddenly breaking his silence of blissful dizziness. "A Roman hill. We do not need the wood and brick of Upper Franconia; we will have a marble theater on a Roman hill."

The sudden opposition of his words seemed to spring from a light, good-natured disdain.

"Do you not admire the work of Richard Wagner?" Donatella Arvale inquired, with a slight frown that for a moment made her Hermes-like face look almost hard.

Stelio looked deep into her eyes; he felt that there was something obscurely hostile in the young girl's manner, and also that he himself experienced against her an indistinct suggestion of enmity. At this moment he again saw her living her own isolated life, fixed in some deep, secret thought, strange and inviolable.

51

"The work of Richard Wagner," he replied, "is founded in the German spirit, and its essence is purely northern. His reform is not without analogy with that attempted by Luther; his drama is the supreme flower of the genius of a race, the extraordinarily powerful summary of the aspirations that have stirred the souls of the symphonists and national poets, from Bach to Beethoven, from Wieland to Goethe. If you could imagine his work on the Mediterranean shores, amid our pale olive-trees, our slender laurels, under the glorious light of the Latin sky, you would see it grow pale and dissolve. Since, according to his own words, it is given to the artist to behold a world as yet unformed resplendent in its future perfection, and to enjoy it prophetically through desire and through hope, I announce to you the coming of a new, or rather a renewed, art which, by the strong, sincere simplicity of its lines, by its vigorous grace, by its ardor of inspiration, by the pure power of its harmonies, will continue and crown the immense ideal edifice of our elect race. I glory in being Latin, and—will you pardon me, most exquisite Lady Myrta, and you, my delicate Hoditz?—in every man of different blood I see a barbarian."

"But Wagner, too," said, Baldassare Stampa, who, having just returned from Bayreuth, was still full of ecstasy, "when he first unwound the thread of his theories, departed from the Greeks."

"It was an uneven and a tangled thread," the poet replied. "Nothing is further from the Orestiades than the tetralogy of the Ring. The Florentines of the Casa Bardi have penetrated much deeper into the true meaning of Greek tragedy. All honor to the Camerata of the Conte di Vernio!"

"I have always thought that the Camerata was only an idle reunion of scholars and rhetoricians," said Baldassare Stampa.

"Did you hear that, Daniele?" exclaimed Stelio, addressing the mystic doctor. "When was there in the world a more fervid intelligence? They sought the spirit of life in Grecian antiquity; they tried to develop harmoniously all human energies, to manifest man in his integrity by every method of art. Giulio Caccini taught that that, which contributed to the excellence of the musician is not only the study of particular things, but of everything in general; the tawny hair of Jacopo Peri and of Zazzerino flamed in their song like that of Apollo. In the discourse that serves as a preface to the Rappresentazione di Anima et di Corpo, Emilio del Cavaliere presents the same ideas on the organization of the new theater that have since been realized at Bayreuth, comprising the rules of perfect silence, an invisible orchestra, and appropriate darkness. Marco da Gagliano, in celebrating a festal performance, eulogizes all the arts that contributed to it 'in such a way that through the intellect all the noblest sentiments are flattered at the same time by the most delightful art that the human mind has discovered.' That is sufficient, I think."

"Bermino," resumed Francesco de Lizo, "presented an opera in Rome, for which he himself built the theater, painted the decorations, carved the ornamental statues, invented the machinery, wrote the words, composed the music, arranged the dances, rehearsed the actors, and in which he, too, danced, sang, and acted."

"Enough! Enough!" cried Prince Hoditz, laughing. "The barbarian is vanquished."

"No, that is not yet enough," said Antimo della Bella; "it remains to us to glorify the greatest of all these innovators; him that was consecrated a Venetian by his passion and death, him whose tomb is in the Church of the Frari, and is worthy of a pilgrimage—the divine Claudio Monteverde."

"There was a heroic soul, of pure Italian essence," warmly acceded Daniele Glauro.

"He accomplished his work in the tempest, loving, suffering, struggling, alone with his faith, his passion, and his genius," said La Foscarina slowly, as if absorbed in a vision of that sad and courageous life that had nourished the creations of its art with its warmest blood. "Tell us about him, Effrena."

Stelio thrilled as if she had suddenly touched him. Again her expressive mouth called up an ideal figure, which rose as if from a sepulcher before the eyes of the poets, with the color and the breath of life. The ancient viola-player, bereaved, ardent, and sorrowful, like the Orpheus of his own fable, seemed to appear before them.

It was a fiery apparition, more fervid and dazzling than that which had glowed in the harbor of San Marco; a flaming force of life, expelled from the deepest recesses of Nature toward the expectant multitude; a vehement zone of light, flashing out from an interior sky to illumine the most secret depths of human will and desire; an unheard word emerging from original silence to say that which is eternal and eternally ineffable in the heart of the world.

"Who could speak of him, even if he himself should speak to us?" said the Inspirer, agitated, unable to conceal the wave of emotion surging in his soul like the troubled waters of a stormy sea.

He looked at the singer, and beheld her as she had appeared during the pauses, when she stood amid the forest of instruments, white and inanimate as a statue.

But the spirit of Beauty they had called up was to manifest itself through her.

"Ariadne!" Stelio murmured, as if to awaken her from a dream.

She arose without speaking, reached the door, and entered the adjoining room. The light sweep of her skirts and her soft footfall were audible; then they heard the sound of the piano being opened. All were silent and expectant. A musical silence filled the vacant place in the supper-room. A sudden gust of wind shook the flames of the candles and swayed the flowers. Then all became motionless in the anxiety of anticipation.

Lasciatemi morire!

53

Suddenly their souls were ravished by a power comparable to the strength of the eagle which, in Dante's dream, bore the poet to the region of flame. They burned together in eternal truth; they heard the melody of the world pass through their luminous ecstasy:

Lasciatemi morire!
Was it Ariadne, still Ariadne, weeping in some new grief, still rising to higher martyrdom?

E che volete
Che mi conforte
In cosa dure sorte,
In cosi gran martire?
Lasciatemi morire!
The voice ceased; the singer did not reappear. The aria of Claudio Monteverde composed itself in the auditors' memories like an immutable lineament.

"Is there any Greek marble that has a perfection of style more sure and simple?" said Daniele Glauro softly, as if he feared to break the musical silence.

"But what sorrow on earth ever has wept like that?" stammered Lady Myrta, her eyes full of tears, that ran down her poor, pale cheeks, which she wiped with her trembling hands, misshaped by gout.

The austere intellect of the ascetic and the sweet, sensitive soul shut within the old, infirm body bore witness to the same power. In the same way, nearly three centuries before, at Mantua, in the famous theater, six thousand spectators had been unable to repress their sobs; and the poets had believed in the living presence of Apollo on the new stage.

"See, Baldassare," said Stelio, "here is an artist of our own race who by the simplest means succeeded in attaining the highest degree of that beauty which the German but rarely approached in his confused aspirations toward the land of Sophocles."

"Do you know the lament of the ailing king?" asked the young man with the sunny locks, which he wore long as a heritage from the Venetian Sappho, the "high Gaspara," unfortunate friend of Collalto.

"All the agony of Amfortas is contained in a mottetto that I know: Peccantem me quotidie, but with what lyric impetus, what powerful simplicity! All the forces of tragedy are there, sublimated, so to speak, like the instincts of a multitude in a heroic heart. The language of Palestrina, much more ancient, appears to me still purer and more virile.

"But the contrast between Kundry and Parsifal, in the second act, the Herzeleide motif, the impetuous figure, that figure of pain drawn from the word of

54

the sacred feast, the motif of Kundry's aspiration, the prophetic theme of the promise, the kiss on the lips of the 'pure fool,' all that rending and intoxicating contrast of desire and horror.... 'The wound, the wound! Now it burns, now it bleeds within me!' And above the despairing frenzy of the temptress, the melody of submission: 'Let me weep on thy breast! Let me unite myself with thee for one hour; then, even if God repel me, through thee I shall be redeemed and saved.' And Parsifal's response, in which the motif of the 'pure fool,' now transfigured into the promised Hero, returns with lofty solemnity: 'Hell would be our fate for all eternity if for one single hour I should permit thee to clasp me in thy arms.' Then the wild ecstasy of Kundry: 'Since my kiss has made thee a prophet, embrace me wholly, and my love will render thee divine! One hour, one single hour with thee, and I shall be saved!' And the last effort of her demoniac will, the last gesture of enticement, the entreaty and the furious words: 'Only thy love can save me! Oh, let me love thee! Mine for a single hour! Thine for a single hour!'"

Perdita and Stelio, entranced, gazed into each other's eyes; for an instant their spirits rushed together and mingled, in all the joy of an actual embrace.

La Marangona, the largest bell of San Marco, sounded midnight, and, as at the eventide, the two enamored ones felt the reverberation of the bronze bell in the roots of their hair, almost like a quiver of their own flesh. Once more they felt, hovering over them, the whirlwind of sound, in the midst of which, in the twilight, they had suddenly become aware of the rising apparition of consoling Beauty, evoked by unanimous prayer. All the beauty of the waters, the timidity of concealed longing, the anxiety, the promise, the parting, the festival, the formidable, many-headed monster, the great, starry sphere, the clamor, the music, the song, and the wonders of the miraculous Flame, the return through the echoing canal, the song of brief youth, the mental struggle and silent agitation in the gondola, the sudden shadow over their three destinies, the banquet illumined by beautiful thought, the presentiments, hopes, pride, all the strongest pulsations of life were renewed between those two, quickened, became a thousand, and again one. They felt that in that one moment they had lived beyond all human limits, and that before them was opening a vast unknown, which they might absorb as the ocean absorbs, for, though they had lived so much, they felt their hearts were empty; though they had drunk so deep, they were still athirst. An overmastering illusion seized upon these rich natures, and each seemed to grow immeasurably more desirable in the other's eyes. The young girl had disappeared. The expression of the despairing, nomadic actress seemed to repeat: "Embrace me wholly, and my love will render thee divine! One hour, one single hour with thee, and I shall be saved! Mine for a single hour! Thine for a single hour!"

The eloquent commentary of the enthusiast still dwelt upon the sacred tragedy. Kundry, the mad temptress, the slave of desire, the Rose of Hell, the original perdition, the accursed, now reappeared in the spring dawn; she reappeared humble and pale in her messenger's attire, her head bent, her eyes cast down; and her harsh, broken voice spoke only the single phrase: "Let me serve! Let me serve!"

The melodies of solitude, of submission, of purification prepared around her humility the enchantment of Good Friday. And behold Parsifal, in black armor and closed helmet, his spear lowered, lost in an infinite dream: "I have come by perilous paths, but perhaps this day I shall be saved, since I hear the murmur of the sacred forest." ... Hope, pain, remorse, memory, the promise, faith panting for the soul's health, and the sacred, mysterious melodies wove the ideal mantle that should cover the Simple One, the Pure, the promised Hero sent to heal the incurable wound. "Wilt thou take me to Amfortas to-day?" He languished and fainted in the old man's arms. "Let me serve! Let me serve!" The melody of submission rose again from the orchestra, drowning the original impetuous motif. "Let me serve!" The faithful woman brings water, kneels humbly and eagerly, and washes the feet of her beloved. The faithful one drew from her bosom a vase of balm, anointed the beloved feet, and wiped them with her flowing hair. "Let me serve!" The Pure One bent over the sinner, sprinkling water on her wild head: "Thus I accomplish my first office; receive this baptism and believe in the Redeemer!" Kundry burst into tears, and knelt with her brow in the dust, freed from impurity, freed from the curse. And then, from the profound final harmonies of the prayer to the Redeemer, rose and spread with superhuman sweetness the melody of the flowery fields: "How beautiful to-day is the meadow! Once I was entwined with marvelous flowers; but never before were the grass and wild blossoms so fragrant!" In ecstasy, Parsifal contemplated the fields and forests, dewy and smiling in the light of morn.

"Ah! who could forget that sublime moment?" cried the fair-haired enthusiast, whose thin face seemed to reflect the light of that joy. "All, in the darkness of the theater, remained motionless, like one solid, compact mass. One would have said that, in order to listen to that marvelous music, the blood had ceased to flow in our veins. From the Mystic Gulf, the symphony rose like a shaft of light, the notes transformed into rays of sunshine, born with the same joy as the blade of grass that pierces the earth, the opening flower, the budding branch, the insect unfolding its wings. And all the innocence of new-born things entered into us, and our souls lived over again I know not what dream of our far-away childhood.... INFANTIA, the device of Carpaccio! Ah, Stelio! how well you brought it back to our riper age! How well you knew how to inspire us with regret for all that we have lost, and with hope of recovering it by means of an art that shall be indissolubly reunited to life!"

Stelio Effrena was silent, oppressed by the thought of the gigantic work accomplished by the barbaric creator, which the enthusiasm of Baldassare Stampa had evoked as a contrast to the fervid poet of Orpheus and of Ariadne. A kind of instinctive rancor, an obscure hostility that did not spring from the intellect, sustained him against the tenacious German who had succeeded, by his own unaided effort, in inflaming the world. To achieve his victory over men and things, he, too, had exalted his own image and magnified his own dreams of dominating beauty. He, too, had approached the multitude as if it were his chosen prey; he, too, had imposed upon himself, as if it were a discipline, an unceasing effort to surpass himself. And now he had the temple of his creed on the Bavarian hill.

"Art alone can lead men back to unity," said Daniele Glauro. "Let us honor the nobler master that has proclaimed this dogma for all time. His Festival Theater,

56

though built of bricks and wood, though narrow and imperfect, has none the less a sublime significance, for within it Art appears as a religion in a living form; the drama there becomes a rite."

"Yes, let us honor Richard Wagner," said Antimo della Bella, "but, if this hour is to be memorable by an announcement and a promise from him who this night has shown the mysterious ship to the people, let us invoke once more the heroic soul that has spoken to us through the voice of Donatella Arvale. In laying the corner-stone of his Festival Theater, the poet of Siegfried consecrated it to the hopes and victories of Germany. The Apollo Theater, which is now rising rapidly on the Janiculum, where eagles once descended, bearing their prophecies, must be the monumental revelation of the idea toward which our race is led by its genius. Let us reaffirm the privilege with which nature has ennobled our Latin blood."

Still Stelio remained silent, deeply stirred by turbulent forces that worked within his soul with a sort of blind fury, like the subterranean energies that swell, rend, and transform volcanic regions for the creation of new mountains and new chasms. All the elements of his inner life, assailed by this violence, seemed to dissolve and multiply at the same time. Images of grandeur and of terror passed through this tumult, accompanied by strange harmonies. Swift concentrations and dispersions of thought succeeded one another, like electric flashes in a tempest. At certain moments, it seemed to him that he could hear songs and wild clamors through a doorway that was opened and closed incessantly; sounds as if a tempestuous wind bore to his ears the alternate cries of a massacre and an apotheosis.

Suddenly, with the intensity of a feverish vision, he saw the scorched and fatal spot of earth whereon he wished to create the souls of his great tragedy; he felt all its parching thirst within himself. He saw the mythical fountain which alone could quench the burning aridity; and in the bubbling of its springs the purity of the maiden that must die there. He saw on Perdita's face the mask of the heroine, quiescent in the beauty of an extraordinarily calm sorrow. Then the ancient dryness of the plain of Argos converted itself into flames; the fountain of Perseia flowed with the swiftness of a stream. The fire and the water, the two primitive elements, rushed over all things, effaced all other traces, spread and wandered, struggled, triumphed, acquired a word, a language wherewith to unveil their inner essence and to reveal the innumerable myths born of their eternity. The symphony expressed the drama of the two elementary Souls on the stage of the Universe, the pathetic struggle of two great living and moving Beings, two cosmic Wills, such as the shepherd Arya fancied it when he contemplated the spectacle from the high plateau with his pure eyes. And, of a sudden, from the very center of the musical mystery, from the depths of the symphonic Ocean, arose the Ode, brought by the human voice, and attaining the loftiest heights.

The miracle of Beethoven renewed itself. The winged Ode, the Hymn, sprang from the midst of the orchestra to proclaim, in phrases absolute and imperious, the joy and the sorrow of Man. It was not the Chorus, as in the Ninth Symphony, but the Voice, alone and dominating, the interpreter, the messenger to the multitude.

"Her voice! her voice! She has disappeared. Her song seemed to move the heart of the world, and she was beyond the veil," said the Animator, who in mental vision saw again the crystal statue within which he had watched the mounting wave of melody. "I will seek thee, I shall find thee again; I will possess myself of thy secret. Thou shalt sing my hymns, towering at the summit of my music!" Freed now from all earthly desire, he thought of that maiden form as the receptacle of a divine gift. He heard the disembodied voice surge from the depths of the orchestra to reveal the part of eternal truth that exists in ephemeral fact. The Ode crowned the episode with light. Then, as if to lead back to the play of imagery his ravished spirit from "beyond the veil," a dancing figure stood out against the rhythm of the dying Ode. Between the lines of a parallelogram drawn beneath the arch of the stage, as within the limits of a strophe, the mute dancer, with her body seemingly free for a moment from the sad laws of gravity, imitated the fire, the whirlwind, the revolutions of the stars. "La Tanagra, flower of Syracuse, made of wings, as a flower is made of petals!" Thus he invoked the image of the already famous Sicilian who had re-discovered the ancient orchestic art as it had been in the days when Phrynichus boasted that he had within himself as many figures of the dance as there were waves on the ocean on a stormy winter night. The actress, the singer, the dancer—the three Dionysian women—appeared to him like perfect and almost divine instruments of his creations. With an incredible rapidity, in word, song, gesture and symphony, his work should crystallize itself and live an all-powerful life before the conquered multitude.

He was still silent, lost in an ideal world, waiting to measure the effort necessary to manifest it. The voices surrounding him seemed to come from a long distance.

"Wagner declares that the only creator of a work of art is the people," said Baldassare Stampa, "and that the sole function of the artist is to gather and express the creation of the unconscious multitude."

The extraordinary emotion that had stirred Stelio when, from the throne of the Doges, he had spoken to the throng seized on him once more. In that communion between his soul and the soul of the people an almost divine mystery had existed; something greater and more exalted was added to the habitual feeling he had for his own person; he had felt that an unknown power converged within him, abolishing the limits of his earthly being and conferring upon his solitary voice the full harmony of a chorus.

There was, then, in the multitude a secret beauty, in which only the poet and the hero could kindle a spark. Whenever that beauty revealed itself by the sudden outburst from a theater, a public square, or an entrenchment, a torrent of joy must swell the heart of him who had known how to inspire it by his verse, his harangue, or a signal from his sword. Thus, the word of the poet, when communicated to the people, was an act comparable to the deed of a hero—an act that brought to birth in the great composite soul of the multitude a sudden comprehension of beauty, as a master sculptor, from the mere touch of his plastic thumb upon a mass of clay, creates a divine statue. Then the silence that had spread like a sacred veil over the completed poem would cease. The material part of life would no longer be typified by immaterial symbols: life itself would be manifested in its perfection by the poet; the word would become flesh, rhythm would quicken in breathing, palpitating form, the idea would be embodied with all the fulness of its force and freedom.

"But," said Fabio Molza, "Richard Wagner believes that the real heart of the people is composed only of those that experience grief in common—you understand, grief in common."

"Toward Joy—still toward eternal Joy," Stelio reflected. "The real heart of the people is composed of those that feel vaguely the necessity of raising themselves, by means of Fiction, Poetry, the Ideal, out of the daily prison in which they serve and suffer."

In his waking dream he beheld the disappearance of the small theaters of the city, where, amid suffocating air heavy with impurities, before a crowd of rakes and courtesans, the actors make public prostitution of their talents. And then, on the steps of the new theater, his mental vision beheld the true people, the great, unanimous multitude, whose human odor he had inhaled, whose clamor he had listened to in the great marble shell, under the stars. By the mysterious power of rhythm, his art, imperfectly understood though it was, had stirred the rude and ignorant ones with a profound emotion, penetrating as that felt by a prisoner about to be released from his chains. Little by little, the sensation of joy at their deliverance had crept over the most abject; the deep-lined brows cleared; lips accustomed to brutal vociferation had parted in amazement; and, above all, the hands—the rough hands enslaved by instruments of toil—had stretched out in one unanimous gesture of adoration toward the heroine who in their presence had wafted toward the stars the spirit of immortal sorrow.

"In the life of a people like ours," said Daniele Glauro, "a great manifestation of art has much more weight than a treaty of alliance or a tributary law. That which never dies is more prized than that which is ephemeral. The astuteness and audacity of a Malatesta are crystallized for all time in a medal of Pisanello's. Of Machiavelli's politics nothing survives but the power of his prose."

"That is true, most true!" thought Stelio; "the fortunes of Italy are inseparable from the fate of the Beauty of which she is the Mother." This sovereign truth now appeared to him the rising sun of that divine, ideal land through which wandered the great Dante. "Italy! Italy!" Throughout his being, like a call to arms, seemed to thrill that name, that name which intoxicates the world. From its ruins, bathed in so much heroic blood, should not the new art, robust in root and branch, arise and flourish? Should it not become a determining and constructive force in the third Rome, reawakening all the latent power possessed by the hereditary substance of the nation, indicating to her statesmen the primitive truths that are the necessary bases of new institutions? Faithful to the oldest instincts of his race, Richard Wagner had foreseen, and had fostered by his own efforts, the aspiration of the German States to the heroic grandeur of the Empire. He had evoked the noble figure of Henry the Fowler, standing erect beneath the ancient oak: "Let warriors arise from every

59

German land!" And at Sadowa and at Sedan these warriors had won. With the same impulse, the same tenacity, people and artist had achieved their glorious aim. The same degree of victory had crowned the work of the sword and the work of melody. Like the hero, the poet had accomplished an act of deliverance. Like the will of the Iron Chancelor, like the blood of his soldiers, the Master's musical numbers had contributed toward the exalting and perpetuating of the soul of his race.

"He has been here only a few days, at the Palazzo Vendramin-Calergi," said Prince Hoditz.

And suddenly the image of the barbaric creator seemed to Stelio to approach him; the lines of his face became visible, the blue eyes gleamed under the wide brow, the lips closed tight above the powerful chin, armed with sensuousness, pride, and disdain. The slight body, bent with the weight of age and glory, straightened itself, appeared almost as gigantic as his work, took on the aspect of a god. The blood coursed like a swift mountain torrent, its breath sighed like a forest breeze. Suddenly the youth of Siegfried filled the figure and permeated it, radiant as the dawn shining through a cloud. "To follow the impulse of my heart, to obey my instinct, to listen to the voice of Nature within myself—that is my supreme law!" The heroic, resounding words, springing from the depths, expressed the young and healthy will that had triumphed over all obstacles and all evil, always in accord with the law of the Universe. And the flames, called forth from the rock by the wand of Wotan, arose in the magic circle: "On the flaming sea a way has opened! To plunge into that fire, oh, ineffable joy! To find my bride within that flaming circle!" All the phantoms of the myth seemed to blaze anew and then vanish.

Then the winged helmet of Brunehilde gleamed in the sunlight: "Glory to the sun! Glory to the light! Glory to the radiant day! My sleep was long. Who has awakened me?" The phantoms fled in tumult, and dispersed. Then arose from the dark shadows the maiden of the song, Donatella Arvale, as she had appeared to him amid the purple and gold of the immense hall in a commanding attitude and holding a fiery flower in her hand: "Dost thou not see me, then? Do not my burning gaze and ardent blood make thee tremble. Dost thou not feel this wild ardor?" Though she was absent, she seemed to resume her power over his dream. Infinite music seemed to rise from the silent, empty place in the supper-room. Her Hermes-like face seemed to retain an inviolable secret: "Do not touch me; do not trouble my repose, and I will reflect forever thy luminous image. Love only thyself and renounce all thought of me!" And again, as on the feverish water, a passionate impatience tortured the Animator, and again he fancied the absent one like a beautiful bow to be drawn by a strong hand that would know how to use it as an instrument to achieve some great conquest: "Awake, virgin, awake! Live and laugh! Be mine!"

Stelio's spirit was drawn violently into the orbit of the magic world created by the German god; its visions and harmonies overwhelmed him; the figures of the Northern myth towered above those of his own art and passion, obscuring them. His own desire and his own hope spoke the language of the barbarian: "I must love thee, blindly, and laughing: and, laughing, we must unite and lose ourselves, each in the other. O radiant Love! O smiling Death!" The joyousness of the warrior-virgin on the flame-circled summit reached the loftiest height; her cry of love and liberty mounted to the heart of the sun. Ah, what heights and what depths had he not touched, that formidable Master of human souls! What effort could ever equal his? What eagle could ever hope to soar higher? His gigantic work was there, finished, amidst men. Throughout the world swelled the last mighty chorus of the Grail, the canticle of thanksgiving: "Glory to the Miracle! Redemption to the Redeemer!"

"He is tired," said Prince Hoditz, "very tired and feeble. That is the reason why we did not see him at the Doge's Palace. His heart is affected." ...

Once more the giant became a man: the slight body, bent with age and glory, consumed by passion, slowly dying. And Stelio heard again in his heart Perdita's words, which had called up the image of another stricken artist—the father of Donatella Arvale. "The name of the bow is BIOS ("life"), and its work is death!"

The young man saw his pathway blazed before him by victory—the long art, the short life. "Forward, still forward! Higher, ever higher!" Every hour, every second, he must strive, struggle, fortify himself against destruction, diminution, oppression, contagion. Every hour, every second, his eye must be fixed on his aim, concentrating and directing all his energies, without truce, without relaxation. He felt that victory was as necessary to his soul as air to his lungs. At the contact with the German barbarian, a furious thirst for conflict awoke in his Latin blood. "To you now belongs the will to do!" Wagner had declared, on the day of the opening of the new theater: "In the work of art of the future, the source of invention will never run dry." Art was infinite, like the beauty of the world. There are no limits to courage or to power. Man must seek and find, further and still further. "Forward, still forward!"

Then a single wave, vast and shapeless, embodying all the aspirations and all the agitations of that delirium, whirling itself into a maelstrom, seemed to take on the qualities of plastic matter, obeying the same inexhaustible energy that forms all animals and all things under the sun. An extraordinary image, beautiful and pure, was born of this travail, lived and glowed with unbearable intensity. The poet saw it, absorbed it with a pure gaze, felt that it took root in the very depths of his being. "Ah, to express it, to manifest it to the world, to fix it in perfection for all eternity!" Sublime moment that never would return! All visions vanished. Around him flowed the current of daily life; fleeting words sounded; expectation palpitated, desire still lived.

He looked at the woman. The stars sparkled; the trees waved, and the dark garden spread out behind Perdita, and her eyes still said: "Let me serve! Let me serve!"

CHAPTER VII
THE PROMISE
Descending the terrace to the garden, the guests had dispersed among the shady paths and under the vine-covered trellises. The night breeze was damp and

61

warm, touching the long lashes on delicate eyelids like lips brushing them in a caress. The invisible stars of the jasmine perfumed the darkness; the rich fragrance of fruit, too, was even stronger than in the island gardens. A vivid power of fertility emanated from this narrow trace of cultivated earth, which appeared like a place of exile, surrounded by a girdle of water, and, like an exiled soul, all the more intense.

"Do you wish me to remain here? Shall I return after the others have gone? Say quickly! It is late!"

"No, no, Stelio, I beg of you! It is late—it is too late! You yourself say it is."

La Fosacarina's voice was full of mortal terror. Her white arms and shoulders trembled in the shadows. She wished at once to refuse and to yield; she wished to die, yet she wished to feel his strong embrace. She trembled more and more; her teeth chattered slightly, for a glacial stream seemed to submerge her, chilling her from head to foot. The strange emotion caused a fancy that her very limbs were ready to break, and she was conscious that the stiffness of her set features had even changed the sound of her voice. And still she longed at once to die and to be loved; still, over her terror, her chill, her body no longer young, hung the terrible sentence the beloved had pronounced, which she herself had repeated: "It is late—it is too late!"

"Your promise, your promise, Perdita! I will not be put off!"

The tide, swelling like a full, fair throat, the estuary, lost in darkness and death, the City, when illumined by the twilight fire, the water flowing in the invisible clepsydra, the bronze bells with their vibrations reaching to the sky, the eager wish, the contracted lips, lowered eyelids, feverish hands, all recurred with the memory of the silent promise. With wild ardor he longed to clasp that being, whose knowledge of all things was immeasurably deep and rich.

"No, I will not be put off!"

His ardor had come to him from far-distant ages, from the most ancient origins, the primitive simplicity of sudden unions, the antique mystery of sacred furies. Like the horde that was possessed by the enchantment of the gods, and descended the mountain side, tearing up trees, rushing on with blind fury, momentarily increasing, its numbers swelled by other madmen, spreading madness in its way, and finally becoming one vast bestial yet human multitude, impelled by a monstrous will, so the crudest of instincts urged him on, confusing all his ideas in a dizzy whirl. And what most attracted him in that wandering and despairing woman, whose knowledge was deep and rich, was the consciousness that she was a being oppressed by the eternal servitude of her nature, destined to succumb to the sudden convulsions of her sex; a being who soothed the fever of stage life in sensuous repose, the fiery actress, who passed from the frenzied plaudits of the multitude to the embrace of a lover; the Dionysian creature who chose to crown her mysterious rites as they were crowned in the ancient orgies.

His amorous madness was now immeasurable, and was a mingling of cruelty, jealousy, poetry and pride. He regretted that he never had sought her after some dramatic triumph, warm from the breath of the people, breathless and disheveled, showing the traces of the tragic soul that had wept and cried in her, with the tears of that alien spirit still damp on her agitated face. As by a flash of light, he had a sudden vision of her reclining, at rest, yet full of the power that had drawn forth a howl from the monster, panting like a Mænad after the dance, athirst and weary.

"Ah, do not be cruel!" entreated the woman, who felt in the voice of the beloved, and read in his eyes, the madness that possessed him. From the burning gaze of the young man she shrank with pathetic modesty. His insistence hurt the sensitive delicacy of her spirit. She recognized in it all that there was of mere selfish impulse; she well knew that he thought of her as something poisonous and corrupt, with memories of many loves, a wandering, implacable temptress. She divined the sudden grudgingness, jealousy and feverish resentment that had blazed up in the long-beloved friend, to whom she had consecrated all of herself that was most precious and most sincere, preserving the perfection of that sentiment by her steadfast refusal to break down all barriers. Now, all was lost; all was suddenly devastated, like a fair domain at the mercy of rebellious and vindictive slaves. Then, almost as if she were passing through the last agonies of death, her whole bitter and stormy past rose before her: that life of struggle and pain, bewilderment, effort, passion, and triumph. She felt all its heavy burden weighing on her, and recalled the ineffable joy, the feeling of mingled terror and freedom, with which, in her far-distant youth, she had given her first, fresh love to the man who had deceived her. And through her mind passed the image of herself, that maiden who had disappeared, who perhaps was still dreaming in some solitary place, or weeping, or promising herself future happiness. "Too late—it is too late!" The irrevocable word rang continually in her ears like the reverberation of the bronze bells.

"Do not be cruel, Stelio!" she repeated, white and delicate as the swansdown that encircled her shoulders. She seemed suddenly to have shorn herself of her power, to have become slight and weak, to have assumed a secret, tender personality, easy to kill, to destroy, to immolate as a bloodless sacrifice.

"No, Perdita, I will not be cruel," he stammered, suddenly discomposed by her face and voice, his heart stirred with human pity, arising from the same depths that had harbored his wilder instincts. "Pardon me! Forgive!"

He would have liked to take her in his arms that moment, to nurse her, console her, let her weep on his breast, and to dry her tears. He felt that he no longer recognized her, that some unknown creature stood before him, infinitely humble and sad, deprived of all strength. His pity and remorse were like the emotion we feel if we unwillingly hurt or offend an invalid or a child—some lonely and inoffensive little being.

"Pardon me!"

63

He would have liked to kneel, to kiss her feet in the grass, to murmur little fond phrases in her ear. He bent toward her and touched her hand. She started violently, opened wide her large eyes upon him; then lowered her eyelids and stood motionless. Shadows seemed to gather under her arched brows, throwing into relief the curve of her cheeks. Again the glacial wave submerged her.

Voices arose from the guests dispersed about the garden, then a long silence followed.

Presently a crunching of gravel, as if trodden by a heavy foot, was heard, followed by another long silence. Soon a confused clamor was heard coming from the canals; the jasmine's fragrance was heavier than before, as a heart in suspense quickens in movement. The night seemed fraught with miracles, and eternal forces worked harmoniously between the earth and the stars.

"Pardon me! If my love oppresses you, I will continue to stifle it; I will even renounce it forever, and obey you. Perdita! Perdita! I will forget all that your eyes said to me a little while ago, in the midst of the idle talk. What embrace, what caress could more wholly unite our souls? All the passion of the night threw us together. I received your soul like a wave. And now it seems that never again can I separate my heart from yours, nor can you separate yours from mine. Together we must go forward to meet I know not what mysterious dawn...."

He spoke in a low tone, with absolute abandon, having become for the moment a vibrating substance that responded to every change in the nocturnal spirit that bewitched him. That which he saw before him was no longer a corporeal form, an impenetrable prison of flesh; it was a soul unveiled by a succession of appearances not less expressive than melody itself, an infinite sensibility, delicate and powerful, which, in that slight frame, created in turn the fragility of the flower, the vigor of marble, the flash of the flame, all shadows and all light.

"Stelio!"

She hardly breathed that name aloud; yet in the sigh that died on her soft lips was as thrilling a note of wonder and exultation as would have been revealed in the most piercing cry. In the accent of the man she had recognized love: love, real love! She, who had so often listened to beautiful and perfect words pronounced by that clear voice, and who had suffered under them as from a torture or a heartless jest, now saw her own life and all the world suddenly transformed at this new accent. Her very soul seemed changed; that which had encumbered it fell away into dim, far-off obscurity, while to the surface rose something free and immaculate, that dilated and curved over her like the sky; and, as the wave of light mounts from the horizon to the zenith with mute harmony, the illusion of happiness mounted to her lips. A smile softly spread over her lips, which quivered like leaves in the breeze, showing a glimpse as pearly as the jasmine's starry flowers.

"All is abolished—all is vanished. I never have lived, I never have loved, I never have suffered. I am renewed. I never have known any love but this. My heart

64

is pure. I should wish to die in the joy of your love. Years and experience have passed over me without reaching that part of my soul which I have kept for you, that secret heaven which has suddenly opened to the unforeseen, has triumphed over all my sadness, and has remained alone to cherish the strength and the sweetness of your name. Your love will save me; the fulness of my love will render you divine!"

Words of wildest transport sprang from her liberated heart, though her lips dared not speak them. But she smiled—smiled her infinite, mysterious, silent smile!

"Is it not true? Speak—answer me, Perdita! Do you not feel too our need of each other—all the stronger from our long renunciation, from the patience with which we have awaited this hour? Ah, it seems to me that all my presentiments and all my hopes would count as nothing, if it were fated that this hour should not come to pass. Say that without me you could not have waited, after life's darkness, for the glorious dawn, as I could not wait without you!"

"Yes, yes!"

In that stifled syllable, she was lost irrevocably. The smile faded, the lines of the mouth became heavy, causing it to appear in sharply drawn relief against the pallor of her face; the lips seemed athirst, strong to attract, to cling, insatiable. And her whole body, which just before had seemed to shrink in sensitiveness and apprehension, now drew itself up again, as if formed anew, recovering all its physical power, and inundated by an impetuous wave of emotion.

"Let us have no more uncertainty. It is late."

He could not disguise his impatience of the social restraints that must be observed on account of the other guests.

"Yes!" La Foscarina repeated, but in a new accent, her eyes dwelling upon his, commanding, imperious, as if she felt certain now of possessing a philter that should bind him to her forever.

Stelio felt his heart-throbs quicken still more at the thought of the love this mysterious being must be able to give. He gazed deep into her eyes, and saw that she was as pale as if all her blood had been sapped by the earth to nourish the rich fruits of the garden; and it seemed to him that the present was part of a dream-life, wherein he and she lived alone in all the world.

65

HE GAZED DEEP INTO HER EYES AND SAW THAT SHE
WAS AS PALE AS IF HER BLOOD HAD BEEN SAPPED
TO NOURISH THE RICH FRUITS OF THE GARDEN

From an Original Drawing by Arthur H. Ewer

La Foscarina was standing under a shrub laden with fruit. The sudden beauty
that had illumined her in the supper-room, made up of a thousand ideal forces,
reappeared in her face with still greater intensity, kindled now from the flame that
never dies, the fervor that never languishes. The magnificent fruits hung over her
head, bearing the crown of a royal donor. The myth of the pomegranate was
revivified in the mystery of midnight, as it had been at the passing of the boat in the
mystic twilight. Who was this woman? Was she Persephone herself, Queen of
Shades? Had she dwelt in that unknown region where all human agitations seem as
trifling as idle winds on a dusty, interminable road? Had she contemplated the
springs of the world, sunk deep in the earth? Had she counted the roots of the
flowers, immobile as the veins in a petrified body? Was she weary or intoxicated
with human tears, laughter, and sensuousness, and with having touched, one after
another, all things mortal, to make them bloom only to see them perish? Who was
she? Had she struck upon cities like a scourge, silenced forever with her kiss all lips
that sang, stopped the pulsation of tyrannous hearts? Who was she—who? What
secret past made her so pale, so passionate, so perilous? Had she already divulged all
her secrets and given all her gifts, or could she still, by new arts, enchant her new
lover, for whom life, love, and victory were one and the same thing? All this, and

66

more, was suggested to him by the little veins in her temples, the curve of her cheeks, the lithe strength of her body.

"All evil, all good, that which I know and do not know, that which you know, as well as that which you are ignorant of—all this had to be, to prepare the fulness of this night." Life and the dream had become one. Thought and sense were as wines poured into the same cup. Even their garments, their faces, their hopes, their glances, were like the plants of the garden, like the air, the stars, the silence.

Sublime moment, never to return! Before he realized it, his hands involuntarily reached out to draw her to himself. The woman's head fell backward, as if she were about to faint; between her half-closed eyelids and her parted lips her eyes and her teeth gleamed as things gleam for the last time. Then swiftly she raised her head again and recovered herself; her lips sought the lips that sought hers.

After a moment they saw each other again in a lucid way. The voices of the guests in the garden were wafted to their ears, and an indistinct clamor from the far-off canal rose from time to time.

"Well?" demanded the young man feverishly, after that burning kiss of body and soul.

The lady bent to lift a fallen pomegranate from the grass. The fruit was ripe; it had burst open in its fall and now poured out its blood from the wound it had received. With the vision of the fruit-laden boat, the pale islet, and the field of asphodels, to the impassioned woman's mind returned the words of the Inspirer: "This is my body.... Take, eat!"

"Well?"

"Yes!"

With a mechanical movement she crushed the fruit in her hand, as if she wished to expel all its juice, which trickled in a stream over her wrist. She trembled, as the glacial wave rushed over her anew.

"Go away when the others go, but then—return! I will wait for you at the gate of the Gradenigo garden."

She trembled still, partly from terror, a prey to an invincible power. As by a flash of light, again he saw her reclining, at rest, panting like a Mænad after the dance. They gazed at each other, but could not bear the fierce light of each other's eyes. They parted.

She went in the direction of the voices of the poets who had exalted her ideal power.

CHAPTER VIII
"TO CREATE WITH JOY!"

Lost! Lost! Now she was lost! She still lived—vanquished, humiliated, as if some one had trampled pitilessly upon her; she still lived, and dawn was breaking, the days were beginning again, the fresh tide was flowing once more into the City Beautiful, and Donatella was still sleeping upon her pure pillow. Into an infinite distance had faded the hour, in reality so short a time before, when she had waited at the gate for her beloved, recognized his step in the funereal silence of the deserted path, and felt her knees weaken as if from a blow, while a strange reverberation rang in her ears. How far-away now seemed that hour! yet the little incidents of her vigil returned to her mind with intensity: the cold iron rail against which she had leaned her head, the sharp, acrid odor that rose from the grass as from a retting-vat, the moist tongue of Lady Myrta's greyhounds that came noiselessly and licked her hands.

"Good-by! Good-by!"

She was lost! He had left her as he would have left some light love, almost with the manner of a stranger, almost impatient even, drawn by the freshness of the dawn, by the freedom of the morning.

"Good-by!"

From her window she perceived Stelio on the bank of the canal; he was inhaling deep breaths of the fresh morning air; then in the perfect calm that reigned over all things, she heard his clear, confident voice calling the gondolier:

"Zorzi!"

The man was asleep in the bottom of his gondola, and his human slumber resembled that of the curved boat that obeyed his movements. Stelio touched him lightly with his foot, and instantly he sprang up, jumped to his place and seized the oar. Man and boat awoke at the same time, as if they had but one body, ready to glide over the water.

"Your servant, Signor!" said Zorzi with a smile, glancing up at the brightening sky. "Sit down, Signor, and I will row."

Opposite the palace, the door of a large workshop was thrown open. It was a stonecutter's shop, where steps were fashioned from the stone of Val-di-Sole.

"To ascend!" thought Stelio, and his superstitious soul rejoiced at the good omen. On the sign, the name of the quarry seemed radiant with promise—the Valley of the Sun. He had already seen, a short time before, the image of a stairway, on a coat-of-arms in the Gradenigo garden—a symbol of his own ascension. "Higher, always higher!" Joy came bubbling up from the depths of his being. The morning awakened all manly energies.

68

"And Perdita? And Ariadne?" He saw them again, as they descended the marble stairway, in the light of the smoking torches. "And La Tanagra?" The Syracusan appeared to his vision, with her long, goat-like eyes, reposing gracefully upon her mother earth, motionless as a bas-relief on the marble in which it is carved. "The Dionysian Trinity!" He fancied them as exempt from all passion, immune from all evil, like creations of art. The surface of his soul seemed covered with swift and splendid images, like sails scattered over a swelling sea. His heart beat calmly, and with the approaching sunrise he felt a renewal of his life-forces, as if he were born anew with the morning.

"We do not need this light any longer," murmured the gondolier slyly, extinguishing the lantern of the gondola.

"To the Grand Canal, by San Giovanni Decollato!" cried Stelio, seating himself.

As the dentellated prow swung into the Canal of San Giacomo dall'Orio, he turned to look once more at the palace, of a leaden hue in the early dawn. One lighted window grew dark at that moment, like an eye suddenly blinded. "Good-by! Good-by!" The woman no longer young was up there alone, sad with the sadness of death; the Song-Maiden was preparing to return to the place of her long sacrifice. He knew not how to pity, he could only promise. From the abundance of his strength, he drew an illusion that he might change those two destinies for his own joy.

"Stop before the Palazzo Vendramin-Calergi!" he ordered the gondolier.

The canal, ancient stream of silence and of poetry, was deserted. The pale green sky was reflected in it with its last fading stars. At first glance, the palace had an aerial appearance, like an artificial cloud hung over the water. The shadows in which it was still wrapped suggested the quality of velvet, the beauty of something soft and magnificent. And, just as in studying a deep-piled velvet, the pattern gradually becomes discernible, the architectural lines revealed themselves in the three Corinthian columns that rose with rhythmic grace and strength to the point where the emblems of nobility, the eagles, the horses, and the amphora, were mingled with the roses of Loredan. NON NOBIS, DOMINE, NON NOBIS.

Within that palace throbbed the great ailing heart. Stelio saw again the image of the barbaric creator: the blue eyes gleaming under the broad brow, the lips compressed above the powerful chin, armed with sensuousness, pride, and disdain. Was he sleeping? Could he sleep, or was he lying sleepless with his glory? The young man recalled strange things that were told of Wagner. Was it true that he could not sleep unless his head rested on his wife's bosom, and that, despite advancing years, he clung to her as a lover to his mistress? He remembered a story told him by Lady Myrta, who, while she was in Palermo, had visited the Villa d'Angri, where the very closets in the room occupied by the master had remained impregnated with an essence of rose so strong that it made her ill. He fancied that slight, tired body,

69

wrapped in sumptuous draperies, ornamented with jewels, perfumed like a corpse ready for the pyre. Was it not Venice that had given him, as long ago it had given Albert Dürer, a taste for luxury and magnificence? Yes, and it was in the silence of her canals that he had heard the passing of the most ardent breath of all his music—the deadly passion of Tristan and Isolde.

And now, within that palace throbbed the great ailing heart, and there its formidable impetuosity was flagging. The patrician palace, with its eagles, its horses, amphora, and roses, was as tightly closed and silent as a great tomb. Above its marble towers the sunrise turned the pale green sky to rosy pink.

"Hail to the Victorious One!" Stelio stood up and cast his flowers at the threshold of the palace door.

"On! On!" he cried.

Urged by this sudden impatience, the gondolier bent to his oar, and the light craft threaded its way along the stream. A brown sail passed silently. The sea, the rippling waves, the laughing cry of the sea-gulls, the sweeping breeze arose before his desire.

"Row, Zorzi, row! To the Veneta Marina, by the Canal dall'Olio!" the young man cried.

The canal seemed too narrow for the expanse of his soul. Victory was now as necessary to his spirit as air to his lungs. After the delirium of the night, he wished to prove the perfection of his physical nature by the light of day and in the sharp breeze of the sea. He did not wish to sleep. He felt a circle of freshness around his eyes, as if he had bathed them with dew. He had no desire for repose, and the thought of his bed in the hotel filled him with disgust. "The deck of a ship, the odor of pitch and of salt, the flutter of a red sail.... Row, Zorzi!"

The gondolier redoubled his efforts. The Fondaco dei Turchi disappeared from their view, a vision of marvelously yellow old ivory, like the only remaining portico of some ruined mosque. They passed the Palazzo of the Cornaro and the Palazzo of the Pesaro, those two giants blackened by time as by smoke from a fire; they passed the Ca' d'Oro, a divine marvel of air and stone; and suddenly the Rialto bridge showed its ample back, laden with shops, already bustling with life, sending forth the odor of vegetables and fish, like a great horn of plenty pouring out upon the shores the fruits of earth and sea to feed the Queen of Cities.

"I am hungry, Zorzi, I am very hungry!" said Stelio, laughing.

"A good sign when a wakeful night makes one hungry; it makes only the old feel sleepy," said Zorzi.

"Row to shore!"

70

He bought at a stall some grapes of the Vignole and some figs from Malamocco, laid on a plate of vine-leaves.

"Row, Zorzi!"

The gondola turned, then sped under the Fondaco dei Tedeschi, making its way toward the Rio de Palazzo. The bells were now ringing joyously in the full daylight, drowning the noises of the market-place with their brazen tongues.

"To the Ponte della Paglia!"

A thought, spontaneous as an instinct, led him back to the glorious spot where it seemed some trace must remain of his lyric inspiration and of the great Dionysian chorus: Viva il forte! The gondola grazed the side of the Palace of the Doge, massive as a monolith cut by chisels not less apt in finding melodies than the bows of the musicians. With all his new-born soul he embraced the mass; he heard once more the sound of his own voice and the bursts of applause. He said again to himself: "To create with joy! That is an attribute of Divinity! Impossible to imagine, in the highest flight of the spirit, a more triumphal act. Even the phrase itself has something of the splendor of the dawn."

Again and again he repeated to the air, the waters, the stones, to the ancient city, to the young dawn: "To create with joy! To create with joy!"

When the prow passed under the bridge and entered the mirror of light, a freer breath gave him fresh realization, with his hope and his courage, of the beauty and strength of the life of the past.

"Find me a boat, Zorzi—a boat that will go out to sea."

He longed for still wider space in which to breathe; he longed to feel a strong wind, salt air and dashing spray; to see the sails swell, and the bowsprit pointed toward a boundless horizon.

"To the Veneta Marina! Find me a fishing-boat, a bragozzo from Chioggia."

He perceived a large red and black sail, just hoisted, and now flapping in the breeze, superb as an ancient banner of the Republic, with the device of the Lion and the Book.

"That one there—that will do. Let us catch it, Zorzi."

In his impatience he waved his hand, to sign to the boat to stop.

"Call out to them to wait for me, Zorzi!"

71

The gondolier, heated and dripping, cried out to the man at the sail. The gondola flew like a canoe in a regatta.

"Bravo, Zorzi!"

But Stelio was panting, too, as if he were in pursuit of fortune, some happy aim, or the certainty of a kingdom.

"We have won the flag!" laughed the gondolier, rubbing his burning palms. "What foolishness!"

The movement, the tone, the good-humor, the astonished faces of the fishermen leaning over the rail, the reflection of the red sail in the water, the cordial odor of fresh bread from a neighboring bake-shop, the smell of boiling pitch from a dock-yard, the voices of workmen entering the arsenal, the strong emanations from the quays, impregnated with the odor of the old rotten vessels of the Serene Republic, the resounding blows of the hammer on the vessels of the new Italy—all these rude and healthful things aroused a wonderful joyousness in the heart of the young man, who laughed aloud for very gladness.

"What do you wish?" demanded the older of the fishermen, bending toward the ringing laughter his bearded bronzed face. "What can I do for you, Signor?"

The mast creaked as if it were alive, swaying from top to bottom.

"You can come on board, if you like," he said. "Is that all you want?"

He brought a ladder and attached it to the stern. It was a simple affair of ropes and pegs, but to Stelio it seemed, like all else in the rough craft, to have a life of its own. As he stepped upon it he felt almost ashamed of his light, glossy shoes. The heavy, calloused hand of the sailor, covered with blue tattoo-marks, helped him to climb up and pulled him on board with a jerk.

"The grapes and the figs, Zorzi!"

From the gondola, Zorzi handed him the vine-leaf plate.

"May it make new blood for you, Signor!"

"And the bread?"

"We have some warm bread," said one of the sailors, "just out of the oven."

Hunger would certainly give that bread a delicious flavor, finding therein all the nourishment of the grain.

"Your servant, Signor, and a fair wind to you!" said the gondolier, taking leave.

72

"Starboard!"

The lateen sail, with the Lion and the Book, swelled crimson. The craft turned toward the open sea, directing its course toward San Servolo. The shore seemed to assume a sharp curve, as if to repel it.

"To the right!"

The boat veered with great force. A miracle met it: the first rays of the sun pierced the fluttering sail and illumined the angels on the campaniles of San Marco and San Giorgio Maggiore, setting on fire the globe of the Fortuna and crowning the five miters of the Basilica with a diadem of light. Venice Anadyomene reigned over the waters, and from her beauty all her veils were ravished.

"Glory to the Miracle!" An almost superhuman feeling of power and of freedom swelled the young man's heart as the wind had swollen the sail transfigured for him. In its crimson splendor, he saw himself as in the splendor of his own blood. It seemed to him that all the mystery of this beauty demanded of him a triumphal act. He felt confident that he was able to accomplish it. "To create with joy!"

And the world was his!

BOOK II
THE EMPIRE OF SILENCE

CHAPTER I
"IN TIME!"

"In time!" In a room of the Academy, La Foscarina had stopped before La Vecchia, by Francesco Torbido—that wrinkled, toothless, flaccid, yellow old woman, who could no longer either smile or weep, that human ruin worse than decay, that species of earthly Parca, who, instead of spindle, thread, or scissors, held in her hand a card bearing that significant warning.

"In time!" she said again, when she and her companion were once more in the open air. She said it to break the pensive silence, during which she had felt her heart sink, like a stone cast into dark waters. She spoke again suddenly:

"Stelio, do you know that closed house in the Calle Gambara?"

"No—which house?"

"The house of the Countess of Glanegg."

73

"No, I don't know it."

"Do you not know the story of the beautiful Austrian?"

"No, Fosca. Tell it to me."

"Will you go with me as far as the Calle Gambara; it is only a short distance?"

"Yes, I will go."

They walked along, side by side, toward the closed mansion. Stelio fell back a step, that he might observe the actress, that he might behold her grace as she walked in that warm, dead air. With his ardent gaze he seemed to embrace her whole person: the line of her shoulders sloping with noble grace, the free and pliant waist on the strong hips, the knees that moved lightly among the folds of her robe, and that pale, passionate face, those eloquent lips, that brow, lofty and beautiful as that of a man, the fringe of dark lashes over the elongated eyes, that sometimes were clouded over, as if tears rose to them and remained unshed—the whole passionate face full of lights and shadows, love and sadness, feverish force and quivering life.

"I love you! I love you! You alone please me! Everything about you pleases me!" he said to her suddenly, whispering the words close to her cheek. He was now walking so close as almost to press against her, as he accommodated his step to hers, his arm passed under her arm. He could not bear to know that she was seized with startled anguish at those terrible warning words.

She trembled, stopped; her eyelids drooped, her cheeks turned pale.

"My friend!" she said, in a tone so faint that the two words seemed modulated less by her lips than by the rare smile of her spirit.

Her sudden sadness melted away, changed into a wave of tenderness that poured in a lavish flood over her friend. Her unbounded gratitude inspired her with an eager desire to find some great gift for him.

"Tell me, Stelio, what can I do for thee?"

She imagined some marvelous test, some unheard-of proof of love. "Let me serve! Let me serve!" cried her heart. She yearned to own the whole earth, that she might offer it to him.

"What dost thou wish? Tell me—what can I do for thee?"

"Love me—only love me!"

"Poor friend, my love is sad."

74

"It is perfect; it crowns my life."

"But you are young."

"I love you!"

"You should possess one with strength equal to your own."

"But it is you, and only you, that each day increases my strength and exalts my hope. My blood runs quicker when I am near you in your mystic silence. At those times things are born in my brain that in time you will marvel to see. You are necessary to me."

"Do not say that!"

"Each day you confirm me in the assurance that all promises made to me will be kept."

"Yes, you will have your own beautiful destiny. For you I have no fear; you are sure of yourself. No peril can surprise you, no obstacle can impede your progress. Oh, to be able to love without fear! One always fears when one loves. It is not for you that I fear. You seem to me invincible. I thank you for that also."

She showed him her faith, deep as her passion, lucid and unlimited. For a long time, even in the heat of her own struggles and the vicissitudes of her wandering life, she had kept her eyes fixed on this young, victorious existence, as on an ideal form born of the purification of her own desire. More than once, in the sadness of vain loves and the nobility of the prohibition imposed between them, she had thought: "Ah, if, some day, from all my courage, hardened in many storms, from all the strong, clear things that grief and revolt have revealed in the depths of my soul, from the best of myself, I could fashion for thee the wings that shall bear thee upward in thy last supreme flight!" More than once, her melancholy had been dissipated in a heroic presentiment. And then she had subjected her soul to restraint, had raised it to the highest plane of moral beauty that she could, had guided it in paths of purity, solely to merit that for which she hoped and feared at once—to be worthy of offering her servitude to him who was so impatient to conquer the world.

And now a sudden violent shock of Fate had thrown her before him in the guise of a mere weak woman, overcome by earthly passion. She had united herself to him by the closest tie; she had watched him at dawn, sleeping; she had had sudden awakenings, alarmed by cruel fear, and had found it impossible to close her tired eyes again, lest he should gaze on her while she slept, and see in her face the lines of care and years.

"Nothing is worth the inspiration you give me," said Stelio, pressing her arm close and seeking her soft wrist under her glove, urged by a longing to feel the

75

pulsation of that devoted life. "Nothing is worth the assurance that nevermore until death shall I be alone."

"Ah, you too feel that, do you—that it is forever?" she cried in a transport of joy at seeing the triumph of her love. "Yes, forever, Stelio—whatever happens, wherever your destiny may lead you, in whatever way you wish me to serve you, either near you or afar...."

In the misty air rose a confused and monotonous sound, which La Foscarina recognized as the chorus of sparrows gathered among the dying trees in the garden of the Countess of Glanegg. The words died on her lips; she made an instinctive movement as if to turn back and to draw her companion with her.

"Where are we going?" Stelio asked, surprised at her sudden movement, and at the unforeseen interruption, that came like a burst of magic music.

She stopped, smiling her faint smile that showed her heart was aching. ("IN TIME!")

"I wished to escape," she replied, "but I cannot."

She looked like a pale flame, as she stood there.

"I had forgotten, Stelio, that I was to take you to the closed house."

Like one lost in a desert, she stood there, helpless, under the gray sky.

"It seemed to me that we were to go somewhere else. But we are already here. 'In time'!"

She appeared to him now as she had in that memorable night, when she had said "Do not be cruel, Stelio!" Clothed in her sweet, tender soul she stood there, so easy to kill, to destroy, to immolate in a bloodless sacrifice.

"Come away—let us go," he said, trying to lead her with him. "Let us go somewhere else."

"I cannot."

"Let us go home—let us go to your house; we will light a fire, the first fire of October. Let me pass this evening with you, Foscarina. It will rain soon. It would be so sweet to sit in your room and talk, or be silent, hand-in-hand. Come! Let us go."

He would have liked to take her in his arms, to nurse her, soothe her, charm away her sadness. The sweetness of his own words augmented his tenderness. Of all her lovable person, he loved most fondly the delicate little lines that radiated from

76

the corners of her eyes to her temples, the little purple veins that made her eyelids look like violets, the curve of her cheeks, the pointed chin, and all that seemed touched by the finger of Autumn, every shadow that overspread that passionate face.

"Foscarina! Foscarina!"

Whenever he called her by her real name, his heart beat faster, as if something more deeply human had entered into his love, as if suddenly her whole past had seized once more the figure he was pleased to isolate in his dream, and as if innumerable threads formed a bond uniting it more closely than ever to implacable life.

"Come! Let us go!"

She smiled pensively.

"But why? The house is very near. Let us pass it by the Calle Gambara. Do you not wish to know the story of the Countess of Glanegg? Look! One would think it a convent."

The street was deserted as the path leading to a hermitage; it was gray, damp, strewn with dead leaves. The east wind had brought a light, warm mist that softened all sounds.

"Behind those walls, a desolate soul survives the beauty of its body," said La Foscarina softly. "Look! The windows are closed, the blinds are nailed, the doors are sealed. Only one door is still open for the servants, and through it they carry the dead woman her nourishment, though she is walled up as if in an Egyptian tomb. The servants feed a body that no longer has the spirit of life."

The naked trees, which rose to the top of the cloister-like enclosure, looked almost smoky in the mist; the sparrows, more numerous than the leaves, twittered incessantly.

"Guess the Countess's name, Stelio. It is beautiful and rare—as beautiful as if you had originated it."

"I do not know."

"Radiana! The prisoner is called Radiana."

"But whose prisoner is she?"

"The prisoner of Time, Stelio. Time stands on guard at her door, with his scythe and hour-glass, as she is shown in old prints."

77

"Are you trying to describe an allegory?"

A boy passed, whistling. When he saw the two strangers looking at the closed windows, he stopped to gaze too, his large eyes full of curiosity and astonishment. They were silent. Presently the little boy grew tired of staring; nothing interesting could be seen; the windows were not opened; everything was motionless, so he ran away. They heard the flight of his little bare feet on the wet stones and rotting leaves.

"Well," said Stelio, "and what did Radiana do? You have not yet told me who is this woman, nor the reason why she is a recluse. Tell me her story. I have already been thinking of Soranza Soranzo."

"The Countess Glanegg is one of the greatest ladies of the aristocratic Viennese world, and perhaps the most beautiful I ever have seen. Franz Lenbach has painted her in the armor of the Valkyries, with the four-winged helmet. Have you ever visited his red studio in the Palazzo Borghese?"

"No, never."

"Go there some day, and ask him to show you that portrait. You will see it unchanged, as I see it now through all those walls. She has wished to remain like that in the memory of those that saw her in the splendor of her beauty. One day, when the sun shone too bright, she saw that the time had come for that beauty to fade, and she resolved to take leave of the world in such a way that men should not be witnesses of the decay and destruction of her famous beauty. Perhaps it was her sympathy with things that disintegrate and fall in ruins that has kept her in Venice. She gave a magnificent farewell banquet, where she appeared, still sovereignly beautiful; then she withdrew forever from the world to this house that you see, in this walled garden, where, alone with her servants, she awaits the end. She has become a legendary figure. They say that there are no mirrors in her house, and that she has forgotten her own face. She has forbidden even her most devoted friends and her nearest relatives to visit her. How does she live? What are her thoughts? By what means does she wile away the time of waiting? Is her soul in a state of grace?"

Every pause in that veiled voice questioning the mystery was filled with deepest melancholy.

"Does she pray? Does she contemplate? Does she weep? Or, perhaps, has she become inert, and suffers no more than a withered apple in the back of some old closet."

"What if she should suddenly show herself at that window?" said Stelio, feeling something like a real sensation, as he fancied he heard a creaking hinge.

Both looked closely at the nailed blinds.

"Perhaps she is sitting behind them, looking at us," he added, in a half whisper.

This thought made them both shudder.

They were leaning against a wall facing the house, and did not wish to move a step. The encircling inertia affected them, the smoke-like mist enveloped them more and more thickly; the chatter of the birds lulled their senses as a drug given to feverish patients. The siren whistles pierced the air from afar. The brown leaves dropped from the trees. How long it took for a floating leaf to reach the earth! All around them was mist, heaviness, slow consumption, ashes.

CHAPTER II
AFTER THE STORM
"I must die, my dear—I must die!" said La Foscarina, in a heart-rending voice, after a long silence, raising her face from the cushions where she had buried it, after a stormy scene of passion, in which the ardent words of her beloved had given her as much pain as pleasure.

She looked at Stelio, who had thrown himself, half reclining, on a divan near the balcony, and now lay silent, his eyes half-closed, his disordered hair touched with a ray of gold from the setting sun. She realized that she was possessed by an incurable madness, spreading throughout her declining body. Lost! Lost! She was irrevocably lost!

"Die?" said her beloved, in a dreamy voice, without moving or opening his eyes, as if he were wrapped in a melancholy trance.

"Yes—die—before you hate me!"

Stelio opened his eyes quickly, raised himself erect and held up one hand, as if to prevent her from saying more.

"Ah, why do you torment yourself in this way?" he said.

He saw that she was ivory pale; her hair fell in wandering wavy locks over her cheeks; she seemed consumed by some corrosive poison; her face was full of terror and misery.

"What are you doing with me? What are we both doing?" she exclaimed in anguish.

"I love you!"

"Not as I wish, not as I have dreamed; I do not wish to be loved thus."

"But you set my heart on fire, and then madness seizes me."

"It is like the madness of hatred."

79

"No, no; do not say that!"

"Your fierceness makes me feel that you hate me—that you even wish to kill me."

"But you make me blind, I tell you, and then I know not what I say or do."

"What is it that maddens you so? What do you see in me?"

"Ah, I know not—I cannot tell!"

"But I know very well what it is!"

"Why do you torment yourself, I say? I love you! This is the love...."

"That condemns me! I must die of it! Call me once more by the name you gave me long ago."

"You are mine! You belong to me, and I will not lose you."

"Yes, you will lose me."

"But why? I do not understand. What wild fancy is this of yours? Does my love offend you? Do you not love me in the same way?"

His irritation and misunderstanding only aggravated her suffering. She covered her face with her hands. Her heart throbbed with hammer-like beating in her rigid breast, seeming to echo in her brain.

Presently she raised her head and looked at him with painful effort.

"I have a heart, Stelio," she said, with trembling lips, as if she were struggling with a sort of fierce timidity in order to force herself to speak those words. "I suffer from a heart, too keenly alive—oh, Stelio, alive and eager and anguished as you never will know...."

She smiled the sweet, faint smile with which she sought to disguise her suffering; hesitated a moment, then reached toward a bunch of violets, which she took and pressed close to her lips. Her eyelids drooped, her classic brow, between her dark hair and the flowers, showed its ivory-like beauty.

"You wound my heart sometimes, Stelio," she said softly, her lips still caressing the violets. "Sometimes you are cruel to it."

It seemed as if those fragrant, humble blossoms helped her to confess her sadness, to veil still more the timid reproach she had made to her beloved. She was

80

silent; Stelio bowed his head. The logs on the hearth crackled; the autumn rain fell monotonously in the fading garden.

"I long for kindness, with a thirst that you never will understand. For that deep, true kindness, dear friend, which does not speak but which comprehends, which knows how to give all in a single look or a single movement; which is strong, sure, always armed against the evil impulse that tempts us. Do you know the sort of kindness I mean?"

Her voice, alternately strong and wavering, was so warm with inner light, was so full of revelation of a soul, that it passed through the young man's blood more like a spiritual essence than a sound.

"In you, yes, Foscarina, I know it."

He took in his own hands the slender hands that lay filled with violets on her lap; he bowed his head low over them and kissed them submissively. Then he knelt at her feet, in the same submission. The delicate perfume seemed to arouse his tenderness. During the long pause the fire and the rain continued their murmured speech.

Suddenly she asked in a clear voice:

"Do you think that I believe myself sure of you?"

"Have you not watched over my slumbers?" he replied, but in an altered tone, for he was suddenly seized by a new emotion: with her query he had seen rise before him her naked soul; and he felt that that soul had penetrated his own, and recognized his secret yearning for the belief and confidence of others in himself.

"Yes, but what does that prove?" was her reply. "Youth sleeps quietly on any pillow. You are young"—

"I love you and I have faith in you! I give myself entirely to you. You are my life's companion, and your hand is strong."

He saw the well known sadness in the lines of that loved face, and his voice trembled with tenderness.

"Kindness!" said she, caressing with light touch the hair on his temples. "You know how to be kind—you even feel a need to comfort at times. But a fault has been committed, and it calls for expiation. Once it seemed to me that for you I could do the humblest as well as the highest things; but now I feel that I can do only one thing—to go away, disappear, and leave you free with your destiny."

He interrupted her by springing to his feet and taking the loved face between his hands.

81

"I can do this, which love alone could not do," she said softly, turning pale, and looking at him with an expression he never had seen before.

Stelio felt that he held her soul in his hands—a living spring, infinitely beautiful and precious.

"Foscarina, Foscarina! my soul, my life! Yes, you can give me more than love—I know it well, and nothing is worth to me that which you give me; no other offer could console me for not having you beside me on my way. Believe me, believe! I have said this to you so often—don't you remember?—even before you became all my own, when the compact still held between us"—

Still holding her face between his palms, he leaned over and kissed her passionately on her lips.

This time she shivered; the glacial flood she felt at times seemed passing over her.

"No! no!" she pleaded, turning away from the young man. Dreamily she bent to gather up the scattered violets.

"The compact!" she said, after an interval of silence. "Why have we violated it?"

Stelio's eyes were fixed on the changeful splendor of the fire on the hearth, but in his open hands lingered the strange sensation, the trace of a miracle—that human face over which, through its sad pallor, had passed a wave of sublime beauty.

"Why?" the woman repeated sadly. "Ah, confess—confess that you, too, before we were seized with the blind madness of that night, felt that the higher life was about to be devastated and lost; that we must not yield if we wished to save the good that remained in us—that powerful, intoxicating thing which seemed to be the only treasure left in my life. Confess, Stelio! speak the truth! I can almost name the exact moment when the better voice spoke to you in warning. Was it not on the water, on the way home, when we had with us—Donatella?"

Before pronouncing that name she had hesitated a second, then she felt an almost physical bitterness—a bitterness that descended from her lips to the depths of her soul, as if the syllables held poison for her. She awaited his reply with suffering. "I do not know how to think about the past, Fosca," the young man replied; "moreover, I do not wish to think about it. I have lost no good attribute that belonged to me. It pleases me that your soul springs to your ripe lips, heavy with sweetness, and that your fair cheek pales when I embrace you."

"Hush, hush!" she begged. "Do not speak like that! Do not prevent me from saying what it is that troubles me! Why do you not help me?"

82

She shrank back among the cushions, and looked fixedly at the fire, to avoid meeting the eyes of her beloved.

"More than once I have seen a look in your eyes that has filled me with horror," she said at last, with a touch of hoarseness in her effort to speak.

Stelio started, but dared not contradict her.

"Yes, with horror," she repeated, in a clearer tone, implacable against herself, having already triumphed over her fear and regained her courage.

Both were now face to face with the truth.

She continued without faltering.

"The first time I saw it was out there in the garden—that night—you know! I understood then what it was you saw in me; all the mire over which I have walked, all the infamy that clung to my feet, all the impurity for which I have so much disgust! Ah, you could not have acknowledged the visions that kindled your thoughts that night! Your eyes were cruel and your mouth was convulsed. When you felt that you wounded my sensitiveness, you took pity on me. But then—but since then"—

Her face was covered with blushes; her voice had grown impetuous, and her eyes were brilliant.

"To have nourished for years, with all the best that was in me, a sentiment of devotion and unbounded admiration, near you or from afar, in joy and in sadness; to have accepted in the purest spirit all the consolation offered by you to mankind through your poetry, and to have awaited eagerly other gifts, even higher and more consoling; to have believed in the great force of your genius since its dawn, and never to have relaxed my watch over your ascent, and to have accompanied it with a wish that has been my morning and evening prayer all these years; to have continued, with silent fervor, the effort to give some beauty and harmony to my own spirit, that it might be more worthy to approach yours; so many times, on the stage, before an ardent audience, to have pronounced with a thrill some immortal phrase, thinking of those which perhaps one day you would communicate to mankind through my lips; to have worked without respite, to have tried always to rise to a higher and simpler form in my art, to have aspired unceasingly to perfection, fearing that nothing less would please you, that otherwise I should seem inferior to your dream; to have loved my fleeting glory only because some day it might serve yours; to have hastened, with the fervent confidence of faith, the latest of your revelations, that I might offer myself to you as the instrument of your victory before my own decay; against all and everything, to have defended this secret ideal in my soul, against all and against myself as much as against others; to have made of you my melancholy, my steadfast hope, my heroic test, the symbol of all things good, strong, and free—ah, Stelio! Stelio!"—

ιe paused an instant, overcome by that memory as by a new shame.

ιnd then to have reached that dawn—to have seen you leaving my house in that way on that horrible morning—Do you remember?"

"I was happy—happy!" cried the young man, in a stifled voice, pale and agitated.

"No, no! Do you remember? You left me as you would have left some light love, some passing fancy, after a few hours of idle pastime."

"You deceive yourself!"

"Confess! Come, speak the truth. Only through truth can we now hope to save ourselves."

"I was happy, I tell you; my whole heart expanded with joy; I dreamed, I hoped, I felt as if I were born anew."

"Yes, yes!—happy to breathe freely, to feel your youth in the breeze and the fresh air. What did you see in her who in her renunciation had so many times suffered keenly—yes, you know it well!—rather than break the vow that she had taken and borne with her in her wanderings over the earth? Tell me! what did you see in me, if you did not believe me a corrupt creature, the heroine of chance amours, the vagabond actress who in her own life, as on the stage, may belong to any man and every man?"

"Foscarina! Foscarina!"

Stelio leaned over her and closed her lips with a trembling hand.

"No, no, do not say that! You are mad! Hush! hush!"

"It is horrible!" murmured the woman, sinking back on the cushions, unnerved by her agitation, submerged in the bitter wave that had flooded her heart.

But her eyes remained wide open, fixed as two crystal orbs, hard as if they had no lashes, fastened on Stelio. They prevented him from speaking, from denying or softening the truth they had discovered. In a moment or two he found that gaze intolerable, and gently pressed the lids down with the tips of his fingers, as one closes the eyes of the dead. She noted the movement, which was full of infinite melancholy; she felt that only tender love and pity were in that touch. Her bitterness passed away, her eyes grew moist. She extended her arms, clasped them around his neck, and raised herself a little. She seemed to be shutting her soul within herself, and became once more gentle and weak, full of silent pleading.

84

"And so I must go," she sighed at last. "Is there no help for it? Is there no pardon?"

"I love you!" her lover repeated.

She disengaged one arm, and held her open hand toward the fire, as if to conjure fate. Then once more she clasped her lover in a close embrace.

"Yes, still a little while! Let me remain with you a little longer. Then I will go away; I will go somewhere, far-away, and die on a stone under a tree. But let me stay with you a little longer."

"I love you!"

The blind and indomitable forces of life were whirling over them in that embrace. And because they realized this with terror their clasp grew closer; and from that embrace sprang an impulse, both good and evil, that stirred them to the soul. In the silent room, the voices of the elements spoke their obscure language, which was like an uncomprehended reply to their mute questioning. The fire, near them, and the rain, from without, discoursed, replied, narrated. Little by little, these voices reached the spirit of the Animator, enticed it, charmed it, drew it into the world of innumerable myths, born of their eternity. His keener spiritual senses heard the deep resonance of the two melodies expressing the intimate essence of the two elementary wills—the two marvelous melodies that he had found, to weave them into the symphonic web of the new tragedy. Of a sudden, all sadness and anxiety left him as in a happy truce, an interval of enchantment. And the woman's clasp relaxed, as if in obedience to some command of liberation.

"There is no help for it!" she repeated to herself, seeming to repeat a formula of condemnation heard by her in the same mysterious way that Stelio had heard the wonderful melodies.

She leaned forward, resting her chin in her hand and her elbow on her knee; and in this attitude she gazed a long time into the fire, with a slight frown on her brow.

As Stelio looked at her, his soul was troubled. He yearned to find some way of breaking the iron band that oppressed her, of dissipating that mist of sadness, of leading his beloved back to joy.

The fire in its sudden burst of flame illumined her face and hair; her forehead was as beautiful as a noble manly brow; something natural and untamed was suggested in the rippling waves and changeful hue of her thick hair.

"What are you looking at so intently?" she said at last, feeling his fixed gaze. "Have you found a gray hair?"

He knelt before his love again, flexible and tender.

"I see only your beauty. In you I always find something that delights me. I was looking then at the strange wave of your hair here—a wave not made by the comb, but by the storm!"

He slipped his fingers through the thick tresses. She closed her eyes, feeling again the spell of his terrible power over her.

"I see only your beauty. When you close your eyes thus, I feel that you are mine to the depth of your heart—lost in me, as the soul is one with the body: a single life, mine and thine."

She listened in the half light, and his voice seemed to come from a long distance, and to be speaking not to her but to another woman; she felt as if she were overhearing a lover's protestations to his mistress, and suddenly fancied herself mad with jealousy, possessed by a desire to kill, filled with a spirit of revenge; but that body must remain motionless, her hands hanging at her sides, nerveless and powerless.

"You are my delight and my inspiration. You have a stimulating power of which you are unconscious. Your simplest act suffices to reveal to me some truth of which I was ignorant. And love is like the intellect: it shines in the measure of the truth it discovers. Why, why do you grieve yourself? Nothing is destroyed, nothing is lost. It was intended that we should be united, so that together we might rise to joy and triumph. It was necessary that I should be free and happy in your true and perfect love in order to create the work of beauty that so many men expect of me. I need your faith; I need to pass through joy and to create. Your presence alone suffices to inspire my mind with incalculable fruitfulness. Just now, when your arms held me close, I heard a sudden torrent of music, a flood of melody, passing through the silence."

To whom was he speaking? Whom did he ask for joy? Was not his imperious demand for music a yearning toward her that sang, transfiguring the universe with her song? Of whom, if not of fresh youth and maidenhood, could he ask joy and creation? While she had held him in her embrace, it was the other woman who had sung and spoken within him! And now, now—to whom was he speaking, if not to that other woman? She alone could give him what was necessary for his art and his life. The maiden was a new force, a closed beauty, an unused weapon, keen and magnificent for the intoxication of war. Malediction! Malediction!

Mingled sorrow and anger stirred her heart, in that vibrating darkness which she dared not leave. She suffered the torments of a nightmare; as if she were rolling toward a precipice with the indestructible burden of her vanished years—years of misery and of triumph—her fading face with its thousand masks, her despairing soul, and the thousand other souls that had inhabited her mortal body. This grand passion of her life, which was to have saved her, seemed now to be pushing her relentlessly toward ruin and death. In order to reach her, and through her to attain

86

to his highest joy, the passion of her beloved was compelled to make its way through what he believed to be a multitude of unknown loves; it would contaminate, corrupt and embitter itself, perhaps even change by slow degrees to disgust. Always that shadowy multitude must keep alive in him that instinct of brutal ferocity which lurked in his strong nature. Ah, what had she done? She herself had armed a furious devastator, and had put him between her friend and herself. No escape was possible. She herself, on that night of the flame, had led before him the fresh and beautiful prey, of whom he had taken possession by one of those looks that are a choice and a promise. To whom was he speaking now, if not to that other woman. Of whom did he ask joy?

"Do not be sad! do not be sad!"

But now she heard his words only confusedly, more faint than before, as if her soul had sunk into a chasm; but she felt his impatient hands as they touched her caressingly. And, in that red darkness, wherein, as it seemed to her, all madnesses and folly were born, she felt a surging revolt in her veins.

"Do you wish me to take you to her? Do you wish me to call her to you?" cried the unhappy woman, suddenly opening her eyes with an expression that astonished Stelio; she seized his wrists and shook him with a grasp so tight that he felt her nails in his flesh. "Go! go! She awaits you! Why do you remain here? Go, run! She awaits you!"

She sprang up, raising him at the same time, and tried to push him toward the door. She was no longer recognizable, transfigured by fury into a dangerous, threatening creature. The strength of her hands was incredible, like the energy of evil intent in her whole being.

"Who awaits me? What did you say? What is the matter with you? Come back to your senses, Foscarina!"

He stammered his appeal, he trembled, fancying he saw madness in that distorted face. But she was like one distraught and heard him not.

"Foscarina!" He called her with all his soul, white with terror, as if to stop with his cry her escaping reason.

She gave a great start, opened her hands, and gazed around as if just roused from a long sleep, of which she remembered nothing.

"Come, sit down."

He led her back to the cushions, and gently made her settle herself among them. She allowed herself to be soothed by his solicitous tenderness. Presently she moaned:

"Who has beaten me?"

87

She felt of her bruised arms, and touched her face lightly, trembling as if she were cold.

"Come; lie down! Put your head here."

He made her lie on the couch; disposed her head comfortably, put a light cushion over her feet, softly and carefully, leaning over her as over a dear invalid, giving up to her all his heart still throbbing with fear.

"Yes, yes," she repeated, in a voice no louder than a sigh, at each movement he made, as if she would prolong the sweetness of these cares.

"Are you cold?"

"Yes."

"Shall I cover you with something?" Stelio inquired.

"Yes."

He sought for some wrap, and found on a table a piece of antique velvet, which he spread over her. She smiled faintly.

"Are you comfortable like that?"

She made an affirmative sign by simply closing her eyelids.

Stelio gathered up the violets, now warm and languid, and laid them on the pillow near her head.

"So?"

Her eyelids drooped even more slightly than before. He kissed her forehead, amid the perfume of the violets; then he turned to stir the fire, putting on more wood and raising a fine blaze.

"Do you feel the heat? Are you getting warm?" he asked softly.

He approached and bent over the poor soul. She slept; the contraction of her face had relaxed, and the lines of her mouth were composed in the equal rhythm of sleep; a calm like that of death spread over her pale face. "Sleep! Sleep!" He was so moved by love and pity that he would have liked to transfuse into that slumber an infinite virtue of consolation and forgetfulness.

He remained standing on the rug, watching her, counting her respirations. Those lips had said: "I can do one thing that love alone cannot do." Those lips had

88

said: "Do you wish me to take you to her? Do you wish me to call her to you?" He neither judged nor resolved, but let his thoughts scatter. Once again he felt the blind, indomitable forces of life whirling over his head, over that sleeping form, and also his terrible desire to cling to life. "The bow is named BIOS, and its work is death."

In the silence, the fire and the rain continued to talk. The voice of the elements, the woman sleeping in her sadness, the imminence of fate, the immensity of the future, remembrance and presentiment, all these things created in his mind a state of musical mystery wherein the yet unwritten work surged anew and illumined his thought. He listened to his melodies developing themselves indefinitely, and heard a personage in the drama say: "This alone quenches our thirst, and all the thirst in us turns eagerly toward this freshness. If it did not exist, none could live here; we should all die of thirst." He saw a country furrowed by the dry, white bed of an ancient river, dotted with bonfires which lighted up the extraordinarily calm, pure evening. He saw a funereal gleam of gold, a tomb filled with corpses all covered with gold, and the crowned corpse of Cassandra among the sepulchral urns. A voice said: "How soft her ashes are! They run between the fingers like the sands of the sea." Another voice said: "She speaks of a shadow that passes over things, and of a damp sponge that effaces all traces." Then night fell; stars sparkled, the myrtles breathed perfume, and a voice said: "Ah! Behold the statue of Niobe! Before dying, Antigone sees a stone statue whence gushes an eternal fountain of tears." The error of the age had passed away; the remoteness of centuries was abolished.

CHAPTER III
A FALLEN GIANT
One afternoon in November, Stelio returned on the steamer from the Lido, accompanied by Daniele Glauro. They had left behind them the thunder of the greenish waves of the Adriatic, the trees of San Niccolò despoiled by a predaceous wind, whirlwinds of dead leaves, heroic phantoms of departures and arrivals, the memory of the archers playing to win the scarlet ensign, and the mad rides of Lord Byron, devoured by the desire to surpass his own destiny.

"I too, to-day, would have given a kingdom for a horse," said Effrena, in self-ridicule, irritated by the mediocrity of life. "Not a cross-bow nor a horse in San Niccolò, not even the courage of an oarsman! Perge andacter! So here we are, on this ignoble gray carcass that smokes and seethes like a kettle. Look at Venice, dancing down there!"

The anger of the waves was extending to the lagoon. The waters were agitated by a violent wind, and the agitation seemed to reach to the foundations of the city, and the palaces, cupolas, and campaniles appeared to heave like vessels on the water. Clusters of floating seaweed showed their white roots; and flocks of sea-gulls circled in the wind, their strange, wild laughter echoing above the crested waves.

"Wagner!" Daniele Glauro said suddenly, in a low tone, touched with emotion, as he pointed at an old man leaning against the railing of a prow. "There he is, with Franz Liszt and Donna Cosima. Do you see him?"

Stelio's heart beat quicker; for him too all other surrounding figures disappeared; his bitter sense of ennui and inertia disappeared; and he felt remaining only the suggestion of superhuman power evoked by that name, and realized that the only reality hovering over all those indistinct phantoms was the ideal world conjured up by that name around the little old man leaning over the troubled waters.

Victorious genius, fidelity of love, unchangeable friendship, the supreme apparitions of heroic nature, were reassembled in silent union beneath the tempestuous sky. The same dazzling whiteness crowned the three heads, whose hair had become blanched through sadness. A troubled sorrow was revealed in their faces and attitudes, as if the same undefined presentiment oppressed their blended spirits. The white face of the woman had a beautiful, strong mouth, with clear-cut lines, revealing a tenacious soul; and her light, steel-like eyes were fixed continually on him who had chosen her for the companion of his noble warfare, watching over him who, having vanquished all hostile forces, would be powerless to vanquish Death, whose menace perpetually pursued him. That feminine vigil, full of fear, opposed itself to the invisible gaze of the other Woman, and threw around the old man a vague, funereal shadow.

"He seems to be suffering," said Daniele Glauro. "Do you not see? He seems almost on the point of swooning. Shall we go to them?"

Effrena looked with inexpressible emotion at those white locks blown about by the sharp wind on the aged neck under the broad brim of the felt hat, and at the almost livid ear, with its swollen lobe. That body, which had withstood the keenest warfare by the proud instinct of its own domination, now looked as limp as some rag which the wind could bear away and destroy.

"Ah, Daniele! what can we do for him?" said Stelio, yielding to an almost religious impulse to manifest in some way his reverence and pity for that great oppressed heart.

"What can we do?" repeated Glauro, to whom that ardent desire to offer something of himself to the hero now suffering the human fate had immediately communicated itself. Their souls were blended in that impulse of fervor and gratitude, that sudden exaltation of their innate nobility; but they could give nothing more than that. Nothing could check the secret ravages of the fatal malady; and both were filled with profound sorrow as they saw the snowy hair tossed about on the old man's neck by the wind coming from afar, and bringing to the quivering lagoon the murmur and the foam of the open sea.

"Ah, glorious sea, thou shalt hear me still! Never shall I find on the earth the health I seek. To thee, therefore, will I remain faithful, O waves of the boundless sea!" The impetuous harmonies of The Flying Dutchman returned to Effrena's

90

memory, with the despairing call that pierces through them from time to time; he fancied that in the rushing wind he could hear again the wild chant of the crew on the ship with the blood-red sails: "Iohohé! Iohohé! come ashore, black Captain! Seven years have passed!" Again his imagination conjured up the figure of Richard Wagner in youth; he saw once more the lonely one wandering in the living horror of Paris, poor yet undaunted, devoured by the fever of genius, his eyes fixed on his star, and his mind resolved to force the world to recognize it. In the myth of the shadowy captain, the exiled one had seen the image of his own breathless race, his furious struggle, his supreme hope. "But some day the pale hero may be delivered, should he meet on earth a woman that will be faithful to him until death."

The woman was there, beside the hero, an ever vigilant guardian. She too, like Senta, knew the sovereign law of fidelity; and death was soon to dissolve the sacred vow.

"Do you think that, steeped as he is in poetic myths, he has dreamed of some extraordinary manner of dying, and that he now prays every day to Nature to conform his end to his dream?" said Glauro, thinking of the mysterious will that induced the eagle to mistake for a rock the brow of Æschylus, and led Petrarch to die alone over the pages of a book. "What would be an end worthy of him?"

"A new melody of unheard-of power, which in his youth had been to him indistinct and impossible to fix, should suddenly rend his soul like a terrible sword."

"True!" said Glauro.

The wind-driven clouds were battling in phalanxes through space; the towers and cupolas seemed swaying in the background; the shadows of city and sky, equally vast and mobile on the troubled waters, alternately changed and blended, as if they had been produced by things equally near dissolution.

"Look at the Magyar, Daniele; there is a generous soul! He has served the hero with boundless faith and devotion; and by this service, more than by his art, he has won glory. But see how this very feeling, so strong and so sincere, inspires him with almost theatrical affectation, because of his continual wish to impose upon his spectators a magnificent image of himself, which shall delude them."

The Abbé Liszt straightened his thin and bony frame, which seemed encased by a coat of mail, and drawing himself to his full height he bared his head to pray, addressing a mute prayer to the God of Tempests. The wind stirred his thick white hair, that leonine mane that at times seemed to emit electric currents which affected his listeners, and many women. His magnetic eyes were raised to heaven, while the words of his inaudible prayer moved his thin lips, lending a mystic air to that face so deeply furrowed with wrinkles.

"What matters it?" said Glauro. "He possesses the divine faculty of fervor and a taste for all-powerful strength and dominating passion. Does not his art aspire

91

toward Prometheus, Orpheus, Dante, Tasso? He was attracted by Richard Wagner as by some great force of nature; perhaps he heard in him the theme he has attempted to express in his symphonic poem: 'That which is heard on the Mountain'."

"That may be," said Effrena.

But both started on seeing the old man turn suddenly, with the gesture of one groping in darkness, and clutch convulsively at his companion, who uttered a cry. They ran toward the group. Everyone on the boat crowded around them, struck by that cry of anguish. A look from the woman prevented the curious from venturing too close to the apparently lifeless body. She herself supported him, laid him on a bench, felt his pulse, and bent over to listen to his heart-beats. Her love and her grief traced an inviolable circle around the stricken one. The bystanders stepped back and waited in silence, anxiously looking on that livid face for signs of either life or death.

The face was still and pale, as it lay on the woman's knees. Two deep furrows descended along the cheeks toward the half-open mouth, deepening near the imperious nose. Puffs of wind ruffled the thin, fine hair on the full forehead, and the white collar of beard below the square chin where the vigor of the jawbone was visible through the wrinkled skin. The temples were covered with perspiration, and one of the feet twitched slightly. The smallest detail of that fallen figure impressed itself forever on the minds of the two young men.

How long did his suffering endure? The shadows continued to float over the dark water, broken at intervals by long shafts of sun-rays that appeared to pierce the air and bury themselves like arrows in the dark waves. The regular cadence of the engine beat upon the air; and now arose the wild laughter of the sea-gulls, and a sort of dull, prolonged moan from the tempest-stricken city.

"We must carry him," said Stelio in his friend's ear; he was intoxicated by the sadness of the situation and by the solemnity of his own visions.

The motionless face gave a slight sign of returning life.

"Yes, let us offer our services," said Glauro, whose face was pale.

They looked at the woman with the snow-white cheeks; then they advanced and offered their arms.

How long did that terrible removal last? The distance from the boat to the shore was not great, but those few steps seemed a long journey. The waves dashed against the posts of the pier; the distant moan came to them from the Grand Canal as if from the winding paths of a cavern; the bells of San Marco rang for vespers; but this confusion of sounds had lost all immediate reality, and seemed infinitely profound and distant, like a lament of the ocean itself.

In their arms they bore the Hero's body—the unconscious form of him who had inundated the world with the flood of melody from his oceanic soul, the mortal being of the Revealer who had translated into infinite song the essence of the Universe for man's adoration. With an ineffable thrill of terror and joy, such as would stir a man who should see a mighty river dashing itself over vast rocks, a volcano bursting into flame, a conflagration devouring a forest, a dazzling meteor obscuring the light of the stars, Effrena felt beneath the hand that he had slipped under the shoulder to sustain the body—and he paused an instant to gather his strength, which was failing him, and gazed at that white head against his breast—he felt the renewed beating of that sacred heart.

CHAPTER IV
THE MASTER'S VISION

"You were strong, Daniele—you who can hardly break a twig! And he was heavy, that old barbarian; his body seemed built over a framework of bronze: well constructed, firm, able to stand on a deck that might rise and fall—the body of a man that nature destined for the sea. Whence came your strength, Daniele? I almost feared for you, but you did not even stagger. Do you realize that we have borne a hero in our arms? This is a day we ought to distinguish and celebrate in some way. His eyes opened again and looked into mine; his pulse revived under my hand. We were worthy to carry him, Daniele, because of our fervor."

"You are worthy not only to carry him, but of gathering and preserving some of the most beautiful promises offered by his art to men who still have hope."

"Ah, if only I am not overwhelmed by my own abundance, and if I can master the anxiety that suffocates me, Daniele!"

The two friends walked on and on, side by side, in exalted and confident mood, as if their friendship had taken on an added nobility.

"It seems as if the Adriatic had overthrown the Murazzi, in this tempest," said Daniele, pausing to look at the waves that had mounted even to the Piazza. "We must return."

"No, let us cross the ferry. Here is a boat. Look at the reflection of San Marco on the water!"

The boatman rowed them to the Torre dell' Orologio. The rising tide soon overflowed the Piazza, looking like a lake surrounded by porticoes, reflecting the greenish-yellow twilight sky.

"EN VERUS FORTIS QUI FREGIT VINCULA MORTIS," read Stelio on the curve of an arch, below a mosaic of the Resurrection. "Did you know that Richard Wagner held his first colloquy with Death in Venice, exactly twenty years ago, at the time he produced Tristan? Consumed by a hopeless passion, he came here to die in silence, and here he composed that wild second act, which is a hymn

93

to eternal night. And now fate has led him back to the lagoons. Fate, it seems, has decreed that here he shall breathe his last, like Claudio Monteverde. Is not Venice full of musical desire, immense and indefinable? Every sound transforms itself into an expressive voice. Listen!"

The city of stone and water seemed indeed to have become as sonorous as a great organ. The hissing and moaning had changed to a sort of choral supplication, rising and falling in regular rhythm.

"Do you not hear the theme of a melody in that chorus of moans? Listen!"

They had debarked from the little boat, and had resumed their walk through the narrow streets.

"Listen!" Stelio repeated. "I can detect a melodic theme, which swells and decreases without power to develop itself. Do you hear it?"

"It is not given to me to hear what you hear," replied the sterile ascetic to the genius. "I will await the time when you can repeat to me the word that Nature speaks to you."

"Ah!" Stelio resumed, "to be able to restore to melody its natural simplicity, its ingenuous perfection, its divine innocence; to draw it, living, from its eternal source, from the true mystery of nature, the inmost soul of the Universe! Have you ever reflected upon the myth connected with the infancy of Cassandra? She had been left one night in the temple of Apollo; and in the morning she was found lying on the marble floor, wrapped in the coils of a serpent that licked her ears. And from that day she understood all the voices of Nature in the air, all the melodies of the world. The power of the great seeress was only a high musical power; and a part of that Apollonian virtue entered the souls of the poets that coöperated in the creation of the tragic Chorus. One of those poets boasted of understanding the voices of all birds; another was able to hold converse with the winds; another comprehended perfectly the language of the sea. More than once I have dreamed that I too was lying on the marble floor, folded in the coils of that serpent. The magic of that old myth must be renewed, Daniele, in order that we may create the new art.

"Have you ever thought what might be the music of that species of pastoral ode sung by the Chorus in Œdipus Tyrannus, Œwhen Jocasta flees, horror-struck, and the son of Laïus still cherishes the illusion of a last hope? Do you recall it? Try to imagine the strophes as if they were a frame, within which an expressive dance-figure is animated by the perfect life of melody. The spirit of Earth would rise before you: the consoling apparition of the great common Mother at the unhappiness of her stricken, trembling children—a celebration, as it were, of all that is divine and eternal above Man, who is dragged to madness and death by blind and cruel Destiny. Try now to conceive how this song has helped me in the writing of my great tragedy to find the means of the highest and at the same time the simplest expression."

94

"Do you purpose, then, to reëstablish the ancient Chorus on the stage?"

"Oh, no! I shall not revive any ancient form; I intend to create a new form, obeying only my instinct and the genius of my own race, as did the Greeks when they created that marvelous structure of beauty, forever inimitable—the Greek drama. For a very long time, the three practicable arts of music, poetry, and dancing have been separated; the first two have developed toward a superior form of expression, but the third is in its decadence, and I think that now it is impossible to combine them in a single rhythmical structure without taking from one or another its own dominant character, which has already been acquired. If they are to blend in one common effect, each must renounce its own particular effect—in other words, become diminished. Among the things most susceptible of rhythm, Language is the foundation of every art that aspires to perfection. Do you think that language is given its full value in the Wagnerian drama? Do you not think that the musical conception itself often loses some of its primitive purity by being made to depend on matters outside the realm of music? Wagner himself certainly realizes this weakness, and shows it when he approaches a friend in Bayreuth, covering his eyes with his hand, that he may abandon his sense of hearing entirely to the virtue of the pure sound of the voice."

"This is all new to me," said Glauro, "yet it rejoices and intoxicates me as we rejoice when we hear something that has been long foreseen and felt by presentiment. Then, as I understand, you will not superpose the three rhythmic arts, but will present them each in its single manifestation, yet all linked by a sovereign idea, and raised to the supreme degree by their own significant energy?"

"Ah, Daniele! how can I give you any idea of the work that lives within me?" Stelio exclaimed. "The words you use in trying to formulate my meaning are hard and mechanical."

They stood at the foot of the Rialto steps. The gale swept over them; the Grand Canal, dark in the shadow of the palaces, seemed to bend like a river hastening to a cataract.

"We cannot remain here," said Glauro, leaning against a door; "the wind will blow us down."

"Go on; I will overtake you. Only a moment," cried the master, covering his eyes with his hand, and concentrating his soul upon sound alone.

Formidable was the voice of the tempest, in the midst of the immobility of centuries, turned to stone. Its unaccompanied song, its hopeless, wailing lamentation, was raised in memory of the multitudes that had become ashes, the scattered pageants, the fallen grandeur, the innumerable days of birth and of death—things of an age without name or form. All the melancholy of the world rushed in the wind over that eager, listening soul.

"Ah! I have seized you!" Stelio cried suddenly, with triumphant joy.

95

The complete and perfect line of the melody had been revealed to him, now belonged to him, and would become immortal in his spirit and in the world.

"Daniele! I have found it!"

He raised his eyes, and saw the first stars in the adamantine sky. He feared to lose the precious treasure he had found. Near, a column he now saw a man with a flickering light at the end of a long pole, and heard the slight sound of the lighting of a lantern. Swiftly and eagerly he jotted down in his notebook, under the lamplight, the notes of the melodic theme, compressing into five lines the message of the elements.

"O day of marvels!" said Daniele Glauro, on seeing Stelio on the steps, as light and agile as if he had robbed the air of some of its elasticity. "May Nature cherish you forever, my brother!"

"Come, come!" said Stelio, taking him by the arm and urging him on with boyish gayety. "I must run!"

He drew him through the narrow streets leading to San Giovanni Elemosinario.

"What you told me one day, Daniele, is quite true. I mean that the voice of things is essentially different from their sound," said Stelio. "The sound of the wind may represent the moans of a frightened throng, the howling of wild animals, the falling of cataracts, the rustle of waving banners, or mockery, threats, and despair. But the voice of the wind is the synthesis of all these sounds: that is the voice which sings and tells of the terrible travail of time, the cruelty of human destiny, the eternal warfare for an illusion eternally born anew."

"And have you never thought that the essence of music does not lie in the sounds alone?" asked the mystic doctor. "It often dwells in the silence that precedes and follows sound. Rhythm makes itself felt in these intervals of silence. Rhythm is the very heart of music, but its pulsation is inaudible except during the intervals between sounds."

This metaphysical law confirmed Stelio in his belief of the justness of his own intuition.

"Imagine," said he, "an interval between two scenic symphonies wherein all the motifs concur in expressing the inmost essence of the characters that are struggling in the drama as well as in revealing the inmost depths of the action, as, for instance, in Beethoven's great prelude in Leonora, or the prelude to Coriolanus. That musical silence, pulsating with rhythm, is like the mysterious living atmosphere where alone can appear words of pure poetry. Thus the personages seem to emerge from the symphonic sea as if from the hidden truth that works within them; their spoken words will possess an extraordinary resonance in that rhythmic silence, will reach the farthest limit of verbal power, because it will be animated by a continuous aspiration to song that cannot be appeased except by the melody which must rise again from the orchestra, at the close of the tragic episode. Do you understand me?"

"Then you place the episode between two symphonies, which prepare it and also terminate it, because music is the beginning and the end of human utterance."

"Thus I bring nearer to the spectator the personages of the drama. Do you recall the figure employed by Schiller in the ode he wrote in honor of Goethe's translation of Mahomet, to signify that, on the stage, only the ideal world seems real. The chariot of Thespis, like the barque of Acheron, is so slight that it can carry only shadows or the images of human beings. On the stage commonly known, these images are so unreal that any contact with them seems as impossible as would be contact with mental forms. They are distant and strange, but in making them appear in the rhythmic silence, accompanied by music to the threshold of the visible world, I shall be able to bring them marvelously close, because I shall illumine the most secret depths of the will that produces them. I shall reveal, in short, the images painted on the veil and that which happens beyond the veil. Do you understand?"

They were now entering the Campo di San Cassiano lonely and deserted on the banks of the gray stream; their voices and their footsteps echoed there as if in an amphitheater of stone, distinct above the sound of the Grand Canal, which made a rushing noise like that of a river. A purple mist rose from the fever-laden waters, spreading like a poisonous breath. Death seemed to have reigned there a long time. The shutter of a high window beat in the wind against the wall, grinding on its hinges, a sign of abandonment and ruin. But, in the mind of the Inspirer, all these appearances produced extraordinary transfigurations. He saw again the wild and solitary spot near the tomb of Mycenæ. Myrtles flourished between the rugged rocks and the cyclopic ruins. Beside a rock lay the rigid, pure body of the Victim. In the death-like silence he could hear the murmuring water and the intermittent breath of the breeze among the myrtles.

"It was in an august place," said he, "that I had the first vision of my new work—at Mycenæ, under the gateway of the Lions, while I was re-reading Orestes. Land of fire, country of thirst and delirium, birthplace of Clytemnestra and of the Hydra, earth forever sterile by the horror of the most tragic destiny that ever has overtaken a human race. Have you ever thought about that barbarian explorer who, after passing the greater part of his existence among his drugs behind a counter, undertook to find the tombs of the Atridæ among the ruins of Mycenæ, and who one day (the sixth anniversary of the event is of recent date) beheld the greatest and strangest vision ever offered to mortal eyes? Have you ever pictured to yourself that fat Schliemann at the moment when he discovered the most dazzling treasure ever held by Death in the dark obscurity of the earth for centuries—for thousands of years? Have you ever fancied that this superhuman and terrible spectacle might have been revealed to some one else—to a youthful and fervent spirit, to a poet, a life-giver, to you, to me, perhaps? Then the fever, the frenzy, the madness—Imagine!"

97

He was on fire and vibrating, suddenly swept away by his own fancy as by a whirlwind. His seer's eyes sparkled with the gleam of the buried treasure. Creative force flowed to his brain as blood to his heart. He was an actor in his own drama, with accent and movement expressing transcendent beauty and passion, surpassing the power of the spoken word, the limit of the letter. And his brother spirit hung upon his speech, trembling before the sudden splendor that proved to him the truth of his own divinations.

"Imagine! Imagine that the earth in which you explore is baleful—it must still exhale the miasma of monstrous wickedness. The curse upon the Atridæ was so terrific that some vestige of it must still have remained to be feared in the dust that they once trod upon. You are bewitched: the dead you seek and cannot find are reincarnated in you, and breathe in your body with the terrible breath with which Æschylus infused them, huge and sanguinary as they appear in the Orestes, pierced perpetually with the darts and flames of their destiny. Hereafter, all the ideal life with which you have nourished yourself must assume the form and impress of reality. And still you go on in this land of thirst, at the foot of the bare mountain, enclosed within the fascination of the dead city, always delving in the earth, with those terrifying phantoms ever before your eyes in the burning dust. At each thrust of the spade you tremble to the very marrow, eager to see the face of one of the Atridæ, still perfect, but with the signs still visible of the violence he suffered, the inhuman carnage. And behold it! the gold, the gold, the bodies, piles of gold, bodies covered with gold"—

The Atridæ princes seemed to be lying there on the stones, a miracle evoked in the obscurity of the pathway. And the one who had evoked these images, as well as his listener, shuddered at the same instant.

"A succession of tombs: fifteen bodies, intact, one lying beside another, on a golden bed, with masks of gold on their faces, their brows crowned with gold and breasts bound with gold; and covering them, on their forms, at their sides, at their feet, everywhere, a prodigality of golden things, countless as the leaves falling in a fairy forest. Do you see? Do you see?"

"Yes, yes, I see! I see!"

"For a second, that man's soul has traversed hundreds and thousands of years, has breathed the terrible legend, has palpitated in the horror of the ancient carnage. For a second, his soul has lived that antique life of violence. The slain ones were all there: Agamemnon, Eurymedon, Cassandra, and the royal escort, and for a moment they lay under his eyes, motionless. Then—they vanished into nothingness—do you see?—like a vapor exhaled, like scattered foam, like flying dust, like I know not what frail and fleeting thing—engulfed in the same fatal silence that surrounded their radiant immobility. And there was only a handful of dust and a mass of gold!" Daniele Glauro, deeply moved, seized his friend's hand; and the Inspirer read in his faithful eyes the mute flame of enthusiasm consecrated to the great work.

They stopped near a door in the dark wall. A mysterious sense of distance possessed the mind of each, as if their souls were lost in the mists of time; and they fancied that behind that door an ancient people lived enthralled by a changeless Destiny. The sound of a rocking cradle came from the house, and the croon of a soft lullaby to a wailing child. The stars glowed in the narrow glimpse of sky; against the walls the sea was moaning. And in another spot a hero's heart suffered while waiting for death.

"Life!" said Stelio, resuming his walk, and drawing Daniele with him. "Here, at this moment, all that trembles, weeps, hopes, breathes, and raves in the immensity of life, gathers itself in your mind, condensing itself there with a sublimation so rapid that you believe yourself able to express it all in a single word. But what word? What word? Do you know it? Who will ever know it well enough to speak it?"

Again he was distressed at his inability to embrace all and express all.

"Have you ever seen, at certain times, the whole universe standing before you, as distinct as a human head? I have, a thousand times. Ah, to cut it off, like him that cut off Medusa's head, at one stroke, and hold it up before the multitude so that it never should be forgotten! Have you ever thought that a great tragedy might resemble the attitude of Perseus? I tell you this: I should like to take the bronze of Benvenuto Cellini from the Loggia of Orcagna and place it in the foyer of the new theater as an admonition. But who will give to a poet the sword of Hermes and the mirror of Athena?

"Perseus!" continued the Inspirer. "In the ravine, below the citadel of Mycenæ, is a fountain called Perseia, and it is the only living thing in that place where all is parched and dead. Men are attracted toward it as to a spring of life in that region where the melancholy whiteness of the dried river-beds is visible late in the twilight. All human thirst ardently approaches that freshness. And throughout my work the music of that stream shall be heard—the water, the melody of the water. I have found it! In that, the pure element, shall be accomplished the pure Act which is the aim of the new tragedy. On its clear, cold waters shall sleep the virgin destined to die 'deprived of nuptials,' like Antigone. Do you understand? The pure Act marks the defeat of antique Destiny. The new soul suddenly breaks the iron band that held it, with a determination born of madness, of a lucid delirium that resembles ecstasy, or a deeper, clearer vision of Nature. In the orchestra, the final ode is of the salvation and liberation of man, obtained through pain and sacrifice. The monstrous Fate is there, vanquished, near the tombs of the Atridæ, before the very corpses of the victims. Do you understand? He that frees himself by means of the pure Act, the brother that kills his sister to save her soul from the horror that was about to seize her, has himself in reality seen the face of Agamemnon!"

The fascination of the funereal gold had taken fresh hold upon his fancy; the evidence of his internal vision gave him a look as of one under a spell of hallucination.

99

"One of the corpses surpasses all the others in height and in majesty: his brow is crowned with a golden diadem, and he wears a cuirass, shoulder-plates, and a girdle of gold, surrounded with swords, lances, daggers, cups, and countless golden discs scattered like petals over his body, more venerable than a demigod. The man bends over this body, while it is vanishing in the light before his very eyes, and lifts the heavy mask. Ah, does he not then see the face of Agamemnon? Is not this corpse perhaps the King of kings? The mouth and the eyes are open. Do you remember that passage of Homer's? 'As I lay dying, I raised my hands to my sword; but the woman with dog-like eyes went away, and would not close my eyes and my mouth, at the moment when I was about to descend to the abode of Hades.' Do you remember? Well, the mouth of this corpse is open, and its eyes are open. He has a high brow, ornamented with a single large golden leaf; the nose is long and straight, the chin oval"—

The magician paused an instant, his eyes fixed and dilated. He was a seer. All about him disappeared, and his fiction remained the only reality. Daniele trembled, for he too was able to see through the eyes of the other.

"Ah, the white spot on the shoulder, too! He has raised the armor. The spot, the spot! the hereditary mark of the race of Pelops 'of the ivory shoulder'! Is he not indeed the King of kings?"

The rapid, half-broken utterances of the seer were like a succession of flashes whereby he himself was dazzled. He had astonished even himself by that sudden apparition, that unexpected discovery which illumined the shadows of his mind, because exterior reality, and almost tangible. How had he been able to discover that spot on Agamemnon's shoulder? From what abyss of his memory had suddenly surged up that detail so strange, yet precise and decisive as a mark that affords recognition of a body dead since the preceding day?

"You were there!" exclaimed Daniele, intoxicated. "It was you yourself that lifted that armor and that mask! If you have really seen what you have just described, you are no longer a man!"

"I have seen! I have seen!"

Again he became an actor in his own drama, and it was with a violent palpitation that he heard, from the lips of a living person, the words of the drama— the very words that were to be spoken in the episode itself: "If you have really seen what you have described, you are no longer a man." From that instant, the explorer of sepulchers took on the aspect of a noble hero fighting against the ancient destiny that had risen from the ashes of the Atridæ to contaminate and overthrow him.

"Not with impunity," he continued, "does a man open tombs and gaze upon the faces of the dead—and what dead! He lives alone with his sister, the sweetest creature that ever has breathed the air of earth—alone with her, in the dwelling full of light and silence, as in a prayer, a consecration. Now, imagine one that unconsciously drinks poison, a philter, I know not what impure thing, which

100

poisons his blood and corrupts his thoughts—suddenly, while his soul is at peace. Imagine this terrible evil, this vengeance of the dead! He is suddenly seized by an unholy passion; he becomes the miserable, trembling prey of a monster; he fights a desperate, secret fight, without truce, without mercy, day and night, every hour, every moment—all the more atrocious the more the innocent pity of the poor creature inclines toward his evil. How can this man be freed? From the very beginning of the tragedy, as soon as the innocent one begins to speak, it is evident that she is destined to die. And all that is said and done in the episodes, all that is expressed by the music, and by the songs and dances of the interludes, serves to lead her slowly but inexorably toward death. She is the equal of Antigone. In her brief, tragic hour, she passes accompanied by the light of hope and the shadow of presentiment; she passes accompanied by songs and tears, by the noble love that offers joy, by the mad love that engenders mourning; and she never pauses except to fall asleep on the cold, clear waters of the fountain that called to her from the solitudes with its continual murmur. Hardly has her brother killed her when he receives from her, through death, the gift of his redemption. 'All stain,' he cries, 'is effaced from my soul! I have become wholly pure! All the sanctity of my former love has reëntered my soul like a torrent of light. Were she here now, all my thoughts of her would be pure as lilies. Were she to rise again, she could walk over my heart as over immaculate snow. Now she is perfect; now she can be adored as a divinity. I will lay her in the deepest of my sepulchers, and around her I will lay all my treasures.' Thus, the act of death, into which he has been drawn by his lucid madness, becomes an act of purification and of liberation, marking the defeat of ancient Destiny. Emerging from the symphonic ocean, the ode shall sing of the victory of man, shall illumine the darkness of the catastrophe with an unknown light, and shall elevate to the summit of music the first word of the Drama renewed."

"The gesture of Perseus!" exclaimed Daniele, still under the spell of exaltation. "At the end of the tragedy you cut off the head of the Moira, and show it to the multitude, ever young and ever-new, which shall bring the spectacle to a close amid great cries of enthusiasm."

Both saw, as in a dream, the marble theater on the Janiculum, the multitude swayed by the idea of truth and of beauty, the illimitable starry Roman sky; they saw the frenzied multitude descending the slope of the hill, bearing in their rude hearts the confused revelation of poetry; they heard the clamor prolonging itself in the darkness of the immortal city.

"And now good-by, Daniele," said the master, reminded of his need to hasten, as if some one waited for him or called him.

The eyes of the Tragic Muse remained immovable in the depths of his dream, sightless, petrified in the divine blindness of statues.

"Where are you going?"

"To the Palazzo Capello."

101

"Does La Foscarina know the thread of your work?"

"Vaguely."

"And what figure shall you give to her?"

"She shall be blind, having already passed into another world, and gone beyond the life of this. She shall see that which others do not see. Her feet shall be in the shadows, but her head in the light of eternal truth. The contrasts of the tragic hour shall reverberate in the darkness of her soul, multiplying themselves there like thunder among the deep circles of solitary rocks. Like Tiresias, she shall comprehend everything, permitted or forbidden, celestial and terrestrial, and she shall know 'how hard it is to know when knowing is useless.' Ah, I shall put marvelous words into her mouth, and silences that shall give birth to infinite beauties."

"On the stage," said Glauro, "whether she speaks or is silent, her power is almost more than human. She reveals to us the existence in our own hearts of the most secret evil and the most hidden hopes; by her enchantment, our past becomes present; and, by the virtue of her aspect, we recognize ourselves in the trials suffered by others throughout time, as if the soul she reveals to us were our own."

They stopped on the Ponte Savio. Stelio was silent, under a flood of love and melancholy, which had suddenly come upon him.

"I wish I had not to leave you to-night, Stelio," confessed the faithful brother, who was also invaded by a peculiar melancholy. "When I am with you, I breathe more freely, and live a swifter life."

Stelio was silent. The wind had abated somewhat. The brown church and the square tower of naked brick seemed to be praying silently to the stars.

"Do you know the green column that stands in San Giacomo dall' Orio?" Daniele resumed, intending to hold his friend a little longer, because he dreaded to say farewell. "What sublimity! It is like the fossilized condensation of an immense green forest. In following its innumerable veins, the eye travels in a dream through sylvan mysteries. When I look at it I fancy myself visiting Sila and Ercinna."

Stelio knew the column. One day Perdita had leaned long against the precious shaft, contemplating the magic frieze of gold that curves above the canvas of Bassano, obscuring it.

"To dream—always to dream," he sighed, with a return of that bitter impatience which had suggested sneering words to him when he had come on the boat from the Lido. "To live on relics! Think of Dandolo, who overthrew the column and an empire at the same time, and who preferred to remain doge when he

102

might have become emperor. Perhaps he lived more than you, who wander in fancy through forests when you examine the marble he pillaged. Good-by, Daniele."

"I shall stop at the Palazzo Vendramin for news," said the faithful brother.

These words recalled afresh the thought of the great ailing heart, the weight of the hero in their arms, the terrible removal.

"He has conquered—he can die," said Stelio.

CHAPTER V

SOFIA

Stelio entered La Foscarina's house like a spirit. His mental exaltation changed the aspect of things. The hall, lighted by a galley lamp, appeared immense to him. The detached cabin of a gondola standing on the pavement near the door, startled him as if he had suddenly seen a coffin.

"Ah, Stelio!" exclaimed the actress, rising with a start and hastening toward him impetuously, with all the spring of her eagerness that had been repressed by expectation. "At last!"

She stopped before him suddenly, without touching him. The swift impulse vibrated in her visibly. She was like a wind when it falls. "Who has detained you from me?" was her thought, while her heart was filled with doubt; for in one instant she had discerned something about the beloved one that rendered him intangible to her—something strange and far-away in his eyes.

But he had found her most beautiful at the very moment when she sprang from the shadows, animated by a violence like that of the tempest sweeping the lagoons. The cry, the gesture, the sudden halt, the vibration of her body, the light in her countenance suddenly extinguished like a fire fallen to ashes, the intensity of her gaze, like the glow of battle, the breath that parted her lips as heat breaks open the lips of the earth—all these aspects of her real self showed a capability of pathos comparable only to the effervescence of natural energies, the power of cosmic force. The artist recognized in her the Dionysian creature, the living material, apt for receiving the rhythms of art, to be modeled according to poetic forms. And, because he saw her character as varying as the waves of the sea, he found inert the blind mask he thought to put on her face; the tragic fable through which she was to pass in sadness seemed narrow, and too limited was the order of sentiment whence she should draw her expressions, almost subterranean the soul she must reveal. His mental images were seized with a sort of panic, a fleeting terror. What could be that single work in the immensity of life? Æschylus composed more than a hundred tragedies, Sophocles still more. They had constructed a world with gigantic fragments lifted by their titanic arms. Their labor was as vast as a cosmogony. The Æschylian figures seemed still warm with ethereal life, shining with sidereal light, humid from the fertilizing cloud. The spirit of the Earth worked in the creators.

103

"Hide me, hide me! Do not ask me anything, and let me be silent!" he implored, incapable of concealing his perturbation, powerless to control the tumult of his disordered thoughts.

The woman's heart beat fast in the ignorance of fear.

"Why? What have you done?"

"I suffer."

"From what?"

"Anxiety, anxiety—from that trouble of mine which you know well."

She clasped him in her arms. He felt that she was trembling in doubt.

"Are you mine—are you still mine?" she asked, in a stifled voice, her lips pressed to his shoulder.

"Yes—always yours."

This woman always suffered a horrible fear every time she saw him depart from her, every time she saw him return. When he went, was it not toward the unknown betrothed? When he returned, was it not to bid her a last farewell?

She clasped him in her arms with the fondness of a lover, a sister, a mother— with all human love.

"What can I do for you? Tell me!"

A continual need tormented her to offer, to serve, to obey a command that urged her toward peril, toward a struggle to seize some good that she might bring to him.

"What can I give you?"

He smiled wearily, overcome by sudden languor.

"What do you wish? Ah, I know!"

He smiled again, allowing himself to be caressed by that voice, by those adoring hands.

"You wish for everything, do you not? You desire everything?"

Still he smiled sadly, like an ailing child listening to descriptions of delightful games.

"Ah, if I only could! But no one in the world can give you anything of any value, dearest friend. Your poetry and your music—they alone can demand everything. I remember that ode of yours beginning 'I was Pan.'"

He leaned against the faithful heart his head now filled with the light of beautiful thoughts.

"'I was Pan.'"

Through his spirit passed the splendor of that lyrical moment, the delirium of that ode.

"Have you seen your sea to-day? Did you see the storm?"

He shook his head, without speaking.

"Was it a great storm? One day you told me that you have many mariners among your forefathers. Have you been thinking to-day of your home on the dunes? Are you homesick for the sand? Do you wish to go back there? You have worked a great deal there, and have done great work. It is a consecrated house. Your mother was with you while you worked. You could hear her stepping softly in the next room. Sometimes she stopped to listen, did she not?"

He embraced her silently. That voice penetrated his very soul, and refreshed it.

"And your sister was with you, too? You told me her name once, and I have not forgotten it. She is called Sofia. I know that she is like you. I should like to hear her speak once, or to watch her walking along the road. Once you praised her hands. They are beautiful, are they not? You told me one day that when she is sad her hands hurt her, as if they were the roots of her soul. That is what you said—'the roots of her soul.'"

He listened, almost happy. How had she discovered the secret of soothing him, the balm for his soul? From what hidden spring did she draw the fluid melody of those memories?

"Sofia never will know the good she has done to the poor traveler. I know little of Sofia herself, but I know that she resembles you, and I have often pictured her to myself. I can see her at this moment. When I have been in distant countries, far-away among strangers, feeling almost lost, she has appeared to me often, and borne me company. She has appeared to me suddenly, when I had neither called nor expected her. Once I saw her at Mürren, where I had arrived after a long, weary journey, made in order to see a poor friend who was at the point of death. Day was breaking; the mountains had that cold, delicate color of beryl that is seen only among glaciers. Why did she come? We waited, together. The sun touched the summits of the mountains. Then a brilliant rainbow crowned them for a moment, then vanished. And Sofia vanished with the rainbow, with the miracle."

He listened, almost happy. Were not all the beauty and all the truth that he himself would like to express contained in a stone, or in a flower of those mountains? The most tragic struggle of human passions was not worth the apparition of that mystic light upon the eternal snows.

"And another time?" he asked softly, for the pause was long, and he feared that she would not continue. She smiled, then looked sad.

"Another time I was at Alexandria in Egypt, in a time of confused horror, as if after a shipwreck. The city had an aspect of putrefaction, like a city in decay. I remember: a street full of muddy water; a white horse, thin as a skeleton, that splashed in the water, its mane and tail of an ochre color; the turrets of an Arabian cemetery, the far-away gleam of the marsh of Mareotis. What misery! What disgust!"

"Oh, dear soul, never, never again shall you be left alone and despairing," said Stelio in his heart, now filled with fraternal tenderness for the nomad woman who recalled the sadness of her continual wanderings.

"And another time?" he said aloud.

"Another time it was in Vienna, in a museum. There was a great, empty hall, the rain whipped against the windows; innumerable precious relics were there in crystal cases; the signs of death were everywhere, exiled things no longer prayed to or adored. Together Sofia and I leaned over a case containing a collection of holy arms, with their metal hands fixed in an immovable gesture. There were martyr's hands sown with agates, amethysts, topaz, garnets, and pale turquoises. Through certain openings, splinters of bone were visible. One hand held a golden lily, another a miniature city, another clasped a column. One was smaller than the others; it had a ring on every finger, and held a vase full of ointment: the relics of Mary Magdalene. Exiled things, become profane, no longer prayed to or adored. Is Sofia devout? Has she the habit of prayer?"

He did not reply. He felt that he should not speak, nor give any visible sign of his own life in the enchantment of that distant life.

"Sometimes your sister used to enter your room while you were at work, and lay a blade of grass on the page newly begun."

The enchantress trembled; a veiled image seemed to be suddenly revealing itself.—Do you know that I began to love her—the girl that sings, the girl whom you cannot have forgotten—because I thought of your sister? Yes—in order to pour into a pure soul the tenderness my soul wished to offer to your sister, from whom so many cruel things separated me! Do you know that?—

Those words quivered with life, but they were not spoken; yet the voice trembled at their mute presence.

106

"Then you would grant yourself a few moments of rest. You went to the window with her, and both gazed out upon the sea. A plowman drove his young oxen over the sand to teach them a straight furrow. When they were finally taught, they no longer plowed the sand, but went up on the hill. Who has told me these things?"

He himself had told her once, almost in the same words, but now these memories came back like unexpected visions.

"Then flocks of sheep passed along the shore; they came from the mountains, and were on the way to the plains of the Puglia. All was still; a golden silence covered the shore. Later, you went with your sister, and followed the tracks left by the sheep along the wet sand.... Who has told me all these things?"

Stelio's fevered mind was calmed. A slow peace, like slumber, descended upon him.

"Then sudden storms sprang up; the sea sometimes overflowed the dunes and the land, leaving foam on juniper and tamarisk trees, on myrtle and rosemary. Heaps of seaweed and jetsam would be thrown on the beach. A boat had been wrecked somewhere. The sea brought firewood to the poor, and mourning to heaven knows whom! The beach would be thronged with people, each trying to collect the largest bundle of wood. Then your sister would bring other aid—bread, wine, vegetables, linen. Blessings would rise louder than the noise of the waves. You looked out of the window, and thought that none of your beautiful images was worth the odor of warm bread. You left the half-finished page, and hurried to help Sofia, speaking to the women, the children and the old men.... Who has told me all these things?"

CHAPTER VI
A BROTHER TO ORPHEUS
From that first evening, Stelio had preferred to go to the house of his beloved through the gate of the Gradenigo garden, making his way through trees and shrubs that had become wild again. The actress had received permission to open a communication between her own garden and that of the long-abandoned palace by means of an opening in the dividing wall. But soon afterward, the Lady Myrta had come to live in the great silent rooms wherein the last guest had been the son of the Empress Josephine, the Viceroy of Italy. The apartments were ornamented with old, stringless musical instruments, and the garden was peopled by graceful hounds, that lacked any prey.

To Stelio, nothing seemed sweeter or more sad than that walk toward the woman that waited for him while counting the hours—so slow, yet so swift in their flight. In the afternoon, the path of San Simeone Piccolo turned a pale golden hue, like a bank of the finest alabaster. The reflected rays of sunlight danced on the iron prows that stood in a row by the pier. A few decaying gondola cabins lay in the shadow of the pavements, with their curtains and cushions stained and spoiled by rain, as if they were catafalques worn out by continual use in funeral ceremonies,

107

grown old on the way to the churchyard. The garden gate opened at the end of the Campiello della Comare, green and mossy like a country cemetery; it spread out between two columns, topped by broken statues, on the limbs of which the dry branches of ivy were outlined like veins.

"Helion! Sirius! Altair! Donovan! Ali-Nour! Nerissa! Piuchebella!"

Seated on a bench near a rose-covered wall, Lady Myrta was calling her dogs. La Foscarina stood near her, in a fawn-colored costume, the material of which resembled that superb textile called rovana, used in ancient times in Venice. The sunlight bathed the women and the roses in the same soft warmth.

"You are dressed like Donovan to-day," said Lady Myrta to the actress, with a smile. "Did you know that Stelio prefers Donovan to all the others?"

A slight blush rose to La Foscarina's cheeks; she looked at the fawn-colored greyhound.

"He is the strongest and the most beautiful," she replied.

"I believe that Stelio would like to have him," added the old lady, with a sweet, indulgent smile.

"What is there that he would not like to have?"

Lady Myrta noted the tinge of melancholy in the tone of the woman in love. She remained silent.

The dogs lay near them, serious and sad, sleepy and dreamy, far from plains, steppes, and deserts, stretched out in the clover, where also grew the gourds, with their greenish-yellow fruit.

"Does your lover grieve you?" the elder woman would have liked to ask of the woman in love, for the silence weighed on her, and she felt her own heart revivified by the fire within that sorrowful soul. But she dared not. She only sighed. Her heart, ever young, still throbbed at the sight of despairing passion and beauty menaced.

"Ah, you are still beautiful, and your lips still attract kisses, and the man that loves you can still be intoxicated with your sweet pallor and your eyes," she thought, as she looked at the pensive actress, toward whom the November roses leaned. "But I am a specter."

She lowered her eyes, gazed upon her own deformed hands lying on her lap, and wondered that those hands were hers, they were so dead and distorted, lamentable monsters that could no longer touch anyone without exciting disgust, that had nothing to caress any more except the dogs. She felt the wrinkles in her face, the false teeth against her gums, the false hair on her head, all the ruin of her poor body, which once was obedient to the graceful will of her delicate spirit; and

108

she wondered at her own persistence in struggling against the outrages of Time, in deceiving herself, in recomposing every morning that ridiculous illusion with essences, oils, unguents, rouge and powder. But, in the perpetual springtime of her dreams, was she not ever youthful? Was it not yesterday, only yesterday, that she had caressed a loved face with her perfect fingers, hunted the fox and the deer in the northern counties, danced with her betrothed in the park to an air of John Dowland's?—There are no mirrors in the house of the Countess Glanegg; there are too many in Lady Myrta's house—was La Foscarina's thought.—One has hidden her decline from herself and from everyone else; the other sees herself growing older day by day. She counts her wrinkles one by one, gathers up her dead hair in her comb, feels her teeth rattling against her pale gums, and tries to repair the damage by artificial devices. Poor tender soul, who wishes still to be smiling and charming! But we must die, disappear, descend into the earth!—She observed the little cluster of violets that Lady Myrta had pinned to her skirt. In all seasons fresh flowers were fastened there, barely visible, hidden among the folds, a sign of her daily illusion of springtime, of the ever-new enchantment she wove about herself by the aid of memory, music, poetry, and all the arts of dreams against old age, infirmity, and solitude.—We should live one supreme, flaming hour, then disappear forever in the earth before all charm has vanished, before all grace is dead!—

She felt the beauty of her own eyes, the careless strength of her hair, blown back by the wind, all the power of rhythm and transport that slumbered in her muscles and her bones. She heard again in fancy the words of her lover, saw him again in his tender transport of love, in the sweetness of languor, the moments of profound oblivion.—Still a little while, still a few days longer I shall please him, and seem beautiful to him, and put fire in his blood. A little while longer!—With her feet in the deep grass, her brow raised to the sunlight, amid the fragrance of fading roses, in the fawn-colored robe that made her seem like the magnificent beast of prey, she glowed with passionate joy of life and hope, a sudden quickening of the blood, as if that future which she had renounced by her resolution to die were flowing back into the present.—Come! come!—Within herself she called to her beloved with a sort of intoxication, sure that he would come, because she already felt that he would, and never had she been deceived by her presentiment.

"Ah, here is Stelio!" said Lady Myrta at that instant, seeing the young man advancing among the laurels.

La Foscarina turned swiftly, with a blush. The greyhounds rose, pricking up their slender ears. The meeting glance of those lovers had something in it like an electric flash. Again, as always, in the presence of that wonderful creature, her lover had the divine sensation of suddenly being enfolded in a cloud of flaming ether, in a vibrant wave that seemed to isolate him from ordinary atmosphere and almost to ravish his senses.

"You were awaited here by all that dwell in this seclusion," said Lady Myrta, with a smile that hid the emotion that stirred the youthful heart in the infirm and aged body at the sight of love and longing. "In coming here, you have responded to a call."

109

"That is true," said the young man, holding the collar of Donovan, which, remembering his caresses, had run to meet him. "The fact is, I have come a long distance. Guess from where?"

"From the country of Giorgione!"

"No, from the cloister of Santa Apollonia. Do you know that place?"

"Is that one of your inventions to-day?"

"Invention? It is a cloister of stone, a real cloister, with a well and with little columns."

"It may be so, but everything that you have once looked at, Stelio, becomes your invention."

"Ah, Lady Myrta, I should like to offer you that gem of a cloister. I wish I might move it here, into your garden. Imagine a small, secret cloister, opening on a sequence of slender columns, set in pairs like nuns when they walk, fasting, in the sun; very delicate, neither white, gray nor black, but that most mysterious tint ever given to stone by the great master colorist—Time. In the midst of these is a well, and on the curb, which is worn by the rope, hangs a pail without a bottom. The nuns have disappeared, but I believe that the shades of the Danaïdes frequent the place."

He stopped speaking suddenly, seeing himself surrounded by the greyhounds, and began to imitate the guttural sounds the kennel-men make to gather the dogs. The animals became excited; their wistful eyes brightened.

"Ali-Nour! Crissa! Nerissa! Clarissa! Altair! Helion! Hardicanute! Veronese! Hierro!"

He knew them all by name, and when he called them they seemed to recognize him for their master. There was the Scottish hound, native of the highlands, with thick, rough coat; the Irish wolf-hound, ruddy and strong, with brown irises showing clearly in their whites; the Tartary hound, spotted with black and yellow, a native of vast Asiatic steppes, where at night he had guarded a tent against hyenas and leopards; the Persian dog, light-colored and small, with ears covered with long silky hair, a fluffy tail, of lighter tint on the sides and legs, more graceful than the antelopes he had killed; there was also the Spanish galgo that had migrated with the Moors, that magnificent animal held in leash by a pompous dwarf in the painting by Velásquez, instructed to course and to force on the naked plains of the Mancha; the Arabian sloughi, illustrious depredator of the desert, with black tongue and palate, a noble animal, all pride, courage, and elegance, accustomed to sleep on rich rugs and to lap pure milk from a pure vase. Assembled in a pack, they quivered around him

110

who knew how to reawaken in their torpid blood their primitive instincts of pursuit and carnage.

"Which among you was Gog's best friend?" he asked, looking from one to another of the pairs of beautiful, eager eyes fixed upon him. "You, Hierro? You, Altair?"

His peculiar accent animated the sensitive creatures, which listened with suppressed and intermittent growls.

"Well, I must tell you all something that I have kept secret till to-day. Gog—do you hear?—who could crush a hare with one snap of his jaws—Gog is crippled."

"Oh, indeed!" exclaimed Lady Myrta, concerned. "Is it possible, Stelio? And Magog—how is he?"

"Magog is safe and well."

These were the names of a pair of greyhounds that Lady Myrta had given to the young man.

"How did it happen?"

"Alas, poor Gog! He had already killed thirty-seven hares. He possessed all the virtues of his fine breed: swiftness, resistance, incredible rapidity in turning, and the constant desire to kill his prey, besides the classical manner of running straight and seizing his prey from behind almost at the same instant. Have you ever watched a greyhound in coursing, Foscarina?"

"Never."

"Then you never have seen one of the rarest spectacles of daring, vehemence, and grace in the world. Look!"

He drew Donovan toward him, knelt beside him, and began feeling the animal with his expert hands.

"No machine in nature exists that is more exactly and powerfully adapted to its purpose. The muzzle is sharp in order to penetrate the air; it is long, so that the jaws can crush the prey at the first snap. The skull is wide between the ears in order to contain the greatest courage and skill. The jowls are dry and muscular, and the lips so short they hardly cover the teeth."

With sure and easy touch, he opened the mouth of the dog, which offered no resistance.

"Look at those white teeth! See how long the eyeteeth are, with a little curve at the top, the better to hold his prey. No other species of dog has a mouth so well constructed for biting."

His hands lingered over the examination, and his admiration for the superb specimen was unbounded. He was kneeling in the clover, and received in his face the breath of the dog, which quietly permitted him to examine it, as if it comprehended and enjoyed the praise of the connoisseur.

"See what elegance in his ribs, arranged with the symmetry of a fine keel, and in that line curved inward toward the abdomen, which is hidden. All point to one aim. The tail, thick at the root and slender at the tip—look! almost like that of a rat—serves as a sort of rudder, necessary to enable him to turn swiftly when the hare doubles. Let us see, Donovan, whether you are perfect also in this respect."

He took the tip of the tail, passed it under the leg, and drew it toward the haunch-bone, where it exactly touched the projecting part.

"Yes, perfect! Once I saw an Arab of the tribe of Arbâa measuring his sloughi in that way. Ali-Nour, did you tremble when you discovered the herd of gazelles? Imagine, Foscarina—the sloughi trembles when he discovers his prey, quivers like a willow, and turns his soft, pleading eyes toward his master, begging to be released. I do not know the reason why this pleases me and stirs me so much. His desire to kill is terrible; his whole body is ready to stretch itself like a bow, yet he trembles! Not with fear, nor with uncertainty, but with sheer desire. Ah, Foscarina! if you could see a sloughi at that moment, you would not fail to learn from him his manner of quivering, and you would render the manner human by the power of your tragic art, and would give mankind a new sensation. Up, Ali-Nour! swift desert arrow! Do you remember? But now you tremble only when you are cold."

Blithe and graceful, he had let Donovan go, and had taken between his hands the serpentine head of the slayer of gazelles; he gazed into those deep eyes, wherein lurked nostalgia for the silent, tropical land; for tents unfolded after a march toward some deceiving mirage; for fires kindled for the evening meal under stars that seemed to throb in the waves of the wind just above the summits of the palm-trees.

La Foscarina had entered into that physical enchantment of love whereby the limits of one's being seem to dilate and be fused in the air, so that every word and movement of the beloved object brings a feeling of happiness sweeter than any caress. Her lover had taken between his hands the head of Ali-Nour, but she felt the touch of those hands upon her own brow. He was gazing into Ali-Nour's eyes, but she could feel that gaze deep in her own soul.

Had he not touched the obscurest mystery of her being? Did he not compel her to feel within herself the animal depths whence had sprung the unexpected revelation of her tragic genius, moving and maddening the multitude as would a splendid spectacle of sea and sky, a gorgeous sunrise, a tremendous tempest. When

112

he had spoken of the trembling sloughi, had he not divined the natural analogies whence she drew the power of expression that amazed peoples and poets? It was because she had re-discovered the Dionysian sense of Nature as a naturalizer, the antique fervor of instinctive and creative energies, the enthusiasm of the multiform god emerging from the fermentation of all sap, that she appeared so new and so great on the stage. Sometimes she felt within herself something like an immanence of the miracle which in the mystic past swelled with divine milk the breasts of the Mænads at the approach of the hungry young panthers.

Stelio began again to imitate the guttural call of the kennel-keeper. The dogs grew more excited; their eyes brightened again; the tense muscles swelled under the coats—tawny, black, white, gray, spotted; the long haunches were curved like bows ready to hurl into space those bodies dry and slender, like a quiver-full of arrows.

"There, Donovan, there!"

Stelio pointed to a reddish-gray object in the grass at the end of the garden; it looked somewhat like a crouching hare with flattened ears. The imperious voice deceived the hesitating hounds, and it was beautiful to see the slender, vigorous bodies quivering in the sunlight.

"There, Donovan!"

The great tawny dog looked him deep in the eyes, gave a formidable bound toward the imaginary prey, with all the vehemence of his reawakened instinct. He reached the spot in an instant, then stopped, disappointed, followed by the whole pack.

"A gourd! a gourd!" cried the deceiver, with shouts of laughter. "Not even a rabbit. Poor Donovan! He bit only a gourd! Poor Donovan! what humiliation! Take care, Lady Myrta, lest he drown himself in the canal for very shame!"

From the contagion of her lover's gayety, La Foscarina laughed too. Her fawn-tinted gown and the tan coats of the hounds shone in the sunlight against the green clover. Her white teeth, revealed by rippling laughter, graced her mouth with a renewal of youth.

"Would you like to own Donovan?" said Lady Myrta, with a touch of graceful, malicious significance. "I know your arts!"

Stelio ceased laughing, and blushed like a boy.

A wave of tenderness filled La Foscarina's heart as she saw the boyish blush. She fairly sparkled with love; she felt a wild wish to clasp him in her arms at that very moment.

Before thanking Lady Myrta, Stelio looked again at the dog, admiring him as he was, strong, splendid, perfect, with the mark of style on his limbs as if Pisanello had drawn him for the reverse of a medal. Then he looked at La Foscarina, who had turned to the group of animals, moving over the grass with a swift undulation, like the movement called the greyhound step by the ancient Venetians. She advanced, with Donovan, holding him by the collar. The chill of evening began to be felt, the shadow of the bronze cupola grew longer on the grass; a purple mist, in which the last flecks of golden sunlight swam, began to spread over the branches that swayed in the breeze.

—See, we are yours!—the woman seemed to be saying mutely, while the animal, beginning to shiver, pressed close against her.—We are yours forever. We are here to serve you!

CHAPTER VII
ONLY ONE CONDITION
Heartrending was the sweetness of that November, smiling like a sick person who fancies himself to have reached a state of convalescence and feels an unusual sense of relief and well-being, knowing not that his hour of agony draws near.

"What is the matter with you to-day, Fosca? What has happened to you? Why are you so distant to me? Speak! Tell me!"

Stelio had entered San Marco by chance, and had seen her there, leaning against the chapel-door that leads to the baptistry. She was alone, motionless, her face devoured by fever and by shadows, with terrified eyes fixed on the fearful figures of the mosaics that flamed in a yellow fire.

"Leave me here alone, I entreat you—I beg of you! I must be alone! I implore you!"

She turned as if to flee, but he detained her.

"But tell me! Speak at least one word that I may understand."

Still she sought to escape, and her movement expressed unspeakable anguish.

"I implore you! If you pity me, the only thing you can do for me now is to let me go."

"But one word—at least one word, so that I shall understand."

A flash of fury passed over the agitated face.

"No! I wish to be alone!"

Her voice was as hard as her glance. She turned, taking a step or two like a person overcome by dizziness seeking some support.

"Foscarina!"

But he dared not detain her longer. He saw the despairing one walk through the zone of sunlight that invaded the basilica like a rushing torrent entering through a door opened by an unknown hand. Behind her the deep golden cavern, with its apostles, martyrs, and sacred beasts, glittered as if the thousand torches of the daylight were pouring in on it.

"I am lost in the depths of sadness.... This violent impulse to revolt against fate, to rush away in search of adventure—to seek.—Who will save my hope? Whence will come a ray of light?... To sing, to sing! But I would sing a song of life at last.... Can you tell me where the Lord of the Flame is at present?"

These words, in a letter from Donatella Arvale, were branded on her eyes and on her soul, with all the characteristics of handwriting, as much alive as the hand that traced them, as throbbing as that impatient pulse. She saw them graved on the stones, outlined on the clouds, reflected in the water, indelible and inevitable as the decrees of Fate.

—Where shall I go? Where shall I go?—Through all her agitation and despair, she had still a sense of the sweetness of things, the warmth of the gilded marbles, the perfume of the quiet air, the languor of human leisure.

She turned with a start, fearing yet hoping to be followed by her lover. She could not see him. She would have fled had she seen him, but her heart ached as if he had sent her to death without a word of recall.—All is over!—

She entered the Porta della Carta, having crossed the threshold. The intoxication of her sorrow led her to the spot where, on a night of glory, the three destinies had come together. She went to the well, the point of that rendezvous. Around that bronze curb the whole life of those few seconds rose again with the distinct outline of reality. There she had said, addressing her companion with a smile: "Donatella, this is the Lord of the Flame!" Then the immense cry of the multitude had drowned her voice, and above their head rose a flight of fiery pigeons against the dark sky.

She approached the well, and gazed into it. She leaned over the curb, saw her own face in the deep mirror, saw in it terror and perdition, saw the motionless Medusa she carried in the depth of her soul. Without realizing it, she repeated the action of him she loved. She saw his face, too, and Donatella's, as she had seen them illumined for an instant that night, close together, lighted by the radiance in the sky.

—Love, love each other! I will go away, I shall disappear! Good-by!—

She closed her eyes at the thought of death, and in that darkness she saw the kind, strong eyes of her mother, infinite as a horizon of peace.—You are at peace, and you await me—you whose life and death were of passion.—

115

She stood erect, then departed by the Molo, stepped into a gondola, and ordered it to be rowed to the Giudecca. The buildings and the water formed a miracle of gold and opal. The image of dead Summer flashed across her memory— dead Summer dressed in gold and shut in a coffin of opalescent glass. She imagined herself submerged in the lagoon, sleeping on a bed of seaweed; but the memory of the promise made on that water, and kept in the delirium of that night, pierced her heart like a knife, and threw her into a convulsion.

—Never more, then? Never more!—

She reached the Rio della Croce. The gondola stopped before a closed door. She landed, took out a small key, opened the door, and entered the garden.

This was her refuge, the secret place for her solitude, defended by the fidelity of her melancholy as by silent guardians.

"Never more?" She walked under the trellises, approached the water, stopped a moment, felt weary, and at last sat down on a stone, held her temples between her hands, and made an effort to concentrate her mind, to recover her self-possession. "He is still here, near me. I can see him again. Perhaps I shall find him standing on the steps of my house. He will take me in his arms, kiss my lips and eyes, tell me again that he loves me, that everything about me pleases him. He does not know— he does not understand. Nothing irreparable has happened. What is it, then, that has so upset and disturbed me? I have received a letter written by a girl who is far-away, imprisoned in a lonely villa near her demented father, who complains of her lot and seeks to change it. That is all. There is no more to say. And here is the letter."

Her fingers trembled, and she fancied she could detect Donatella's favorite perfume, as if the young girl were sitting beside her.

—Is she beautiful? Really beautiful? How does she look?—

The lines of the image were indistinct at first. She tried to seize them, but they eluded her. One particular above all others fixed itself in her mind—the large, massive hand.—Did he see her hand that night? He is very susceptible to the beauty of hands. When he meets a woman, he always looks at her hands. And he adores Sofia's hands.—She allowed herself to dwell on these childish considerations, then she smiled bitterly. And suddenly the image became perfect, lived, glowing with youth and power, overwhelmed and dazzled her.—Yes, she is beautiful! And hers is the beauty he desires.—

She kept her eyes fixed on the silent splendor of the waters, with the letter on her lap; she was nailed there by the inflexible truth. And involuntary thoughts of destruction flashed upon her inert discouragement; the face of Donatella burned by fire, her body crippled by a fall, her voice ruined by an illness! Then she had a horror of herself, followed by pity for herself and the other woman.—Has she not too the right to live? Let her live, let her love, let her have her joy.—She imagined for the

116

young girl some magnificent adventure, a happy love, an adorable betrothed, prosperity, luxury, pleasure.—Is there only one man on this earth, then, that she can love? Is it impossible that to-morrow she might meet some one who would win her heart? Is it impossible that her fate should suddenly turn her in another direction, take her far from here, lead her through unknown paths, separate her from us forever? Is it necessary that she should be loved by the man I love? Perhaps they never will meet again.—She tried thus to escape her presentiment. But a contrary thought whispered: "They have met once; they will seek each other, they will meet again. Her soul is not obscure—not one that can be lost in the multitude. She possesses a gift that shines like a star, and it will always be easily recognizable even from afar—her song. The marvel of her voice will serve her as a signal. She will surely avail herself of this power; she too will pass among mankind leaving a wake of admiration behind her. She will have glory as she has beauty—two attributes that will easily attract Stelio. They have met once; they will meet again."

The sorrowing woman bent as if under a yoke. A clear, pearly light bathed the lagoon in radiance. The islands of La Follia, San Clemente, and San Servilio were enveloped in a light mist. From a distance came at intervals a faint cry, as of shipwrecked sailors becalmed, answered by the harsh voice of a siren whistle or by the raucous call of the sea-gulls. At first the silence seemed terrible, then it grew sweet.

The woman, little by little, recovered her deep goodness of heart, felt again her old tenderness for the beautiful creature in whose personality she had once deceived her desire to love the good sister, Sofia. She thought again of the hours passed in the lonely villa on that hill of Settignano, where Lorenzo Arvale created his statues in the fulness of his strength and fervor, ignorant of the blow that was about to fall. She lived again in those days, saw again those places; she sat once more in memory for the famous sculptor who modeled her in clay, while Donatella sang some quaint old song; and the spirit of melody animated at once the model and the effigy, and her thoughts and that pure voice and the mystery of Art composed an appearance of a life almost divine in that great studio open on all sides to the light of heaven, whence Florence and its river was visible in the springtime valley.

In addition to fancying the girl a reflection of Sofia, had she not been attracted otherwise to her—the sweet Donatella, who never had known a mother's caress since her birth? She saw her again, grave and calm beside her father, the comfort for his hard work, guardian of the sacred flame, and also of a resolve of her own—a secret resolve, which preserved itself as bright and keen as a sword in its sheath.

—She is sure of herself; she is mistress of her own power. When at last she knows she is free, she will reveal herself as one made to rule. Yes, she is made to subjugate men, to excite their curiosity and their dreams. Even now, her instinct, bold and prudent as experience itself, directs her.—La Foscarina remembered Donatella's attitude toward Stelio on that night; her almost disdainful silence, her brief, dry words, her manner of leaving the table, her disappearance, leaving the image of herself framed within the circle of an unforgettable melody. Ah, she knows the art of stirring the soul of a dreamer. Certainly he cannot have forgotten her. And

117

just as certainly he awaits the hour when it shall be given him to meet her again—not less impatiently than she, who asks me where he is.—

Again she lifted the letter and ran her eyes over it, but her memory traveled faster than her eyes. The enigmatic query was at the foot of the page, like a half-veiled postscript. Looking at the written words, she felt again the same sharp pang as when she read them the first time, and once more her heart was shaken as if the danger were imminent, as if her passion and her hope were already lost beyond recall.—What is she about to do? Of what is she thinking? Did she expect him to search for her without delay, and, disappointed in that, does she now wish to tempt him? What does she intend to do?—She struggled against that uncertainty as against an iron door which she must force in order to find again behind it the light of her life.—Shall I answer her? Suppose I reply in such a way as to make her understand the truth, would my love necessarily be a prohibition of hers?—But here her soul rose with a mingled feeling of repugnance, modesty, and pride.—No, never! Never shall she learn of my wound from me—never, not even should she question me!—And she realized all the horror of an open rivalry between a woman no longer young and a girl strong in her maiden youth. She felt the humiliation and cruelty of such an unequal struggle. "But if not Donatella, would it not be some one else," again whispered the contrary spirit "Do you believe you can bind a man of his nature to your melancholy passion? The only condition under which you should have allowed yourself to love him, and to offer him a love faithful unto death, was in keeping the compact that you have broken."

"True, true!" she murmured, as if answering a distinct voice, in formal judgment, pronounced in the silence by invisible Fate.

"The only condition on which he can now accept your love, and recognize it, demands that you leave him free, that you give up all claim on him, that you renounce all, forever, and ask for nothing—the condition of being heroic. Do you understand?"

"True, true!" she repeated aloud, raising her head.

But the poison bit her. She remembered all the sweetness of caresses—the lips, the eyes, the strength and ardor of the lover had re-animated all her being.

A far-away monotonous sound of song floated in the air—a song of women's voices, that seemed to rise from bosoms oppressed, from throats as slender as reeds, like the sound evoked from the broken wires of old spinets at a touch on the worn keys; a shrill, unequal tone, in a lively and vulgar rhythm, which sounded sadder in that light and silence than the saddest things of life.

"Who is singing?"

With obscure emotion she arose, approached the shore, and listened.

"The madwomen of San Clemente!"

From the isle of La Follia, from the barred windows of the light, lonely hospital, came the lively yet melancholy chorus. It trembled, hesitated in the immensity of space, grew fainter and almost died away, then rose again and swelled to a piercing shriek, diminished once more, and finally sank to silence.

CHAPTER VIII
ILLUSIONS
Yes, heart-rending was the sweetness of that November, smiling like a sick person who has become free from suffering, knowing it is the last, and tasting again the sweetness of life, which reveals to him new charms when just about to leave him.

"Look at the Euganean hills below us, Foscarina; if the wind should come they will rise and float in the air like gauzy veils, and pass over our heads. I never have seen them so transparent. Some day I should like to go with you to Arquà; the villages there are as pink as the shells we find in myriads in the earth. When we arrive there, the first drops of a sudden shower will be robbing the peach-blossoms of their petals. We will wait under one of the arches of the Palladio to avoid getting wet. Then, without inquiring the way of anyone, we will look for the fountain of Petrarch. We will carry with us his poems in the small edition of Misserini's, that little book you keep beside your bed and cannot close any more because it is so full of pressed leaves and grasses. Would you like to go to Arquà some spring day?"

She did not reply, but gazed silently at the lips that said these graceful things; and, without hope, she simply took a fugitive pleasure in their movement and accent. For her there was in his image of the Spring the same enchantment as in a stanza of Petrarch's; but she could lay a bookmark in the one and find it again, while the poetic fancies must be lost with the passing hour.

She wished to say: "I will not drink at that fountain," but kept silence, that she might still enjoy the caress.—Oh, yes, intoxicate me with illusions! Play your own game; do with me as you will.—

"Here we are at San Giorgio in Alga. We shall reach Fusina in a few minutes."

The little walled islet passed before them, with its marble Madonna, perpetually admiring her reflection in the water, like a nymph.

"Why are you so sweet, my beloved? I never have seen you like this before. I know not where I am with you to-day. I cannot find words to tell you with what a sense of melody your presence inspires me. You are here beside me, I can hold your hand, yet you are diffused in the horizon, you yourself are the horizon, blended with the waters, with the islands, with the hills. When I was speaking just now, it seemed that each syllable created in you infinitely dilating circles, like those round that leaf just fallen from the gold-leaved tree. Is it true? Tell me that it is. Oh, look at me!"

119

He felt himself enveloped in this woman's love as by the air and the light; he breathed in that soul as in a distinct element, receiving from it an ineffable fulness of life as if a stream of mysterious things were flowing from her and from the glory of the daylight at the same time, and pouring itself into his heart. The desire to make some return for the happiness she gave him lifted him to an almost religious height of gratitude, and suggested to him words of thanks and of praise which he would have spoken had he been kneeling before her in the shadows. But the splendor of sky and sea around them was so great that he could only be as silent as she. And for both this was a moment of marvelous communion in the light; it was a journey brief yet immense, in which both traversed the dizzy distances they had within themselves.

The boat reached the shore of Fusina. They roused themselves, and gazed at each other with dazzled eyes.

—Does he love me, then?—

Hope and pain revived in the woman's heart. She did not doubt the sincerity of her beloved, nor that his words expressed the ardor of his heart. She knew how absolutely he abandoned himself to every wave of emotion, how incapable he was of deception or of falsehood. More than once she had heard him utter cruel truths with the same feline, flexible grace that some men adopt when they wish to appear charming. She knew well the direct, limpid gaze which sometimes became hard and icy, but which never was otherwise than straight; but she knew also the rapidity and marvelous diversity of emotion and thought that rendered his spirit unseizable. There was always in him something flexible and vigorous that suggested to the actress the double and diverse image of flame and of water. And it was this man she wished to fix, to captivate, to possess! There was always in him an unlimited ardor of life, a sense of euphoria, or joy in existence, as if every second were the supreme instant, and he were about to tear himself from the pleasure and pain of living, as from the tears and embraces of a last farewell. And it was for this insatiable avidity that she wished to remain the only nourishment!

What was she to him, if not an aspect of that "life of the thousand and thousand faces," toward which the poet's desire, according to one of his own images, continually shook all its thyrsi? For him she was a theme for visions and inventions, like the hills, the woods, the storms. He absorbed mystery and beauty from her as from all forms of the universe. Even now he had withdrawn his thoughts from her, and was occupied with a new quest; his changeful, ingenuous eyes sought for some miracle to marvel at and adore.

She looked at him, but he did not turn his face toward her; he was studying the damp, foggy region through which they were driving slowly. She sat beside him, feeling herself deprived of her strength, no longer capable of living in and for herself, of breathing with her own breath, of following a thought that was unknown to her beloved, hesitating even in her enjoyment of natural objects that he had not pointed out.

120

Her life seemed to be alternately dissolving and condensing itself. An instant of intensity would pass, and then she waited for the next, and between them she was conscious of nothing save that time was flying, the lamp was flickering, the body was fading, and that all things were perishing, dying.

"My dear, my friend," said Stelio, suddenly turning and taking her hand, impelled by an emotion that had overcome him, "why did we come to these places? They seem very sweet, but they are full of terror."

He looked at her keenly.

"You suffer," he said, with a depth of pity in his tone that made the woman turn pale. "Do you too feel this terror?"

She looked around with the anxiety of one pursued, and fancied she saw a thousand ominous phantoms rising from the earth.

"Those statues!" said Stelio, in a tone that changed them in her eyes into witnesses of her own wasting life.

The country around them was as deserted and silent as if its former inhabitants had been gone for centuries, or were sleeping in graves new-made the day before.

"Do you wish to return? The boat is still there."

She seemed not to hear.

"Speak, Foscarina!"

"Let us go—let us go on," she replied. "Wherever we may go our fate will not change."

Her body swayed to the slow, lulling roll of the wheels, and she feared to interrupt it; she shrank from the least effort, the smallest fatigue, overcome by heavy inertia. Her face was like the delicate veil of ash that covers a live coal, hiding its consumption.

"Dear, dear soul!" said Stelio, leaning toward her and lightly touching the pale cheek with his lips. "Lean on me; give yourself entirely to me; have confidence in me. Never will I fail you, never will you fail me. We shall find it—we shall find the true secret on which our love can rest forever, immovable. Do not be reserved with me. Do not suffer alone, nor hide your sorrows from me. When your heart swells with grief, speak to me. Let me believe that I can comfort you. Let us not hide anything from each other. I shall venture to recall to you a condition that you yourself made. Speak to me, and I will always answer you truthfully. Let me help you—me, who have received from you so much of good. Tell me that you do not fear to suffer. I believe your soul capable of supporting all the sadness of the world. Do not let me lose faith in that force of passion, whereby more than once you have

121

seemed to me divine. Tell me you do not fear suffering.... I don't know.... I may be mistaken. But I have felt a shadow around you, like a desperate wish to withdraw yourself, to leave me, to find some end. Why? Why? And, just now, looking at all this terrible desolation that smiles at us, a great fear suddenly filled my heart—I thought that perhaps even your love might change like all things, and pass away into nothingness. 'You will lose me.' Ah, those words were yours, Foscarina! They fell from your own lips."

She did not answer. For the first time since she had loved him, his words seemed vain, useless sounds, moving powerless through the air. For the first time, he seemed to her a weak and anxious creature, bound by inexorable laws. She pitied him as well as herself. He asked her to be heroic, a compact of grief and of violence. At the moment when he attempted to console and comfort her, he predicted a difficult test, prepared her for torture. But what was courage worth, of what use was any effort? What were all miserable human agitations worth, and why think of the future, even of the uncertain morrow?

The Past reigned supreme around them, and they themselves were nothing, and everything was nothing.—We are dying; both of us are dying. We dream, and then we die.—

"Hush! Hush!" was all she said, softly, as if they were in a cemetery. A slight smile touched her lips, and rested there as fixedly as the smile on the lips of a portrait.

The wheels rolled on over the white road, along the shores of the Brenta. The stream, sung and praised in the sonnets of the gallant abbés in the days when gondolas laden with music and pleasure had glided down its current, had now the humble aspect of a canal, where the iris-necked ducks splashed in flocks. On the damp, low plain the fields smoked, the bare trees showed plainly, their leaves rotting on the damp earth. A slow, golden mist floated above an immense vegetable decay that seemed to encroach even upon the walls, the stones, the houses, seeking to destroy them like the leaves. The patrician villas—where a pale life, delicately poisoned by cosmetics and perfumes, had burned itself out in languid pastimes— were now in ruins, silent and abandoned. Some had an aspect like a human ruin, with empty spaces that suggested hollow orbits and toothless mouths; others were crumbling, and looked as if ready to fall in powder, like a dead woman's hair when her tomb is opened; and here, there, everywhere, rose the still surviving statues. They seemed innumerable, like a scattered people. Some were still white, others were gray or yellow with lichens, or green and spotted with moss. They stood in all sorts of attitudes: goddesses, heroes, nymphs, seasons, hours, with their bows and arrows, their wreaths, cornucopias, and torches, with all the emblems of power, riches and pleasure, exiled now from fountains, grottoes, labyrinths, arbors, and porticoes: friends of the greenwood and the myrtle, protectors of fleeting loves, witnesses of eternal vows, figures of a dream far more ancient than the hands that had carved them, and the eyes that had contemplated them in the ruined gardens. And, in the sweet sunlight of the dying season, their shadows were like the shadows of the irrevocable Past—all, all that loves no longer, laughs and weeps no more,

122

never will live, never will return. And the unspoken word on their marble lips was the same that was expressed in the fixed smile on the lips of the world-weary woman—NOTHING!

CHAPTER IX
THE LABYRINTH
But that day they were to pass through other shadows, to know other fears.

Henceforth the tragic meaning of life filled both their minds, and they tried in vain to banish the physical sadness which from moment to moment made their spirits more clear yet more disturbed. They clasped each other's hand, as if they were groping in dark, dangerous places. They spoke little, but often they gazed into each other's eyes, and the look of the one poured into that of the other a wave of confused emotion, the mingling of their love and horror. But it did not calm their hearts.

"Shall we go farther?"

"Yes, let us go on."

Still they clasped each other's hand closely, as if they were about to go through some strange test, and were resolved to experiment as to what depths could be reached by the combined force of their melancholy. At the Dolo, the wheels made the chestnut-leaves rustle and crackle beneath them, and the tall changing trees flamed over their heads like crimson draperies on fire. At a distance was the Villa Barbariga, silent, deserted, of a reddish hue in its denuded garden, showing vestiges of old paintings in the cracks of its façade, like streaks of rouge on the wrinkled cheeks of an old woman. And, at every glance, the distances of the landscape seemed fainter and bluer, like things slowly submerged.

"Here is Strà."

They alighted before the Villa Pisani, and, accompanied by its guardian, they visited the deserted apartments. They heard the sound of their own footsteps on the marble that reflected them, the echoes in the historic arches, the creaking of the doors, the tiresome voice of the keeper awakening the memories of the place. The rooms were vast, hung with faded draperies and furnished in the style of the Empire, with Napoleonic emblems. The walls of one room were covered with portraits of the Pisani, procurators of San Marco; of another, with marble medallions of all the Doges; of a third, with a series of flowers painted in water-colors and mounted in delicate frames, pale as the dry flowers that are laid under glass, in memory of love or death.

As La Foscarina entered one room, she said:

"In time! Here, too!"

123

There, on a bracket, stood a transformation into marble of La Vecchia by Francesco Torbido, made even more repulsive by the relief, by the subtle skill of the sculptor, to bring out with his chisel each tendon, wrinkle, and hollow place in the old woman's face. And at the doors of this room seemed to appear the ghosts of the crowned women that had hidden their unhappiness and their decay in that vast dwelling, at once like a palace and a monastery.

"Maria Luisa di Parma, in eighteen hundred and seventeen," continued the monotonous voice.

"Ah, the Queen of Spain, wife of Charles the Fourth, and mistress of Manuel Godoï," said Stelio. "She attracts me more than all the others. She came here when they were in exile. Do you know whether she stayed here with the King and the favorite!"

But the guardian knew only that name and the date.

"Why does she attract you?" La Foscarina asked. "I know nothing of her history."

"Her end, the last years of her life of exile, after so much struggle and passion, are extraordinarily full of poetry."

And he described that violent and tenacious character, the weak, credulous King, the handsome adventurer who had enjoyed the smiles of the Queen, and had been dragged through the streets by the infuriated mob; the agitations of the three lives bound together by Fate, and swept before Napoleon's will like leaves in a whirlwind; the tumult at Aranjuez, the abdication, the exile.

"And Godoï—the Prince of Peace, as the King called him—faithfully followed the sovereigns into exile; he remained faithful to his royal mistress, and she to him. They all lived together under the same roof thenceforth, and Charles never doubted the virtue of Maria Luisa. Even to the day of his death, he lavished all manner of kindness on the two lovers. Imagine their life in this place; imagine here such a love coming safely through a storm so terrible. All was broken down, overthrown, reduced to powder by the destroyer. Bonaparte had passed that way, but had not smothered that love, already old, beneath the ruins. The faithfulness of those two violent natures moves my heart not less than the credulity of the kindly King. Thus they grew old. Imagine it! The Queen died first, then the King; and the favorite, who was younger than they, lived a wandering life a few years more."

"This is the Emperor's room," said the guardian solemnly, flinging open a door.

The great shade seemed omnipresent in the villa of the Doge Alvise. The imperial eagle, symbol of his power, dominated all the faded relics. But in the yellow room, the shade seemed to occupy the vast bed, to rest under the canopy,

124

surrounded by the four bedposts ornamented at the top with golden flames. The formidable sigla inscribed within the laurel crown shone upon the polished side of the bed. And this species of funereal couch seemed to be prolonged in the dim mirror hanging between the two figures of Victory that supported the candelabra.

"Did the Emperor sleep in this bed?" inquired the young man of the custodian, who pointed out to him on the wall the portrait of the great condottiere mantled in ermine, wearing a crown of laurel and holding a scepter, as he appeared at the coronation blessed by Pius VII. "Is it certain?"

He was surprised at himself at not feeling the emotion experienced by ambitious spirits at the sight of the traces of heroes—that strong throb he knew so well.

He lifted the edge of the yellow counterpane, and let it fall as suddenly as if the pillow under it had been full of vermin.

"Let us go away from this place; let us go!" said La Foscarina, who had been looking through the windows at the park, where the golden bars of the setting sun alternated with bluish-green zones of shade. "We cannot breathe here," she added.

The air, in truth, was like that of a vault.

"Now we pass into the room of Maximilian of Austria," said the droning voice, "he took the dressing-room of Amélie de Beauharnais for his bedroom."

They crossed this apartment in a flood of crimson light. The sunlight struck on a crimson couch, flashed rainbows from a frail chandelier with crystal drops that hung from the ceiling and kindled perpendicular red lines on the wall. Stelio stopped on the threshold, evoking in his fancy as he did so, the pensive figure of the young Archduke, with blue eyes, that fair flower of Hapsburg fallen in a barbaric land one summer morning!

"Let us go!" begged La Foscarina again, seeing him still delay.

She hastened through the immense salon, painted in fresco by Tiepolo; the Corinthian bronze gate closing behind her gave forth a clang as resonant as the stroke of a bell, sending prolonged vibrations through space. She flew along, terrified, as if the whole palace were about to crumble and fall, and the light to fail, and she dreaded lest she should find herself alone among the shadows with these phantoms of unhappiness and death. As Stelio followed, through the space wherein the air was moved by her flight, between those walls enclosing relics, behind the famous actress who had simulated the fury of deadly passions, the desperate efforts of will and of desire, and the violent conflict of splendid destinies on the stage of all lands, the warm blood in his veins grew chill, as if he were passing through a freezing atmosphere; he felt his heart grow cold, his courage flag; his reason for being lost its hold on his mind, and the magnificent illusions with which he had fed his soul, that it might surpass itself and his destiny, wavered and were dispersed.

125

"Are we still living?" he asked, when they found themselves in the air without, in the park, far from the unwholesome odor.

He took La Foscarina's hand, shook her gently, gazed into her eyes and tried to smile; then he drew her into the sunlight in the middle of the green meadow.

"What heat! Do you feel it? How sweet the grass is!"

He half-closed his eyes, that he might feel the sun's rays on his eyelids, and was once more filled with the joy of living. The woman imitated him, calmed by the pleasure her beloved showed; and she looked from under her half-closed eyelids at his fresh, sensuous mouth. They sat thus for some time, hand-in-hand, their feet resting on the warm grass. Her thoughts turned back to the Eugenean hills, which he had described, to the villages pink as the buried shells, to the first drops of rain on the tender leaves, Petrarch's fountain, to all things fair and pleasant.

"Life might still be sweet!" she sighed, in a voice wherein was the miracle of hope born anew.

The heart of her beloved became like a fruit suddenly ripened by a miraculous ray. Joy, delight, and tenderness spread through his whole being. Once more he reveled in the joy of the moment, as if it were the last of life. Love was exalted above Destiny.

"Do you love me? Tell me?"

She made no answer, but she opened wide her eyes, and the vastness of the universe was within the circle of those pupils. Never was boundless love more powerfully signified by mortal woman.

"Ah, life with thee is sweet, sweet—yesterday as well as to-morrow!"

He seemed intoxicated with her, with the sunlight, the grass, the divine sky, as with something never before seen or possessed. The prisoner leaving his stifling cell, the convalescent who beholds the sea after looking death in the face, are not more intoxicated.

"Would you like to go now? Shall we leave our melancholy behind us? Would you like to go to a country where there is no autumn?"

—The autumn is in myself, and I carry it everywhere—she thought; but she smiled the slight smile with which she veiled her sadness.—It is I—It is I that must go away alone; I will disappear; I will go far-away and die, my love, O my love!—

During this moment of respite, she had not succeeded either in conquering her sadness or reviving her hope; but her anguish was softened, and she had lost all bitterness and rancor.

"Do you wish to go away?"

—To go away, always to be going away, to wander throughout the world, to go long distances!—thought the nomad woman.—Never to stop, never to rest! The anxiety of the journey is not over yet, but already the truce has expired. You wish to comfort me, my friend, and, to console me, you propose that I should go far-away once more, although I returned to my home, as it were, but yesterday.—

Suddenly her eyes looked like two sparkling springs.

"Leave me in my home a little while longer. And remain here, too, if that is possible. Later, you will be free, you will be happy. You have so long a time before you! You are young. You will win what you deserve. They will not lose you, even if they must wait for you."

Her eyes had two crystal masks before them; they glittered in the sunshine, and seemed almost fixed in her fevered face.

"Ah, always the same shadow!" Stelio exclaimed, with an impatience he could not conceal. "But what are you thinking of? What do you fear? Why not tell me what it is that troubles you? Explain yourself. Who is it that must wait for me?"

She trembled with terror at that question, which seemed new and unexpected, although he only repeated her own last words. She trembled to find herself so near danger, as if, in walking across this fair meadow, a precipice had suddenly opened under her feet.

And suddenly, in that unfamiliar place, on that beautiful grass, at the end of the day, after all those specters, sanguinary or bloodless, rose a living image of will and desire, which filled her with far greater terror. Suddenly, above all the figures of the Past, arose the figure of the Future, and again the aspect of her life was changed; and the sweetness of the respite was already lost, and the fair meadow with its sweet grass was worth nothing.

"Yes, let us talk, if you wish."

But she was obliged to lift her face a little to keep her tears from falling.

"Do not be sad!" pleaded the young man, whose soul was suspended on those eyelids, whence the tears would not fall. "You hold my heart in your hand. I never will fail you. Then why torment yourself? I am wholly yours."

127

For him, too, the image of Donatella was there, with her rounded figure, her body as robust and agile as a wingless Victory, armed with the glory of maidenhood, attractive yet hostile, ready to struggle, and then to yield. But his soul was suspended from the eyelids of the other woman, like the tears that veiled the eyes in which he had seen the vastness of the universe, the infinity of love.

"Foscarina!"

At last the warm tears fell, but she did not let them course down her cheeks. With one of those movements that sometimes sprang from her sadness with the swift grace of a freed wing, she checked them, moistened her finger-tips with them, and touched her temples without drying them. And, while she still kept her tears upon herself, she tried to smile.

"Forgive me, Stelio. I am so weak!"

"Ah, dear fingers—beautiful as Sofia's! Let me kiss them as they are, still wet."

Within his caressing arm, he drew her across the field to a zone of golden green. Lightly, with his arm supporting hers, he kissed her finger-tips, one after another, more delicate than the buds of the tuberose. She startled, and he felt her tremble at each touch of his lips.

"They are salt!"

"Take care, Stelio! Some one may see us."

"No one is here."

"Perhaps down there, in the hothouses."

"There is not a sound. Hark!"

"What a strange silence! It is ecstasy."

"We might hear the falling of a leaf."

"And the keeper?"

"He has gone to meet some other visitor."

"Does anyone ever come here?"

"The other day Richard Wagner came here with Daniela von Bülow."

"Ah, yes, the niece of the Countess Agoult, of 'Daniel Stern.'"

128

"And, among all those phantoms, with which did that great stricken heart converse?"

"Who can tell?"

"Only with himself, perhaps."

"Perhaps."

"Look at the glass windows and walls of the conservatories—how they sparkle! They appear iridescent. Rain, sunshine and time have painted it in that way. Does it not seem to reflect a distant twilight? Perhaps you have sometimes stopped on the Pesaro quay, to look at the beautiful pentafore window of the Evangelists. If you raised your eyes, you could see the windows of the palace marvelously painted by the changes of weather."

"You know all the secrets of Venice!"

"Not all yet."

"How warm it is here! See how tall those cedars are. There is a swallow's nest hanging on that limb."

"The swallows went away very late this year."

"Will you really take me to the Euganean hills in the spring?"

"Yes, Foscarina, I should like to do so."

"Spring is so far-away!"

"Life can still be sweet."

"We are living in a dream."

"Look at Orpheus with his lyre, all dressed in lichens."

"Ah, what a land of dreams! No one comes here any more. Grass, grass everywhere! There is not a single human footstep."

"Deucalion with his stones, Ganymede with his eagle, Diana with her stag—all the gods of mythology."

"How many statues! But these, at least, are not in exile. The ancient hornbeams still protect them."

129

"Here strolled Maria Luisa di Parma, between the King and the favorite. From time to time she would pause to listen to the click of the blades that cut the hornbeams to form arches. She would let fall her handkerchief, perfumed with jessamine, and Don Manuel Godoï would pick it up with a graceful gesture, hiding the pain he suffered when he stooped—a souvenir of the outrages he had endured at the hands of the mob in the streets of Aranjuez. How warm the sun was, and how excellent the snuff in its enameled box, when the King said with a smile: 'Certainly, our dear Bonaparte is not so well off at Saint Helena as we are here.' But the demon of power, of struggle, and of passion was still alive in the Queen's heart. Look at those red roses!"

"They fairly burn. One would think each had a live coal at its heart. Yes, they seem actually to burn."

"The sun is growing red. This is the hour for the Chioggia sails on the lagoon."

"Gather a rose for me."

"Here is one."

"Oh, but its leaves are falling."

"Well, here is another."

"These leaves are falling too."

"They are all at the point of death. Perhaps this one is not."

"Do not break it off."

"Look! These seem to be redder still. Bonifazio's velvet—do you remember it? It has the same strength."

"'The inmost flower of the flame.'"

"What a memory!"

"Listen! They are closing the doors of the conservatories."

"It is time to go," said Stelio, abruptly yet gently.

"The air is beginning to be cooler."

"Do you feel cold?"

"No, not yet."

"Did you leave your cloak in the carriage?"

"Yes."

"We will wait at Dolo for the train, and return to Venice by the railway."

"Yes."

"We still have time to spare."

"What is this? Look!"

"I don't know."

"What a bitter odor! It is a sort of shrubbery of box and hornbeams."

"Ah, it is the labyrinth!"

A rusty iron gate barred the entrance to the labyrinth between two columns that bore two Cupids riding on stone dolphins. Nothing was to be seen on the other side of the gate, except the beginning of the path, and a kind of solidly built and intricate thicket, dark and mysterious. In the center of the maze rose a tower, at the summit of which stood the statue of a warrior, as if reconnoitering from that point.

"Have you ever been in a labyrinth?" Stelio inquired.

"No, never," she replied.

They lingered to examine the entrance to the deceptive playground, composed by an ingenious gardener for the amusement of ladies and their cavaliers in the days of hoops and flowered waistcoats. But age and neglect had rendered it mournful and wild, had deprived it of all appearance of grace and regularity, and had changed it into thick yellowish-brown woodland, full of inextricable turns through which the slanting rays of the setting sun shone so red that some of the shrubs looked like smokeless fire.

"It is open," said Stelio, feeling the gate yield as he leaned on it. "Do you see?"

He pushed back the rusty iron gate, took a step forward, and crossed the threshold.

"Where are you going?" asked his companion, with instinctive fear, putting out a hand to detain him.

"Do you not wish to go in?"

She was perplexed. But the labyrinth attracted them with its mystery, illumined by deep flames.

131

"Suppose we should lose ourselves?"

"You can see for yourself that it is very small. We can easily find the gate again."

"And suppose we don't find it?"

He laughed at this childish fear.

"We might remain in there through all eternity!" he said.

"No, no! No one is anywhere near. Let us go away."

She tried to draw him back, but he defended himself, stepping backward toward the path. Suddenly he disappeared, laughing.

"Stelio! Stelio!"

She could see him no longer, but she heard his ringing laughter in the midst of the wild thicket.

"Come back! come back!"

"No, no! Come in and find me."

"Stelio, come back! You will be lost," she called.

"I shall find Ariadne."

At that name, she felt her heart throb suddenly, then contract, then palpitate confusedly. Was not that the name he had called Donatella, that first night? Had he not called her Ariadne down there, in the gondola, while seated at the young girl's feet? She even remembered his words: "Ariadne possesses a divine gift, whereby her power transcends all limits." She recalled his accent, his attitude, his look.

Tumultuous anguish seized upon her, obscured her reason, prevented her from realizing the spontaneity of the happening, and the simple careless jest in her friend's speech. The terror that lay hidden in the depths of her love rose in rebellion, mastered her, blinded her with misery. The trifling little accident assumed an appearance of cruelty and derision. She could still hear that laugh ringing from the melancholy maze.

"Stelio!"

In her frantic hallucination, she cried out as if she had seen him embraced by the other woman, torn from her arms forever.

132

"Stelio!"

"Come and find me!" he answered laughing, still invisible.

She rushed into the labyrinth to find him, and advanced straight toward the voice and the laugh, guided by her impulse. But the path turned; a wall of bushes rose before her, impenetrable, and stopped her. She followed the winding, deceiving path; but one turning followed another, and all looked alike, and the circle seemed to have no end.

"Look for me!" cried the voice from a distance, through the living hedges.

"Where are you? Where are you? Can you see me?"

She looked about for some opening in the hedge through which she might see. But all she saw was thick, interlacing branches, and the redness of the setting sun which lighted them on one side, while shadows darkened them on the other. The box-bushes and the hornbeams were so closely mingled that they increased momentarily the bewilderment of the breathless woman.

"I am losing myself! Come and meet me!"

Again that boyish laugh came from the maze.

"Ariadne, Ariadne! the thread!"

Now the words came from the opposite side, striking her heart as if with a blow.

"Ariadne!"

She turned back, ran, turned again, tried to break through the hedge, to see through the undergrowth, to break the branches. She saw nothing but the maze, always the same in every direction. At last she heard a step, so close that she thought it must be just behind her, and she started. But she was deceived. Again she explored her green prison; she listened, waited; she could hear no sound but her own breathing and the beating of her heart. The silence had become absolute. She gazed at the clear sky, curving in its immensity over the two green walls that held her prisoner. She felt that that immensity and narrowness were the only things in the world. And she could not succeed in separating in her thoughts the reality of that place from the image of her mental torture, the natural aspect of things from that kind of living allegory created by her own anguish.

"Stelio, where are you?"

No reply. She listened and waited in vain. The seconds seemed like hours.

133

"Where are you? I am afraid!"

No reply. But where was he, then? Had he found the way out? Had he left her there all alone? Would he continue to play this cruel game?

A mad desire to scream, to sob, to throw herself on the ground, to hurt herself, to make herself ill, to die, assailed the distracted woman. Again she raised her eyes to the silent sky. The tops of the tall hornbeams were reddened, like logs when they have ceased to blaze and are about to fall in ashes.

"I can see you!" suddenly said a laughing voice, in the deep shadows, very near her.

"Where are you?"

He laughed among the leaves, but without revealing himself, like a faun in hiding. This game excited him; his body grew warm and supple by this exercise of his agility; and the wild mystery, the contact with the earth, the odor of autumn, the strangeness of this unexpected adventure, the woman's bewilderment, even the presence of the marble deities mingled with his physical pleasure an illusion of antique poetry and grace.

"Where are you? Oh, do not play any more! Do not laugh in that way! Enough!"

He had crept, bareheaded, into the bushes on his hands and knees. He felt the dead leaves, the soft moss. And as he breathed among the branches, and felt his heart throb with the strange delight of the situation, with the communion between his own life and the vegetable life around him, the spell of his fancy renewed among those winding ways the industry of the first maker of wings, the myth of the monster that was born of Pasiphaë and the Bull, the Attic legend of Theseus in Crete. All that ancient world became real to him. In that glowing autumn evening, he was transfigured, according to the instincts of his blood and the recollections of his mind, into one of those ambiguous forms, half animal and half divine, one of those glittering genii whose throats were swollen with the same gland that hangs from the neck of the goat. A joyous voluptuousness suggested strange surprises to him, suggested the swiftness of pursuit, of flight, capture, and a fleeting embrace in the shadows of the wood. Then he desired some one like himself, fresh youthfulness that could share his laughter, two light feet to fly before him, two arms to resist him, a prize to capture at last. Donatella with her curved figure recurred to his mental vision.

"Enough, Stelio! I cannot run any more. I shall fall."

La Foscarina uttered a scream on feeling her skirt pulled by a hand that had reached through the shrubbery. She bent down, and saw in the shadows the face of a laughing faun. The laughter struck her ear without calming her distress, without

134

breaking the sense of suffering that overpowered her. As she looked at his boyish face, she saw at the same instant the face of the singer, who seemed to be stooping with her, imitating her movement as if she were a shadow. Her mind became more confused, and she could not distinguish between illusion and reality. The other woman seemed to overthrow her, oppress her, suffocate her.

"Leave me! Leave me! It is not I whom you seek!"

Her voice was so changed that Stelio broke off his laughter and his sport, withdrew his arm, and rose to his feet. She could not see him; the leafy, impenetrable wall was between them again.

"Take me away from this place. I cannot bear any more. My strength is gone. I suffer."

He could find no words to comfort her. The simultaneous coincidence of his recent thought of Donatella, and her sudden divination of it, impressed him deeply.

"Wait a little! I will try to find the way out. I will call some one."

"Are you going away?"

"Don't be afraid! There is no danger."

But while he spoke thus to reassure her, he felt the inaneness of his words— the incongruity between that laughable adventure and the obscure emotion born of a far different cause. And now he too felt the strange ambiguity whereby the trifling event appeared in two confusing aspects: a suppressed desire to laugh persisted under his concern for her, so that his perturbation was new to him, like wild agitations born of extravagant dreams.

"Do not go away!" she implored, a prey to her hallucinations. "Perhaps we can meet there at the next turning. Let us try. Take my hands."

Through an opening, he took her hands; he started on touching them; they were icy cold.

"Foscarina, what is the matter? Are you really ill? Wait! I will try to break through."

He attempted to break down the hedge, and snapped off a few twigs, but its thickness resisted him, and he scratched his hands uselessly.

"No, it is impossible."

"Cry out! Call some one."

He cried aloud in the silence.

135

The top of the hedge had lost its deep color, but a red light now spread over the sky above them. A triangle of wild ducks passed in sweeping flight.

"Let me go, Foscarina. I shall find the tower easily, and will call from there. Some one will be sure to hear me."

"No! No!"

But she heard him move away, followed the sound of his steps, and was once more bewildered by the maze, once more alone and lost. She stopped, waited, listened, and looked at the sky. She lost all sense of time; the seconds seemed hours.

"Stelio! Stelio!"

She was no longer capable of an effort to control her disordered and exasperated mind. She felt the approach of a crisis of mad fear, as one feels the approach of a whirlwind.

HE WATCHED THE WOMAN TURNING AND RUNNING LIKE A MAD CREATURE ALONG THE DARK, DELUSIVE PATHS

136

From an Original Drawing by Arthur H. Ewer

"Stelio!"

He heard that cry full of anguish, and hastened his search along the winding paths that first seemed to lead him toward the tower and then away from it. The laughter had frozen in his heart. His whole soul shook to its foundation every time his name reached him, uttered by that invisible agony. And the gradual lessening of the light brought up an image of blood that is flowing away, of slowly fading life.

"I am here! I am here!"

One of the paths brought him at last to the open space where the tower stood. He ran furiously up the winding stairs, felt dizzy when he reached the top, closed his eyes while grasping the railing, opened them again, and saw a long zone of fire on the horizon, the disk of the rayless moon, the gray plain, and the labyrinth below him, black and spotted with box-bush and horn-beam, narrow in its endless convolutions, looking like a dismantled edifice covered with wild vines.

"Stop! Stop! Do not run like that! Some one has heard me. A man is coming. I can see him coming. Wait! Stop!"

He watched the woman turning and running like a mad creature along the dark, delusive paths, like something condemned to vain torture, to some useless but eternal fatigue, like a sister of the fabulous martyrs.

"Stop!"

It seemed that she did not hear him, or that she could not control her fatal agitation, and that he could not rescue her, but must always remain there, a witness of that terrible chastisement.

"Here he is!"

One of the keepers had heard their cries, had approached them, and now entered by the gateway. Stelio met him at the foot of the tower, and together they hastened to find the lost woman. The man knew the secret of the labyrinth, and Stelio prevented any chatter and jests by surprising him with his generosity.

"Has she lost consciousness—has she fallen?" The darkness and the silence were sinister, and he felt alarmed. She did not answer when he called her, and he could not hear her footsteps. Night had already fallen on the place, and a damp veil was descending from the purple sky.

"Shall I find her in a swoon upon the ground," he thought.

137

He started at seeing a mysterious figure appear at a turning, with a pale face that attracted all the last rays of daylight, white as a pearl, with large, fixed eyes, and lips closely compressed.

They turned back toward the Dolo, taking the same route beside the Brenta. She never spoke, never opened her lips, never answered, as if she could not unclose her teeth. She lay in the bottom of the carriage, wrapped in her cloak, and now and then she shook with a deep shudder, as one attacked by malarial fever. Her friend tried to take her hands in his to warm them, but in vain—they were inert and lifeless. And as they drove along, the statues passed and passed beside them.

The river flowed black between its banks, under the purple and silver sky; the moon was rising. A black boat came down the stream, towed by two gray horses with heavy hoofs, led by a man who whistled cheerfully, and the funnel smoked on the deck like a chimney on a hut. The yellow light of a lantern flashed, and the odor of supper floated on the air; and here and there, as they drove along, the statues passed and passed beside them.

It was like a Stygian landscape, like a vision of Hades, a region of shadows, mist, and water. Everything grew misty and vanished like spirits. The moon enchanted and attracted the plain, as it enchants and attracts the water, absorbing the vapors of earth with insatiable, silent thirst. Solitary pools shone everywhere; small, silvery canals were visible, glittering at uncertain distances. Earth seemed to be gradually losing its solidity, and the sky seemed to regard its own melancholy reflected in innumerable placid mirrors.

And here and there, along the banks of the stream, like the ghosts of a people disappeared, the statues passed and passed!

CHAPTER X
THE POWER OF THE FLAME
"Do you think often of Donatella, Stelio?" La Foscarina inquired suddenly, after a long silence, during which neither had heard anything but the sound of their own footsteps along the canal path of the Vetrai, illumined by the multi-colored lights from the fragile objects that filled the windows of the neighboring shops.

Her voice sounded harsh and strained. Stelio stopped suddenly, as one who finds himself confronted by an unexpected difficulty. His spirit had been roaming over the red and green isle of Murano, begemmed with flowers in her present desolate poverty, which seemed to blot out the memory of the joyous time when poets had sung her praises as "a sojourn for nymphs and demigods." He had been thinking of the famous gardens where Andrea Navagero, Cardinal Bembo, Aretino, Aldo, and their learned followers, rivaled one another in the elegance of their Platonic dialogues, lauri sub umbra. He had been thinking of convents, luxurious as boudoirs, inhabited by little nuns dressed in white camelot and laces, with curls on their temples, and necks uncovered, after the fashion of the ancient honored courtesans, given to secret loves, much sought after by wealthy patricians, with such

138

euphonious names as Ancilla Soranzo, Cipriana Morosini, Zanetta Balbi, Beatrice Falier, Eugenia Muschiera, pious instructors in the ways of love. His changeful dreams were accompanied by a plaintive little air, a forgotten dance measure, in which the faint soul of Murano tinkled and whispered.

At this abrupt question, the air fled from his memory, all imaginings were dispersed, the enchantment of the old life vanished. His wandering mind was called back, and came with reluctance. He felt beside him the throbbing of a living heart, which he must inevitably wound. He looked at his friend.

She was walking beside the canal, calm, with no sign of agitation, between the green water and the iridescence of the rows of delicate vases. Only her slender chin trembled slightly, between her short veil and fur collar.

"Yes, sometimes," he replied, after an instant of hesitation, recoiling from falsehood, and feeling the necessity to elevate their love above ordinary deceptions and pretensions, so that it should remain for him a cause of strength, not of weakness, a free agreement, not a heavy chain.

She pursued her way without wavering, but she had lost all consciousness of movement in the terrible throbbing of her heart, which shook her from head to foot. She saw nothing more: all she was aware of was the nearness of the fascinating water.

"Her voice is unforgettable," Stelio went on, after a pause, having found his courage. "Its power is amazing. From that first evening, I have thought that that singer might be the marvelous instrument for my great work. I wish she would consent to sing the lyric parts of my tragedy, the odes that arise from the symphonies and resolve themselves into figures of the dance at the end, between episodes. La Tanagra has consented to dance. I have confidence in your good offices, dear friend, to obtain also the consent of Donatella Arvale. Thus the Dionysiac trinity would be reëstablished in a perfect manner on the new stage, for the joy of mankind."

Even while he spoke he realized that his words had a false ring, that his unconscious air contrasted too crudely with the dark shadow on the woman's face. In spite of himself, he had exaggerated his frank tone in speaking of Donatella merely as an instrument of art, a purely ideal force to be drawn into the circle of his magnificent enterprise. In spite of himself, disturbed by the anxiety in that soul so near his own, he had leaned slightly toward deception. Certainly what he had said was the exact truth, but his friend had demanded from him another truth. He broke off suddenly, unable to endure the sound of his own words. He felt that at that hour, between the actress and himself, art had no meaning, no vital value. Another force dominated them, more imperious, more disquieting. The world created by intellect seemed inert as the ancient stones on which they trod. The only real and formidable power was the poison running in their human blood. The will of the one said: "It is my will that you shall love and serve me, wholly, mine alone, body and soul." The will of the other said: "It is my will that you shall love and serve me, but

139

while I live I shall renounce nothing that may appeal to my wish and fancy." The struggle was bitter and unequal.

As she remained silent, unconsciously hastening her steps, he prepared himself to face the other truth.

"I understand, of course, that that was not what you wished to know."

"You are right: it was not that. Well?"

She turned to him with a sort of convulsive violence that reminded him of her fury one far-off evening, when she had cried madly: "Go! Run! She awaits you!"

At this moment a workman met them, and offered to show them over the neighboring glass factory.

"Yes, let us go in there," said La Foscarina, hurriedly following the workman. Presently they reached the furnace room, and were enveloped in its fiery breath, as they gazed at an incandescent altar, the glow from which dazzled their eyes with a painful glare.

—To disappear, to be swallowed up, to leave no sign!—cried the woman's heart, intoxicated with the thought of destruction.—In one second that fire could devour me like a dry stick, a bundle of straw.—And she went nearer to the open mouths in which she could see the molten flame, more resplendent than a midsummer sun, rolling around the earthen pots in which the shapeless mass was melting; the workmen, standing around, awaited the right moment to approach with iron tubes to shape that mass with the breath from their lips and the instruments of their art.

—O virtue of Fire!—thought the Inspirer, turned from his anxiety by the miraculous beauty of the element that had become to him as familiar as a brother, since the day he had found the revealing melody.—Ah, that I might give to the life of the creatures that love me the perfection of the forms to which I aspire! That I might fuse all their weaknesses in some white heat, and make of the product obedient matter in which to impress the commandments of my heroic will and the images of my pure poetry! Why, my friend, why will you not be the divine living statue molded by my spirit, the work of faith and sorrow whereby our lives might surpass even our art? Why are we so near resembling ordinary lovers, who lament and curse? When I heard from your lips those admirable words: 'I can do one thing that love alone cannot do,' I believed indeed that you could give me more than love. You must be able always to do those things that love can do, besides those it cannot do, in order to meet my insatiable nature.—

Meanwhile, work was going on about the furnace. At the end of the blow pipes the molten glass swelled, twisted, became silvery as a little cloud, shone like the moon, cracked, divided into a thousand infinitesimal fragments, glittering and thin as the threads we see at daybreak stretching from tree to tree. The glass-blowers

140

were making harmonious vases. The apprentices placed a small, pear-shaped mass of burning paste on the spot chosen by the master-workmen; and the pear lengthened, twisted, transformed itself into a handle, a rim, a spout, a foot, or a stem. The glowing heat slowly died out under the instruments, and the half-formed cup was again exposed to the heat, then drawn from it docile, ductile, sensitive to the lightest touches that ornamented and refined it, conforming it to the model handed down by their ancestors, or to the free invention of a new creator.

Extraordinarily light and agile were the human gestures that produced these elegant creatures of the fire, of breath and iron; they were like the movements of a silent dance. The figure of La Tanagra appeared to the Inspirer among the perpetual undulations of the flame, like a salamander. Donatella's voice seemed to sing to him the powerful melody.

—To-day, again, I myself have given you the thought of her for a companion—thought La Foscarina—I myself have called her up between us, and evoked her shadow when perhaps your thoughts were elsewhere; I have suddenly led her to you, as on that night of delirium.—

It was true, it was true! From the instant when the singer's name had been spoken on the water by Foscarina, she herself had unconsciously exalted the new image in the poet's mind, had nourished it with her jealousy and fear, had strengthened and increased it day by day, and had at last illumined it with certainty. More than once she had said to the young man, who perhaps had forgotten: "She awaits you!" More than once she had presented to his imagination that distant, mysterious figure of expectancy. As on that Dionysian night, when the conflagration of Venice had lighted up the two youthful faces with the same reflection, it was now her own passion that illumined them, and they glowed only because she herself had made them.—Certainly, he now possesses that image, and it possesses him. My anguish only augments his ardor. It is a joy to him to love her before my despairing eyes!—

"As soon as the vase is shaped, we put it in the furnace room to be tempered," replied one of the men to a query from Stelio. "If it were exposed to the air immediately it would crack in a thousand pieces."

They could see the radiant vases, still slaves of the fire, still under its empire, gathered in a receptacle joined to the furnace in which they had been fused.

"They have been there ten hours," said the workman, pointing to his graceful family. "Is this our great Foscarina?" he added in an undertone to Stelio. He had recognized her when she had lifted her veil, suffocating with the heat.

Revealing ingenuous emotion, the master workman took a step toward her and bowed respectfully.

141

"One evening, my lady, you made me tremble and weep like a child. Will you allow me, in memory of that evening, which I never shall forget, to offer you a little work from the hands of the poor Seguso?"

"A Seguso, are you?" said the poet, leaning toward the little man, to look at him closer; "are you of the great family of glass-blowers, one of the genuine race?"

"At your service, master."

"A prince, then."

"Yes, a harlequin playing the prince."

"You know all the secrets of the art, eh?"

The Muranese made a mysterious gesture which seemed to call up all the deep ancestral knowledge of which he affirmed himself the last heir.

"Then, mistress, will you deign to accept it?"

La Foscarina had not spoken, fearing to trust her voice, but now all her affable grace rose above her sadness and accepted the gift while compensating the giver.

The vase held by the little bent man that had created it was like a miraculous flower blooming on a twisted shrub. It was a thing of beauty, mysterious as natural things are mysterious; it held the life of a human breath in its hollow; its transparence equaled that of sky and water; its purple rim was like a floating seaweed; no one could have told the reason why it was so beautiful; and its value was either slight or beyond price, according to the eyes that looked at it.

La Foscarina chose to take it with her, without having it packed, as one carries a flower.

CHAPTER XI
REMINISCENCE
They left the factory, and walked along a road that was enclosed between the walls of silent gardens. The bronze-like laurels were touched with gold at the tops by the setting sun. The air was filled with sparkling gold-dust.

"How sweet and terrible was the fate of Gaspara Stampa," said Stelio. "Do you know her Sonnets? Yes, I saw them one day on your table. She was a strange mingling of ice and fire. Sometimes her mortal passion, above the Petrarchism of Aretino, lifted a glorious cry. I remember a magnificent verse of hers:

Vivere ardendo e non sentire il male!"

142

"Do you remember, Stelio," said La Foscarina, with that peculiar slight smile of hers which gave her face the look of one walking in her sleep, "do you remember the sonnet that begins:

Signore, io so che in me non son più viva,
E veggo omai ch'ancor in voi son morta?"
"I don't remember, Fosca."

"Do you remember your beautiful fancy about the dead Summer? Summer was lying on a funeral barge, dressed in gold like a dogaressa, and the procession was bearing her toward the Island of Murano, where a master of the flame was to enclose her in a shroud of opalescent glass, so that when she should be submerged in the depths of the lagoon, she could at least watch the waving seaweed. Do you remember?"

"It was an evening in September."

"The last night of September, the night of the Allegory. There was a great light on the water. You were in an exalted mood, and talked and talked. What things you said! You had come from solitude, and your overcharged soul broke forth. You poured a sparkling wave of poetry over your companion. A bark passed, laden with pomegranates. I called myself Perdita. Do you remember?"

As she walked she felt the extreme lightness of her step and felt that something in her was vanishing, as if her body were on the point of being changed to an empty chrysalis.

"My name was still Perdita. Stelio, do you recall another sonnet of Gaspara's beginning:

Io vorrei pur che Amor dicesse come
Debbo seguirlo....
And the madrigal beginning:

Se tu credi piacere al mio signore?"
"I did not know you were so familiar with the unhappy Anasilla, my dear."

"Ah, I will tell you. I was hardly fourteen years old when I played in an old romantic tragedy called Gaspara Stampa. I played the leading part. It was at Dolo, where we passed the other day on our way to Strà. We played in a small rustic theater—a kind of tent. It was the year before my mother died. I remember it very well. I can remember the sound of my own voice, which was weak then, when I forced it in the tirades because some one in the wings kept whispering to me to speak louder, louder!... Well, Gaspara was despairing; she wept and raved for her cruel Count. There were many things about it all that my small, profaned soul did not know or understand, and I know not what instinct and comprehension of sorrow led me to find the accent and the cries that could stir the miserable crowd from which we expected to gain our daily bread. Ten hungry persons used me as a

143

breadwinner; brutal necessity cut and tore away from me all the dream-flowers born of my trembling precocity. Oh, it was a time of weeping and suffocation, of terror, of unthinking weariness, of mute horror. Those that martyrized me knew not what they were doing, poor creatures, made stupid by poverty and work. God pardon them and give them peace! Only my mother—she, too, who 'for having loved too well and been too little loved, unhappy lived and died'—only my mother had pity on my pain, and knew how to take me in her arms, how to calm my horrible trembling, to weep when I wept, to console me. My blessed mother!"

Her voice changed. Her mother's eyes once again looked upon her, kind and firm and infinite as a peaceful horizon.—Tell me, tell me what I must do! Guide me, teach me, you who know!—Her heart felt again the clasp of those arms, and from the distance of years the old pain came back, but not harshly; it was almost sweet. The memory of her struggles and her sufferings seemed to bathe her soul in a warm wave, to sustain and comfort it. The test had been hard and the victory difficult, obtained at the price of persistent labor, against brutal and hostile forces. She had witnessed the deepest misery and ruin, she had known heroic efforts, pity, horror, and the face of Death.

"I know what hunger is, Stelio, and what the approach of night seems like when a place of rest is uncertain," she said softly.

She stopped between the high walls, and lifted her little veil, looking deep into her friend's eyes. He grew pale under that look, so sudden was his emotion and surprise at her words. He felt confused, as if in the incoherence of a dream, incapable of applying the true significance of those words to the woman who was smiling at him, holding the delicate glass in her ungloved hand. Yet he had heard what she said, and she stood there before him in her rich fur cape, looking at him with beautiful soft eyes, misty with unshed tears.

"And I have known other things."

It relieved her heart to speak like this; his humility gave her strength, as if she had accomplished some proud and daring deed. She never had felt conscious of her power and worldly glory in the presence of her beloved, but now the memory of her obscure martyrdom, her poverty and hunger, created in her heart a feeling of real superiority over him she believed invincible.

"But I have no fear of suffering," she said, remembering the words he had spoken once: "Tell me you do not fear to suffer.... I believe your soul capable of bearing all the sorrow of the world." And her hand stole up to his cheek and caressed it, and he understood that she had answered those words spoken long ago.

He was silent, as intoxicated as if she had presented to his lips the very essence of her heart pressed out into that crystal cup like the blood of the grape. He waited for her to go on.

144

They reached a crossroads where stood a miserable hut, falling into ruin. La Foscarina stopped to look at it. The rude, unhinged windows were held open by a stick laid across them. The low sun struck the smoked walls within, and revealed the furniture—a table, a bench, a cradle.

"Do you remember, Stelio," said La Foscarina, "that inn at Dolo where we waited for the train. Vampa's inn, I mean. A great fire burned on the hearth, the dishes glittered on the shelves, and slices of polenta were toasting on the gridiron. Twenty years ago everything was exactly the same—the same fire, the same dishes, the same polenta. My mother and I used to go in there after the performance, and sit on the bench before a table. I had wept, cried, raved, and had died of poison or by the sword, on the stage. I still heard in my ears the resonance of the verses I had uttered, in a voice that was not my own, and a strange will still possessed my soul, and I could not shake it off—it was as if another person, struggling with my inertness, persisted in performing over again those movements and actions. The simulation of an outside life remained in the muscles of my face, and some evenings I could not calm them. Already, even then, the mask, the sensation of the living mask, was beginning to grow. My eyes would remain fixed, and a chill crept at the roots of my hair. I had difficulty in recovering full consciousness of myself and my surroundings.

"The odors from the kitchen sickened me; the food on our plates seemed too coarse, heavy as a stone, impossible to swallow. My disgust at everything sprang from something indescribably delicate and precious, of which I was conscious under all my weariness—a vague feeling of nobility beneath my humiliation. I hardly know how to express it. Perhaps it was the obscure presence of that power which later developed in me, of that election, of that difference wherewith Nature has marked me. Sometimes the consciousness of that difference from others became so strong that it almost raised a barrier between my mother and myself—God forgive me!— almost separated me from her. A great loneliness possessed me; nothing around me had power to touch me any more. I was alone with my destiny. My mother, even though she was with me, gradually receded into an infinite distance. Ah, she was to die soon, and was already preparing to leave me, and perhaps this withdrawal was the forerunner. She used to urge me to eat, with the words only she knew how to say. I answered: 'Wait! Wait!' I could only drink; I had a great craving for cold water. At times, when I was more tired and trembling than usual, I smiled a long-continued smile. And even that dear woman herself, with her deep heart, could not understand whence came my smile!

"Incomparable hours, wherein it seemed that the bodily prison was being broken through by the soul that wandered to the extremest limits of life! What must your youth have been, Stelio! Who can imagine it? We have all felt the weight of sleep that descends upon us after fatigue or intoxication, heavy and sudden as a stroke from a hammer, and it seems to annihilate us. But the power of dreams sometimes seizes upon us in waking hours with the same force; it holds us and we cannot resist it, though the whole thread of our existence seems on the point of being destroyed. Ah, some of the beautiful things you said that night in Venice come back to my mind, when you spoke of her marvelous hands weaving her own lights and shadows in a continuous work of beauty. You alone know how to describe the indescribable.

"Well, ... on that bench, in front of that rustic table, in Vampa's inn at Dolo, where destiny led me again with you, I had the most extraordinary visions that dreams ever have called up in my brain. I saw that which is unforgettable; I saw the real forms around me obliterated by the dream-figures born of my instinct and my thoughts. Under my fixed eyes, dazzled and scorched by the smoky petroleum lamps of the improvised stage, the world of my expression began to throb with life. The first lines of my art were developed in that state of anguish, of weariness, fever, disgust, in which my sensibility became, so to speak, plastic, after the manner of the incandescent material we saw the workmen holding at the end of the tube. In it was a natural aspiration to be modeled, to receive breath, to fill a mold. On certain evenings, in that wall covered with copper utensils, I could see myself reflected as in a mirror, in attitudes of grief or rage; with an unrecognizable face; and, in order to escape from this hallucination, to break the fixity of my gaze, I opened and shut my eyes rapidly. My mother would say, over and over: 'Eat, my daughter, at least eat this.' But what were bread, wine, meat, fruits, all those heavy things, in comparison with what I had within me? I said to her: 'Wait!' and when we rose to go, I used to take only a large piece of bread with me. I liked to eat it in the country the next morning, under a tree, or sitting on the bank of the Brenta.... Oh, those statues! They did not recognize me the other day, Stelio, but I recognized them!

"It was in the month of March, I remember. I went out into the country very early with my bread. I walked at random, though I meant to go to the statues. I went from one to another, and stopped before every one, as if I were paying a visit. Some appeared very beautiful to me, and I tried to imitate their poses. But I remained longer with the mutilated ones, as if to console them. In the evening, on the stage, I remembered some of them while I was acting, and with so deep a feeling of their distance and their solitude that I felt as if I could not speak any more. The audience would grow impatient at these pauses too prolonged. At times, when I had to wait for my companion in the scene to finish his tirade, I used to stand in the attitude of one of those statues, and remain as motionless as if I had been made of stone. I was already beginning to carve my own destiny.

"I loved one of them tenderly; it had lost its arms, which once balanced a basket of fruit on its head. But the hands still remained attached to the basket, and the sight of them always aroused my pity. This statue stood on its pedestal in a flax-field; a little canal of stagnant water was near it, in which the reflected sky repeated the tender blue of the flowers. And always, since that time, in my most glowing moments on the stage, visions of some landscape rise in my memory, particularly when by the mere force of silence I succeed in producing a thrill in the listening throng."

Her cheeks had flushed a little, and as the sun wrapped her in a radiant garment, drawing sparkles from her furs and from the crystal cup, her animation seemed like an increase of light.

146

"What a spring that was! In one of my wandering journeys I saw a great river for the first time. It appeared to me suddenly, swollen, and flowing rapidly between two wild banks. I felt then how much of divinity there is in a great stream running through the earth. It was the Adige, flowing down from Verona, from the city of Juliet."

An ambiguous emotion filled her heart while she recalled the poverty and poetry of her youth. She was impelled to continue, though she did not know how she had arrived at these confidences, when she had intended to speak to her friend of another young life, not belonging to the past, but to the present. By what surprise of love had she been turned from an effort of her will, from her firm decision to face the painful truth, from the concentration of her slumbering energy to linger in the memory of the past, and to cover with the image of her own lost virgin self that other image which was so different?

"We reached Verona one evening in May. I was devoured by anxiety. I clasped close to my heart the book in which I had copied the lines of Juliet, and continually repeated to myself the words of my first entrance: 'How now? Who calls? I am here. What is your will?' My imagination was excited by a strange coincidence: on that very day I was fourteen years old—the age of Juliet. The Nurse's gossip sounded in my ears; and, little by little, my own destiny seemed mingled with that of the Veronese. At the corner of every street I thought I could see a throng approaching me, accompanying a coffin covered with white roses. When I saw the Arche degli Scaligeri behind its iron bars, I cried to my mother, 'Here is Juliet's tomb!' And I burst into sobs, and had a desperate desire to love and to die. 'O thou too early seen unknown, and known too late!'"

Her voice, repeating the immortal words, penetrated the heart of her lover like a heart-rending melody. She paused a moment, then repeated:

"Too late!"

They were the ominous words spoken by her lover, which she herself had repeated in the garden, when both were on the brink of being swept away on the flood of their passion: "It is late; too late!" The woman that was no longer young now faced the former image of herself, in her maidenhood, throbbing in the form of Juliet before her first dream of love. Having reached the limit of experience, had she not at the same time preserved the dream intact—but to what purpose? If to-day she looked at the image of her far-distant youth, it was only to trample upon it in leading her beloved to the other woman, to her who lived and waited.

With her smile of inimitable sadness, she said:

"I was Juliet! One Sunday in May, in the immense arena in the amphitheater under the open sky, before an audience that had breathed in the legend of love and death, I was Juliet herself. No thrill from the most responsive audience, no applause, no triumph, ever has had from me the fulness and intoxication of that unique hour.

147

Actually, when I heard Romeo say: 'O, she doth teach the torches to burn bright,' my whole being kindled. With great economy, I had managed to buy a large bunch of roses, and these were my only ornament. I mingled the roses with my words, my gestures, with every attitude. I dropped one at Romeo's feet when we first met; I strewed the petals of another on his head, as I stood on the balcony; and I covered his body with them as he lay in the tomb. The words came with the strangest ease, almost involuntarily, as in delirium, and I could feel the throbbing in my veins accompanying them.

"I could see the great amphitheater, half in sunlight, half in shadow, and in the lighter part a sparkling from thousands of eyes. The day was as calm as this. Not a breath of air disturbed the folds of my robes, or the hair that floated on my uncovered neck. I felt my strength and animation momentarily increasing. How I spoke of the lark and the nightingale! I had heard them both a thousand times in the country. I knew all their songs of the woods, the meadows, and the sky. Every word, as it left my lips, seemed to have been steeped in the warmth of my blood. There was no fiber in me that did not give forth harmonious sound. Ah, the grace, the state of grace! Every time it is given to me to rise to the highest summit of my art I live again in that indescribable abandon. Yes, I was Juliet! I cried out in terror at the approach of dawn. The breeze stirred my hair. I could feel the extraordinary silence on which my lamentation fell. The multitude seemed to have sunk into the ground. I spoke of the terror of the coming day, but already I felt in reality 'the mask of night upon my face.' Romeo had descended. We were already dead; already both had entered the vale of shadows. Do you remember? My eyes sought the fading light of the sky. The people were noisy in the arena; they were impatient for the death scene; they would listen no more to the mother, the nurse, or the friar. The quiver of that impatience quickened my throbbing heart. The tragedy swept on. I recall the odor of the pitch from the funeral torches, and of the roses that covered me, and I remember the sound of far-off bells, and of the sky that was losing its light, little by little, as Juliet was losing her life, and a star, the first star, that swam in my eyes with my tears. When I fell dead on Romeo's body, the cry of the multitude in the shadows was so violent that I was frightened. Some one lifted me and dragged me toward that cry. Some one held the torch close to my tear-stained face, which must have been the color of death.... And thus, Stelio, one night in May, Juliet came to life again, and appeared before the people of Verona."

Again she paused, and closed her eyes as if she were dizzy, but her sorrowful lips still smiled at her friend.

"And then? Then came the need to move, to go no matter where, to traverse space, to breathe in the wind. My mother followed me in silence. We crossed a bridge, walked beside the Adige, and went on and on. My mother asked at times where we were going. I wished to find the Franciscan convent where Juliet's tomb was hidden, since, to my great regret, she was not buried in one of those beautiful tombs behind the great iron gates. But I did not wish to say so, and I could not speak. My voice seemed to have been lost with the last word of the dying Juliet. 'Where are we going?' again asked that indefatigable kindness. Ah, then the last word of Juliet came to me in reply. We were again near the Adige, beside a bridge. I think

148

I began to run, because soon afterward I felt myself seized by my mother's arms, and I stood leaning against the parapet, choking with sobs. 'There let me die!' I wished to say, but could not. The river carried with it the night and all its stars. I felt that the desire to die was not mine alone. Ah, blessed mother!"

She became very pale; her whole heart felt once more the embrace of those arms, the kiss of those lips, those tender tears, the depth of that suffering.

With a mingled feeling of surprise and alarm, Stelio watched the great waves of life that passed over her, the extraordinary expressions, the alternating lights and shadows; but he dared not speak, dared not break in upon the occult workings of that great, unhappy soul. He could only feel confusedly in her words the beauty and sadness of things unexpressed.

"Speak to me still," he said. "Draw nearer to me, sweet soul! No moment since I first loved you has been worth the steps that we have taken together to-day."

Again her first sudden question returned to her mind: "Do you think often of Donatella?"

A short path led to the Fondamenta degli Angeli, whence the lagoon could be seen, smooth and luminous.

"How beautiful that light is!" she said. "It is like that night when my name was still Perdita, Stelio."

She now touched a note that she had touched in an interrupted prelude.

"The last night of September," she added. "Do you remember?"

Her heart was filled with exaltation to such a degree that she almost feared it would fail her. But she resolved that her voice should utter firmly the name that must break the silence between her friend and herself.

"Do you remember the ship anchored before the gardens? A salute greeted the flag as it slid down the mast. Our gondola touched the ship as we passed under its shadow."

A moment's pause. Her pallor was animated by a wonderful vitality.

"Then, in that shadow, you first spoke Donatella's name."

She made a new effort, as a swimmer, submerged by a wave, rises again and shakes his head free of the foam.

"She began then to be yours!"

149

She felt as if she were growing rigid from head to foot. Her eyes stared fixedly at the glittering water.

"She must be yours," she said at last, with the sternness of necessity in her voice, as if to repel with a second shock the terrible things that were ready to surge up from her fiery heart.

Seized by sudden anguish, incapable of interrupting by a word the lightning-like apparitions of her tragic soul, Stelio halted, and laid his hand on his companion's arm to make her stop also.

"Is it not true?" she asked with a sweetness almost calm, as if her tension had suddenly relaxed, and her passion had quietly accepted the yoke laid upon it by her will. "Speak! I do not fear to suffer. Let us sit down here. I am a little tired."

They sat down on a low wall, facing the water.

"What can I say to you?" said the young man in a stifled voice, after a pause, unable to overcome the agitation arising from the certainty of his present love and the consciousness of his desires, inexorable as fate. "Perhaps what you have imagined is true; perhaps it is only a fancy of your own mind. I am certain to-day of only one thing, and that is that I love you and recognize in you all that is noble. I know one other thing that is noble—that I have a work to do and a life to live according to the dictates of Nature. You, too, must remember. On that September evening I spoke to you a long time of my life and of the genii that are leading it to its final destiny. You know that I can renounce nothing."

He trembled as if he held in his hand a sharp weapon, with which, as he was compelled to move it, he could not avoid wounding the defenseless woman.

"No, nothing; and especially your love, which ceaselessly exalts my strength and my hope. But did you not promise me more than love? Can you not do for me things that love alone cannot do? Do you not desire to be the constant inspiration of my life and my work?"

She listened motionless, with fixed eyes.

"It is true," he continued, after an anxious pause, recovering his courage, and feeling that on the sincerity of this moment depended the fate of that free alliance whereby he had hoped to be broadened, not confined. "It is true; that evening, when I saw you descend the stairs in the midst of the throng in company with her who had sung, I believed that a secret thought guided you from the moment that you did not come alone to meet me."

The woman felt a chill run through the roots of her hair. Her fingers trembled round the crystal cup, wherein the colors of sky and water were blended.

150

"I believed that you yourself had chosen her. Your look was that of one who knows and foresees. I was struck by it."

By her keen torture, the woman realized how sweet a falsehood would have been. She wished that he would either lie or be silent. She measured the distance that lay between her and the canal—the water that swallows and lulls to sleep.

"There was something about her that was hostile to me. She remained to me obscure, incomprehensible. Do you remember the way she disappeared? Her image faded, and only the desire of her song remained. You yourself, who led her to me, have more than once revived the remembrance of her. You have seen her shadow even where she was not."

She saw Death itself. No other wound had gone deeper, had hurt her so cruelly.—I alone! I alone have brought it on myself!—And she remembered the cry that had brought this misery: "Go! She awaits you!" Suddenly the internal tempest seemed to become a mere hallucination. She thought herself non-existent, and wondered to see the glass shining in her hand; she lost all corporeal sense. All that had happened was only a trick of the imagination. Her name was Perdita. The dead Summer was lying in the depths of the lagoon. Words were words, that was all.

"Could I love her? Were I to see her again, should I desire to turn her destiny toward mine? Perhaps. But of what use would that be? And of what use would all the vicissitudes and necessities of life be against the faith that links us? Could you and I resemble commonplace lovers who pass their days in quarreling, weeping, and cursing?"

The woman gnashed her teeth. She had a wild instinct to defend herself, and to hurt him as in a hopeless struggle. A murderous desire flashed across her maddened brain.

—No, you shall not have her!—And the brutality of her tyrant seemed monstrous to her. Under the measured and repeated blows, she felt that she was like a man she had once seen on the dusty road of a mining town, prostrated by repeated blows on his head from a mallet in his enemy's hand. That hideous memory mingled with her mental torture. She sprang up, impelled by the savage force that filled her being. The glass broke in her convulsed hand, cut her, fell in a sparkling shower at her feet.

Stelio startled. The woman's motionless silence had deceived him, but now he looked at her and saw her at last; and once more he saw, as on that night in her room when the logs had crackled on the hearth, the expression of madness on her agitated face. He stammered some words of regret, but impatience boiled under his concern.

151

"Ah," said La Foscarina, mastering her agony with a bitterness that convulsed her mouth, "how strong I am! Another time have a care that your wounds are not made so slowly, since my resistance is so slight, my friend."

She saw that blood was dripping from her fingers; she wrapped them in her handkerchief. She looked at the sparkling fragments on the grass.

"The cup is broken! You had praised it too highly. Shall we raise a mausoleum for it here?"

She was very bitter, almost mocking, her lips opening slightly to utter a mirthless laugh. Stelio stood silent, chagrined, his heart full of rancor at beholding the destruction of so beautiful an effort as that perfect cup.

"Let us imitate Nero, since we have already imitated Xerxes!"

She felt even more keenly than he the harshness of her sarcasm, the insincerity of her voice, the malignity of the laugh that was like a muscular spasm. But she was unable to conquer her soul at that moment. She felt a bitter, irresistible necessity to scorn, to devastate, to trample under foot, invaded by a sort of perfidious demon. Every vestige of tenderness and benevolence had vanished, every hope, every illusion. The bitter hatred that lurks under the love of ardent natures was dominant. On the man's face she could discern the same shadow that darkened her own.

"Do I irritate you? Do you wish to return to Venice alone? Would you like to leave the dying season behind you? The tide is falling, but there is always enough water for one who has no intention of returning. Would it suit you to have me try it? Am I not as docile as you could wish?"

She said these insensate things in a hissing tone, and became almost livid, as if suddenly burned by some corroding poison. And Stelio remembered having seen the same mask on her face on a distant day of love, madness and sadness. His heart contracted, then softened.

"Ah, if I have hurt you, I ask for pardon," he said, trying to take her hand and soothe her by a gentle act. "But did we not begin together to approach this matter? Was it not you that"—

She interrupted him, exasperated by his gentleness.

"Hurt me? And what does that matter? Have no pity, no pity! Do not weep over the beautiful eyes of the wounded hare!"

The words broke between her teeth. Her contracted lips opened in a convulsion of wild laughter that was like heart-rending sobs. Her companion shuddered, spoke to her in a low tone, aware of the curious eyes of the women who sat at the thresholds of their cabins.

"Calm yourself! Calm yourself! Oh, Foscarina, I beg of you! Do not act so, I entreat! We shall soon be at the quay, and then we shall go home. I will tell you— You will understand me then. Come, now we are in the street. Do you hear me?"

He feared she would fall in her hysterical convulsion, and stood ready to support her. But she only walked faster, unable to speak, smothering that wild laughter with her bandaged hand.

"What ails you? What do you see?" Stelio inquired anxiously.

Never could he forget the change in those eyes. They were dull, staring, sightless, yet they seemed to see something that was not there; they were filled with an unknown vision, occupied by some monstrous image which without doubt had generated that mad and anguished laughter.

"Shall we stop here a little while? Would you like some water?"

They found themselves now on the Fondamenta dei Vetrai. How long was it since they had walked beside the stagnant canal? How much of their life had vanished in the interval? What profound shadow were they leaving behind them?

Having descended into the gondola, and wrapped herself in her cloak, La Foscarina tried to control her hysteria, holding her face with both hands, but from time to time the terrible laugh would escape; then she pressed her hands closer to her mouth, as if she were trying to suffocate herself.

The lagoon and the deep twilight obliterated all forms and colors; only the rows of posts, like a file of monks on a path of ashes, showed against the dark background. When the bells began their clamor, her soul remembered, her tears gushed forth; the horror was vanquished.

She took her hands from her face, leaned toward her friend's shoulder, and found again her voice in saying:

"Forgive me!"

CHAPTER XII
CASSANDRA'S REINCARNATION
She humbled herself with shame. From that day every action of her silently begged for pardon and oblivion.

A new grace seemed born within her. She became more cheerful, spoke more gently, walked softly about the house dressed in quiet colors, veiling her beautiful eyes with the deep shadow of her lashes, because she dared not look at her friend. The fear of tiring him, of displeasing or boring him, gave her the wings of

153

divination. Her ever watchful sensibility listened at the inaccessible door of his dreams.

Her spirit, determined to create a new feeling capable of conquering the violence of instinct, revealed in her face with marvelous signs the difficulty of her task. Never before had her supreme art found expressions so singular. Looking at her one day, Stelio spoke to her of the infinite power concentrated in the shadow produced by the helmet on the face of Il Pensieroso.

"Michelangelo," he said, "has, in a small cavity in the marble, concentrated all the effort of human meditation. Just as the stream fills a hollowed palm, so the eternal mystery that surrounds us fills the small space made by the Titan's chisel in the material from the mountains; and there it has remained, growing denser through all the centuries. I know only the mobile shadow of your face, Fosca, that equals that shadow in intensity, and sometimes even surpasses it."

Eager for poetry and knowledge, she yearned for the Inspirer's presence. She became for him the ideal figure of one that listens and understands. The strange, unique arrangement of her hair suggested fluttering, impatient wings round her pure forehead.

She read aloud to him pages from the sovereign poets. The august form of the Book seemed magnified by the attitude she assumed in holding it, by her way of turning the pages, by her religious gravity of attention, and the harmony of the voice that changed the printed symbols into vocal cadences. While reading Dante, she was as severe and noble as the sibyls in the dome of the Sistine Chapel, sustaining the weight of the sacred volumes with all the heroism of their bodies moved by the breath of prophecy.

When the last syllable had been spoken, she saw Stelio rise impetuously, feverishly, and roam about the rooms, stirred by the dart of the god, panting in the excitement roused by the confused tumult of his own creative force. Sometimes he approached her with glowing eyes transfigured by a sudden beatitude, kindled by an inner flame, as if an immortal truth had just been revealed. With a shudder that drove away from her heart the memory of every caress, she saw him lay his head upon her knees, overwhelmed by the tremendous struggle he carried on within himself, by the shock that accompanied some hidden metamorphosis. She suffered, yet she was happy, though she knew not whether he too suffered or was happy; her heart was filled with pity, fear, and reverence to feel that vigorous form laboring thus in the genesis of the idea. She kept silence; she waited, adoring that head that lay upon her knees, filled with thoughts unrevealed.

But she comprehended his great emotion better when one day, after she had been reading to him, he spoke of the exile of Dante.

"Imagine, Fosca, if you can without bewilderment, the transport and ardor of that great soul, when uniting itself with elementary energies in order to conceive his words! Imagine Alighieri, his mind already filled with his incomparable vision, on

154

the way to exile, an implacable pilgrim, driven by his passion and his poverty from country to country, from refuge to refuge, across plains, over mountains, beside rivers and seas, in all seasons, suffocated by the sweetness of spring, shivering under the harshness of winter, always alert, attentive, with wide, voracious eyes, anxious with the inner travail whereby his gigantic work was formed. Imagine the fulness of that soul in the contrast between common necessities and the flaming apparitions that rose suddenly before him at a turn in the road, on the bank of a stream, from a hollow in the rocks, on the slope of a hill, in the depths of the forest, or in a meadow where the larks were singing. By means of his senses, life multiform and multiplex poured into his spirit, transfiguring into living images the abstract ideas that filled his brain. The sound, the appearance, and the essence of the very elements themselves entered into his occult labor, developing it with voices, lines, color, movement, and with innumerable mysteries. Fire, air, earth, and water worked in collaboration at the sacred poem, penetrated the sum of its doctrine, warmed it, aërated it, watered it, covered it with leaves and flowers. Open this Christian book, and imagine at the same time the face of a Greek god. Do you not see, springing from both, shadows and light, the flashes or the wind from the heavens?"

She began to feel that her own life was becoming one with the all-absorbing work, that her own personal self was entering, drop by drop, into the personage of the drama, that her look, her poses, her gestures and voice were going to the composing of the figure of the heroine "living beyond life." She fancied that she was dissolving into her elements in the fire of that other intellect, only to be re-formed by the necessity of a heroism that should dominate Fate.

Sometimes it seemed to her that she was losing her human sincerity, and that she would always remain in the state of fictitious excitement into which she threw herself while studying a tragic rôle she was to create. Thus she experienced a new torment. She tried to shut and contract her soul under his keen glance, as if to prevent his intellect from penetrating her mind and robbing her of her secret life. She grew afraid of the seer.—He will read in my soul the silent words that he will put in the mouth of his creation, and I shall only speak them on the stage, under my mask.—Sometimes she felt a sudden need to break the spell, to withdraw from the image that was to be like her, to spoil those lines of beauty, which forced her to a determined sacrifice. Was there not also in the tragedy a maiden thirsting for love and eager for joy, a maiden in whom a great mind recognized the living incarnation of his most exquisite dream, the Victory that was to crown his life? And was there not also an impassioned woman no longer young, who had one foot already in the dark shadow, and who had but a few steps more to take in order to disappear? More than once she was tempted to contradict her seeming resignation by some violent act. Then, like a penitent, she redoubled her fervor to ward off the peril, hardened herself to discipline, sharpened her vigilance, repeating with a sort of intoxication the act of supreme renunciation that had risen from the depths of her sadness at the aspect of the purifying flame.—You must have all; I shall be content with seeing you live, seeing your joy. And do with me as you will!—

Then Stelio loved her for the unexpected visions she brought him. He trembled and turned pale one day when she entered the room with her soft step, her

155

face fixed in calm sorrow, as if she were emerging from depths of wisdom whence all human agitations seem but a puff of wind on a dusty road.

"Ah, at last! I have created you! I have created you!" he cried, thinking he saw his heroine herself standing on a threshold of the distant chamber filled with treasure taken from the tombs of the Atrides. "Stand still a moment! Do not move your eyelids—keep your eyes motionless, as if they were petrified! Now you are blind. But you can see things that others do not see, and nothing can be hidden from you. Here in this place the man you love has declared his love to another, who trembles at the revelation. They are still here, they have just let go each other's hands, and their love quivers in the air. The room is full of funeral treasure, and on two tables are laid out the riches that covered the bodies of Agamemnon and Cassandra. There are the coffers filled with necklaces, and there are the urns full of ashes. The balcony looks out upon the plain of Argos and on the distant mountains. It is twilight, and all that terrible gold glitters in the creeping shadows. Do you understand? And you are there, on the threshold, led by the nurse. You are blind, yet nothing is hidden from you. Stop a moment!"

He spoke in the sudden fever of invention. The scene appeared before him, then disappeared, submerged in a flood of poetry.

"What shall you do? What shall you say?"

The actress felt a chill at the roots of her hair. Her very soul vibrated. She became blind and prophetic. The cloud of Tragedy descended and hung over her head.

"What shall you say? You will call them. You will call both of them by name in that silence where the great royal spoils repose."

The actress felt the coursing of her blood; her voice was to resound through the silence of thousands of years, to revive the ancient suffering of men and heroes.

"You will take their hands; you will feel their two lives stretching toward each other."

The blindness of the immortal statues was in her eyes. She could see herself sculptured in the great silence, and feel the thrill of the mute throng, seized with awe at the sublime power of her attitude.

"And then? And then?"

The Inspirer rushed impetuously toward the actress, as if he wished to strike her in order to draw sparks from her.

"You must awake Cassandra from her sleep; you must feel her ashes revive in your hands; she must be present in your mental vision. Will you? Do you understand? Your living soul must touch her ancient soul, and blend into one soul

156

and one grief, so that the flight of time seems annihilated. Cassandra is in you, and you are in her. Have you not loved her, and do you not love Priam's daughter also? Who that once shall hear it can ever forget, who can ever forget the deep notes of your voice and the convulsion of your lips at the first cry of fatalistic fury: 'O Earth! O Apollo!' I see you once more, deaf and dumb, on your chariot with the look of a wild beast just captured. But among so many terrible cries, some were infinitely sweet and sad. The old men compared you to the nightingale. What were the words you used when you spoke of your beautiful river? And when the old men questioned you about the love of the god—do you remember your answer?"

The Tragic Muse palpitated as if the breath of the god again invaded her. She had become ardent, ductile material, subject to all the inspirations of the poet.

"Do you remember your answer?"

"O espousals, espousals of Paris, fatal to the beloved! O you, paternal waters of the Scamandros! Once, on your shores, my youth was nourished by you!"

"Ah, divine woman, your melody does not make one regret the syllables of Æschylus! I remember. The soul of the multitude, seized by the lamentation 'of discordant sounds,' relaxed and was soothed by that melodious sigh, and each of us received the vision of years long past and our innocent happiness. You can say: 'I was Cassandra.' In speaking of her, you will remember a former life. Her mask of gold will be in your hands."

He seized both her hands; both were intent on the flashes generated by their blended forces; the same electric spark ran through their nerves.

"You are there, near the spoil of the slave-princess, and you feel the mask. What shall you say?"

In the pause that followed, both seemed to be waiting for a flash. The actress's eyes again became fixed and blind, her face became like marble. The Inspirer let go her hands, and they made the gesture of feeling the sepulchral golden mask. In a voice that created the tangible form, she said:

"How large her mouth is!"

"You see her, then?"

"Yes, I too can see her. The mouth is large; the terrible effort of prophecy dilated it; she cried aloud, cursed, and lamented without ceasing. Can you imagine her mouth in silence?"

Still in the same attitude, as if in ecstasy, she said slowly:

"What profundity in her wonderful silence!"

She seemed to be repeating words suggested to her by mysterious genii, and, while the poet listened to her, he fancied that he himself had been about to speak them. A profound tremor shook him, as if he were witnessing a miracle.

"And her eyes?" he demanded, agitated. "Of what color were her eyes?"

She made no reply.

The marble lines of her face changed slightly, as if under a wave of suffering. A furrow appeared between her eyes.

"Her eyes," continued the revealer, "were as sweet and sad as two violets."

She paused again, panting, as one who suffers in a dream. Her lips were dry, her temples moist.

"Thus they were before they closed forever!"

Sometimes Stelio came to his friend's house breathless and excited, as if pursued by an Erinni. La Foscarina never questioned him, but her personality soothed that restless spirit.

"Sometimes I am afraid of the vastness of my conceptions," he said. "I am afraid of being suffocated by them. You believe me to be a little mad, do you not? Do you remember that stormy evening when I returned from the Lido? How sweet you were that evening! A short time before that, standing on the Bridge of the Rialto, I found a Motive. I had translated the words of the Elements into notes. Do you know what a Motive is? It is a small spring, from which may be born many other springs, a tiny seed that may give birth to a crown of forests; a little spark that may kindle an endless chain of conflagration—a nucleus that produces infinite force. A few days ago I began to develop the Motive of that stormy evening, which I shall call the Pipes of Æolus. Listen to it."

He went to the piano, and struck a few notes with one hand.

"It contains no more than that, but you cannot imagine the generating force of those few notes. A tempest, a whirlwind of music has been born of them, but I have not yet been able to master it. I am almost vanquished, suffocated, constrained to fly."

He laughed a little; but his soul was swaying like the sea.

"The Pipes of Prince Æolus, opened by the companions of Ulysses. Do you remember it? The imprisoned winds arise and push back their vessel, and the men tremble with terror."

His spirit could not rest long, and nothing could divert him from his mental work. He kissed his friend's hand, paced to and fro, stopping before the piano that Donatella had played when she sang Claudio's melody. He wandered to the window, and gazed upon the leafless garden. His aspiration reached out toward the musical creature, toward her that must chant his hymns at the summit of his tragic symphonies.

In a low, clear voice the woman said:

"If Donatella were here with us!"

He turned, approached her, and gazed at her fixedly, silently. She smiled her slight, mask-like smile at seeing him so near her, yet so far removed. She felt that he loved no one at that moment—not herself, not Donatella, but that he regarded both simply as instruments of his art, forces to employ, bows to bend. He was on fire with poetry, and she, with her poor wounded heart, her secret torture, her mute plea—she was there, intent on nothing but her sacrifice, ready to pass beyond love and life, as the heroine of the future drama. Meanwhile, each day must make its mark on her face, discolor her lips, fade her hair; each day, in the service of old age, would hasten the work of destruction in her miserable flesh. And then?

She recognized that it was love, after all, unquenchable passion, that created all the illusions and all the hopes which seemed to aid her in accomplishing "what love alone cannot do."

She realized that the torturing restraint of those days had not succeeded in creating in her even a symptom of the new feeling whereby love was to be made sublime. Her secret task, therefore, meant simply continual dissimulation. Was it worth while to live for this?

If once the young man's madness and ardor had caused her to suffer, she now suffered far more in seeing that that ardor had grown calm, and that a sort of reserve had taken its place—a reserve that sometimes repelled the gentlest caress. She felt shame at her regret, knowing that he was possessed by his great idea, and was concentrating all his energies upon it. But a dark rancor often mastered her in the evening, after he had departed, and blind suspicions nightly tortured her sleepless soul.

—To go away!—The necessity to do this came suddenly, urgently. She had said to her beloved once, on a memorable day: "There is only one thing I can do— go away, and leave you free with your fate. This thing I can do, which love alone could not do." Henceforth, delay was no longer possible; she must break off with all hesitation, and emerge finally from that kind of fatal suspension of movement, in which she had lived so long in agitation.

Since that October dawn, their outward life had been unchanged. Nevertheless, she felt that it was impossible for her to continue to live in that way

159

any longer. She felt a consciousness of something fully accomplished, as in the tree that has yielded all its fruit, as in the river that has reached the sea.

Her courage revived; her soul grew stronger, her energies awoke once more, and the virile qualities of the leader again came to life. In a few days she had arranged her professional route, reassembled her dramatic company, and fixed the date of departure.—You must go and work over there among the barbarians across the ocean. You must wander still from town to town, from hotel to hotel, from theater to theater, and every night you will draw howls from the crowd that pays you. You will gain much money; you will return laden with gold and with wisdom, unless it happens that you are crushed by a wheel some misty day on a crowded street. Who knows? From whom have you received the order to depart? From some one within yourself—deep, deep within you—who sees that which you cannot see, like the blind woman in the tragedy. Who knows whether over there, on one of those wide, peaceful rivers, your soul will not find its harmony and your lips will not learn that smile they have attempted so many times in vain! Perhaps you will discover a few white hairs and that smile in your mirror at the same time!—

And she went on preparing for her journey.

CHAPTER XIII
THE STORY OF THE ARCHORGAN
From time to time a breath of Spring passed across the February sky.

"Do you feel the Spring?" said Stelio to his friend, inhaling deep breaths of the new air.

La Foscarina fell behind him a step or two, because her resolute heart was weakening; she lifted her face to the sky, now flecked with white clouds like floating plumes. The raucous shriek of a siren whistle prolonged itself in the estuary, becoming fainter by degrees until the sound was as soft as the note of a flute. It seemed to the woman that something rose from the depths of her heart and escaped with that prolonged note, as a poignant grief gradually changes into a tender memory.

"Yes, Spring has already arrived at the Tre Porti."

Once more they floated aimlessly along the lagoon, that water as familiar to their thoughts as is the web to the weaver.

"Did you say at the Tre Porti?" the young man cried, enthusiastically, as if his soul were reawakened. "It is there, near the lower bank, at the setting of the moon, that the sailors take the Wind prisoner, and bring it, chained, to Dardi Seguso. Some day I will tell you the story of the Archorgan."

160

His air of mystery in describing the action of the sailors made La Foscarina smile.

"What story?" she asked, enticed by his significant tone. "And what does Seguso do here? Has the story anything to do with the master glassblower?"

"Yes, but a master of a former day, who knew Latin and Greek, music and architecture, who was admitted to the Academy of the Pellegrini, whose gardens are at Murano; he was often invited to sup with Titian in his house in the Contrada dei Biri; was a friend of Bernardo Cappello, of Jacopo Zane, and other ancient Petrarchists. At Caterino Zeno's house he saw the famous organ built for Matthias Corvinus, King of Hungary, and his magnificent idea came to him in the course of a discussion with that Agostino Amadi who succeeded in adding to his collection of instruments a true Grecian lyre, a great Lesbian heptachord, rich with gold and ivory. Ah, imagine it, that relic of the school of Mitylene, brought to Venice by a galley which, in passing through the waters of Santa Maura, caught and dragged the body of Sappho as far as Malamocco, like an armful of dead grass! But that, too, is another tale."

Again the nomad woman recovered her youthful spirits enough to smile, pleased as a child to whom one shows a picture-book. How many marvelous stories, how many delightful fancies had not the Visionary conjured up for her on those waters, during the long hours of the afternoon? How many enchantments had he not known how to weave for her, to the rhythm of the oar, in words that made all things seem reality? How many times, seated beside her beloved in the light boat, had she not enjoyed that sort of waking dream in which all cares were banished, carried away on waves of poetry?

"Tell it to me," she begged.

She wished to add:—This story will be the last.—But she restrained herself, because up to this time she had not spoken to him of her fixed resolution.

He laughed.

"You are as eager for stories as Sofia."

At that name, as when she heard the name of Spring, she felt her resolution weaken; the cruelty of her fate pierced her heart, and her whole being turned with yearning toward her escaping happiness.

"Look!" he said, pointing to the mirror-like lagoon, rippled here and there by a light breeze. "Do not those infinite lines of silence aspire to become music?"

Silvery-white in the calm afternoon, the estuary seemed to bear the islets on its breast as lightly as the softest clouds hung from the sky.

161

"Well, the master glassblower heard at Zeno's house praises of the famous organ of the King of Hungary, and cried: 'Corpo di Bacco! You shall see what an organ I will build, with my stick, liquida musa canente! I will make the god of organs! Dant sonitum glaucæ per stagna loquacia cannæ. The waters of the lagoon shall give it its tone, and in it the stones, the buoys, and the fish also shall sing. Multisonum silentium. You shall see, by the body of Diana!' All his hearers laughed, save Giulia da Ponte—because she had black teeth! And the Sansovino gave a dissertation on hydraulic organs. But the boaster, before taking his leave, invited the company to hear his new music on the day of the Sensa, and promised that the Doge on his Bucentaur should halt in the middle of the lagoon to listen. That evening the news that Dardi Seguso had lost his senses spread to Venice, and the Council, which had a tender regard for its famous workmen, sent a messenger to Murano to learn the truth about the report. The messenger found the artisan with his sweetheart, Perdilanza, who was very loving to him because she was anxious, and feared that Dardi was insane. The master, after looking at the messenger with fiery eyes, burst into a hearty laugh, which reassured her as to his state of mind; then, quite calm again, Seguso ordered the messenger to report to the Council that, on the day of the Sensa, Venice, San Marco, the Grand Canal, and the Palace of the Doges should possess yet another miracle. On the following day, he made a formal request for the possession of one of the five little islets that circled Murano like the satellites of a planet, but have now disappeared, or have dwindled to mere sandbanks. After exploring the waters around Temòdia, Trencòre, Galbaia, Mortesina, and La Folèga, he chose Temòdia as one chooses a bride, and Perdilanza entered the shadow of affliction. Look, Fosca; perhaps even now we are passing over the memory of Temòdia. The organ-pipes are sunk deep in the mud, but they never will decay. There are seven thousand of them. We are passing over the ruins of a forest of melodious glass. How delicate the seaweed is here!"

"Tell me the reason why Perdilanza entered the shadow of affliction," said La Foscarina, as both leaned over and looked deep into the beautiful clear waters.

"Because her name had been driven from the lips and the heart of her lover by the name of Temòdia, which he constantly uttered with vehement ardor, and because the island was the only place to which she might not follow him. There he had constructed his new work-rooms, and there he stayed the greater part of the day, and almost all night, assisted by his workmen, whom he had bound to silence by a solemn oath before the altar. The Council, in ordering that the master should be provided with everything necessary for his tremendous task, had decreed that he should lose his head should his work prove inferior to his proud boast. Then Dardi tied a scarlet thread around his bare neck."

La Foscarina felt as if she were in a dream. Stelio seemed to have been speaking of himself in those strange figures of speech, as on that last night of September when he had explained the myth of the pomegranate, and the name of the imaginary woman began with the first two syllables of the name he had given her in those days! Was any personal significance veiled behind this story? Why had he, deliberately, in the vicinity of the place where she had been seized with that terrible laughter, called up, by that fanciful tale, the memory of the broken vase? In

162

trying to understand, she made for herself an instrument of torture, with the dream-fancies of Stelio's brain. She did not remember that as yet he was ignorant of her approaching departure. Instinctively she said within herself:—I am going far-away; do not wound me.—

She wished to hear the remainder of the story, however, for she longed to understand him fully.

"Well, what happened then to the man with the scarlet thread?" she inquired.

"More than once he felt his head was insecure on his shoulders," Stelio replied laughingly. "He had to blow pipes as large as the trunk of a tree, and he had to do it with his own mouth, unaided by bellows. He blew and blew with all his might, without ceasing. Fancy it! The lungs of a Cyclops would hardly be strong enough for that. Ah, some day I shall describe the fever of that existence hanging between the ax and the production of a miracle, in colloquy with the elements. He had Fire, Water, and Earth, but lacked Air—the movement of the Air. But every day the Council of Ten sent to him a red-haired man to wish him good morning—you know, that red-haired man, with a cap over his eyes, who embraces the column in the Adoration of the Magi of the second Bonifazio. After colossal labors, Seguso had a brilliant idea. He found a magician, who was said to have power over the Wind in favor of long navigations. He said to the wizard: 'I need a little wind, not too light nor too strong, but steady and gentle, which I could manage as I wish: only a little breeze with which to blow some glass that I have in my head. Lenius aspirans aura secunda venit. Do you understand, old man?'"

The story-teller burst into a ringing laugh, for he could fancy the scene with all its details in a house on the Calle della Testa, at San Zanepolo, where the Schiavone lived with his daughter.

La Foscarina tried to join in his gayety; but his boyish laughter pained her as it had once before when she was lost in the labyrinth.

"It is a long story," Stelio went on. "Some day I shall use it, but I am keeping it for a time when I have more leisure. Now fancy! The magician works the spell. Every night Dardi sent his sailors to the Tre Porti to spread a snare for the little Wind. At last, one night, or rather just before dawn, when the moon was about to set, they caught it asleep on a sandy bank in the midst of a flock of tired swallows it had borne thither.

"There it lay, on its back, breathing as lightly as a child in the salty aroma of the waters, almost covered by innumerable little forked tails. The rising tide rocked it in its slumber, and the black-and-white travelers fluttered about it, weary with their long flight."

"What a charming fancy!" exclaimed La Foscarina at this fresh picture. "Where have you seen that?"

163

"Here begins the real charm of the story," he answered. "They seize the sleeping Wind, bind it with osier withes, carry it aboard their boat, and set sail for Temòdia. The bark is invaded by the flock of swallows, which will not abandon the leader of their flight."

Stelio paused, because the details of the fantasy crowded his imagination to such a degree that he knew not which to choose to relate.

"And then?" urged his companion, with interest.

"I can tell no more now, Fosca. I know too many things.... Well, imagine that Dardi falls in love with his prisoner. It is called Ornitio, because it leads flights of migrating birds. A continual twittering of swallows surrounds Temòdia; nests hang from the posts and the scaffolding that surround the great structure; wings are singed in the flames of the furnace, when Ornitio blows through the tube to create a light and luminous column with that ball of burning paste. But before he had tamed it and taught it what to do, he had much trouble with it. The Master of the Flame began by speaking Latin to it, and reciting lines of Virgil to it, believing it would understand. But the azure-haired Ornitio spoke Greek, naturally, with a slightly sibilant accent. It knew Sappho's odes by heart, and while it breathed through the unequal tubes, it remembered the pipes of Pan."

"And what did it eat?"

"Pollen and salt."

"Who gave it the food?"

"No one. It was sufficient to inhale the pollen and salt scattered on the breeze."

"And did it never try to escape?"

"Always. But Seguso took infinite precautions, like the lover he was."

"And did Ornitio return his love?"

"Yes, it began to love him after a time, particularly because of the scarlet thread that the master wore continually around his bare neck."

"And Perdilanza?"

"She was left alone, and languished in her grief. I will tell you more of her some day. Some day I shall go to the seashore of Palestrina, and I will write this fable for you in the golden sand."

164

"But how does the story end?"

"The miracle is accomplished. The Archorgan is raised at Temòdia with its seven thousand glass pipes, resembling one of those frozen forests which Ornitio— who was a little inclined to boast of the wonders it had met in its travels—declared it had seen in the land of the Iporborrei. At last comes the day of the Sensa. The Serenissimo, between the Patriarch and the Archbishop of Spalatro, goes out of the harbor of San Marco on the Bucentaur. So great is the pomp that Ornitio believes it must be the triumphal return of the son of Chronos. The fountains are set playing all around Temòdia; and animated by the eternal silence of the lagoon, the gigantic organ peals forth, under the magic fingers of the new musicians, a wave of harmony so vast that it reaches as far as the mainland and even to the Adriatic. The Bucentaur stops, because its forty oars have suddenly fallen at its sides, abandoned by the astonished crew. But suddenly the wave of harmony breaks into discordant sounds, and at last it dies away in a faint murmur. Dardi feels the instrument becoming dumb under his fingers, as if his own soul had failed. What has happened? The master hears only great shouts of jeers and scorn that come to him through the silent pipes—the sound of firing and the uproar of the populace. A group embarks from the Bucentaur, bringing the red-haired man, who bears a block and an ax. The blow is aimed exactly at the scarlet thread; the head falls, and is thrown into the water, where it floats like the head of Orpheus."

"But what had happened?"

"Perdilanza had thrown herself into the cataract! The water dragged her into the machinery of the organ. Her body, with its famous hair, lay across the great delicate instrument, and silenced its musical heart."

"But Ornitio?"

"Ornitio rescued the head from the water and flew away with it toward the sea. The swallows heard of its flight and followed it, and very soon a cloud of black wings and white surrounds the fugitive. All the nests in Venice remain empty after this sudden flight."

"And Dardi's head?"

"Where it is, no one knows," concluded the story-teller, laughing.

The woman bent her head in thoughtful silence.

"Perhaps there is a hidden meaning in your tale," she said, after a pause. "Perhaps I have understood."

"Alas, yes! if there were any resemblance between my audacity and that of the master workman. Perhaps I too should wear a scarlet thread around my neck, as a sort of warning."

165

"You will have your great destiny. I have no fear for you."

He ceased to laugh.

"Yes, my friend, I must conquer. And you shall help me. Every morning I too receive my menacing visitor—the expectation of those that love me and those that hate me. Expectation should wear the dress of the executioner, for nothing on earth is so pitiless."

"But it is the measure of your power."

He felt the vulture's beak in his breast. Instinctively he straightened himself up, seized with an impatience of even their slow idling on the water. Why did he live in such idleness? Every hour and every minute he ought to be trying, struggling, fortifying himself against destruction, diminution, violation, contagion. Every hour and every minute his eyes should be fixed on his aim, and all his energies should be concentrated upon it.

"Do you know this saying of the great Herodotus: 'The name of the bow is Bios, and its work is death'? This saying is one that excites our spirits even before communicating to it its exact meaning. I heard it continually within myself, that evening last autumn, when I was sitting at your table—the night of the Epiphany of the Flame. That night I had an hour of true Dionysian life, an hour of secret though terrible delight, as if I held in my breast the burning mountain where the Tiades howl and shriek. Sometimes I could really hear songs and clamor, and the cries of distant battle. It astonished me that I could remain motionless, and the sense of my bodily immobility increased my mental frenzy. I could see only your face, which suddenly appeared extraordinarily beautiful, revealing all the strength of your soul; and behind it I could see other countries and other peoples. If I could only tell you how I saw you! In the tumult, at the passage of marvelous images, accompanied by floods of music, I called to you as in the thick of battle; I made appeals which perhaps you heard—not for love alone, but for glory; not for one thirst, but for two, and I know not which was the more ardent. And the face of my great work appeared to me then the same as your face. I saw it, I tell you! And with incredible rapidity my work took form in words, song, movement, and symphony, and was so real that if I succeed in infusing a part of it into that which I wish to express, I shall surely inflame the world.

"To express oneself! That is the necessity. The greatest vision has no value if it is not manifested and condensed in vital forms. And I have everything to create. I am not pouring my substance into hereditary molds. My work is entirely my own invention. I must not, and I will not, obey anything but my instinct and the genius of my race. Nevertheless, like Dardi, who saw the famous organ at the house of Caterino Zeno, I too have another work before my mind—a work accomplished by a formidable creator, a gigantic work in the eyes of man."

The image of the barbaric creator reappeared to him: the blue eyes gleamed under the vast forehead, and he saw once more the white hair tossed by the wind

166

about that aged neck. He remembered his own indescribable thrill of joy and fear when he had so unexpectedly felt beneath his hand the throbbing of that sacred heart.

"I should say not before but around my spirit. Sometimes it is like a stormy sea trying to draw me down and swallow me. My Temòdia is a granite rock in the open sea, and I am like an artisan trying to erect upon it a pure Doric temple. Compelled to defend the order of his columns from the violence of the waves, his spirit is always strained in order never to cease to hear, in the midst of the clamor, the secret rhythm which alone must regulate the intervals between lines and spaces. And in this sense too my tragedy is a battle."

He took one of his friend's hands.

"Do you hear the song?" he asked.

"Where is it?" she said, raising her face to the sky. "Is it in heaven or on the earth?"

An infinite melody seemed to be flowing through the peaceful, silvery atmosphere.

She felt Stelio's hand quiver.

"When Alessandro enters the illuminated chamber where the virgin has been reading the lament of Antigone," he said, "he tells how he has come on horseback across the plain of Argos, where the song of the larks fills the sky. He says that one lark fell at his horse's feet, like a stone, and lay there silent, overcome by its own frenzy of joy in its song. He picked it up. 'Here it is.' Then you hold your hand toward him, you take the bird, and murmur: 'Ah, it is still warm!' And while you speak the virgin trembles. You can feel her quivering."

The actress felt the mystic chill steal over her once more, as if the soul of the blind woman reëntered her own soul.

"At the end of the Prelude, the impetuosity of the chromatic progressions expresses this growing joy, this fever of delight.... Listen, listen!... Ah, what a miracle! This morning, Fosca, this morning I was at work upon my melody, and now it is developing itself in the air! Are we not in a state of grace?"

A spirit of life seemed indeed running throughout the solitude; a vehement inspiration filled the silence with emotion. La Foscarina gave up her whole soul to it, as a leaf yields itself to the whirlwind, ravished to the very summit of love and faith.

But a feverish impatience to act, to work, to accomplish seized the young man. His capacity for work seemed multiplied. He thought of the plenitude of the hours

167

to come; he saw his work in concrete form—the pages, the scores, the variety of needs, the richness of material adaptable to rhythm.

"In a week, Fosca, if grace assists me, my Prelude will be finished, and I should like to try it immediately with an orchestra. Perhaps I shall go to Rome to do this. Antimo della Bella is even more impatient than I; I receive a letter from him almost every day. I believe that my presence in Rome is necessary for a few days in order to prevent certain errors that may arise in the building of the theater. Antimo writes about the possibility of tearing down the old stone stairs leading from the Corsini Garden to the Janiculum. The street that will lead to the theater, after one passes the Arch of Septimius, will continue beside the Palazzo Corsini, cross the garden, and extend to the foot of the hill. The hill is green and mossy, covered with cypress, laurel, and flags. The Paulina fountain rises at the left. A flight of stone steps leads to a terrace from which open two paths bordered by Apollo-like laurels, and worthy of leading the people toward Poetry. Can anyone imagine a nobler entrance? Centuries have wrapped it in mystery; no sound is heard but the song of birds, the tinkling of fountains, the whisper of the forest. And I believe that poets and innocents can even hear there the fluttering of the Hamadryads and the breath of Pan!"

The ugly shores, crumbling stones, decaying roots, traces of ruined buildings, the odor of dissolution, the funereal cypresses, the black crosses, in vain recalled to him the words the statues beside the Brenta had spoken with their marble lips. Only the great song of victory and liberty, stronger than all other signs, now touched the heart of him who was to create with joy. "On! on! Higher! ever higher!"

And the heart of Perdita, purified from all cowardice, ready for any test, betrothed itself once more to Life! As in that distant hour of the delirious night, she repeated: "Let me serve! Let me serve!"

CHAPTER XIV
THE WORLD'S BEREAVEMENT
The gondola entered a canal enclosed between two green shores, which reached the line of vision so precisely that the numerous reeds were perceptible, the newer ones discernible by their paler tint.

From the fulness of her soul, and the abundance of her nature, La Foscarina sought everywhere for living things to love; her glance became child-like once more, and all things were reflected in it as in the peaceful water, and some seemed to reappear from the distant past, like apparitions.

When the gondola touched the shore, she was surprised at having arrived.

"Do you wish to land, or do you prefer to go back?" asked Stelio, coming out of his reverie.

168

For a moment she hesitated, because her hand lay in his, and to move would have meant a lessening of sweetness.

"Yes," at last she said, with a smile. "Let us walk on this grass a little while."

They landed on the Island of San Francesco. A few slender young cypress shrubs greeted them timidly. Not a human face was to be seen. The invisible myriad filled the desert with their canticle of praise. The mists rose in clouds near the sunset hour.

"How many times we have walked together on the grass, have we not, Stelio?"

"But now comes the steep rock," he replied.

"Let the rock come, no matter how steep and rough it may be," said La Foscarina.

Stelio was surprised at the unusual gayety in his companion's voice. He looked at her, and saw a sort of intoxicated joy deep in her beautiful eyes.

"Why do we feel so joyous and free on this lonely island?"

"And do you know the reason why?"

"To others, this is a melancholy pilgrimage. Most persons, when they come to this place, leave it with the taste of death on their lips."

"But we are in a state of grace," said La Foscarina.

"The more we hope, the more we live," was the reply.

"And the more we love, the more we hope."

The rhythm of the aerial song continued, drawing from them their ideal essences.

"How beautiful you are!" said Stelio.

A sudden flush flowed over that impassioned face. She was silent, but her breath came quick, and she half-closed her eyes.

"A warm current of air is passing," she said in a half whisper. "Did you not feel on the water an occasional breath of warmer air?"

She drew deep breaths.

"There is an odor like that of new-mown hay. Don't you detect it?"

169

"That is the odor that comes from the banks of seaweed that are beginning to be uncovered."

"See how beautiful the country is!"

"That is Le Vignole. Down there is the Lido. And over there is the Island of Sant' Erasmo."

The sun had now thrown aside its veil and was showering gold upon the estuary. The damp banks emerging from the fog suggested the opening of flowers. The shadows of the slender cypresses began to grow longer and of a deeper blue.

"I am certain," said La Foscarina, "that almond trees are in blossom somewhere near. Let us go on the dyke."

She shook her head, tossing back her hair with one of those instinctive movements that seemed to break a bond or to free her of some fetter.

"Wait!"

And quickly withdrawing from her hat two large pins that held it in place, she uncovered her head. She turned back to the landing and tossed the sparkling hat into the gondola; then she rejoined her friend, running her fingers lightly through the waves of her hair, through which the air passed, while the sun shone on it warmly. She seemed to feel relieved, as if she breathed more freely.

"Did the wings hurt?" Stelio asked with a laugh.

And he regarded the ripples, roughened not by the comb but by the wind.

"Yes, the least weight annoys me. If I should not appear eccentric, I should always go without a hat. But when I see the trees I cannot resist my impulses. My hair remembers that it was born wild and free, and it wishes to breathe in its natural way—in the desert, at least."

Frank and gay in her manner, she glided over the grass with her graceful, swaying movement. And Stelio recalled the day when, in the Gradenigo garden, she had appeared to his eyes like the beautiful tawny greyhound.

"Oh, here comes a Capuchin!"

The friar-guardian approached them, and greeted them with affability. He offered to conduct Stelio within the walls of the monastery, but said that the rules forbade the admission of his companion.

"Shall I go in?" said Stelio, with a look at La Foscarina, who was smiling.

"Yes, go."

"But you will be all alone."

"Never mind; I will stay here alone."

"I will bring you a bit from the sacred pine."

He followed the friar under the portico with a raftered roof, whence hung the empty swallows' nests. Before he crossed the threshold, he turned once more to wave his hand at his friend. Then the door closed after him.

O BEATA SOLITUDO!
O SOLA BEATITUDO!
Then, as a change in the stops of an organ changes its whole tone, the woman's thoughts were suddenly transfigured. The horror of absence, to her the worst of all evils, bore down upon her loving soul. Her beloved was no longer there; she no longer heard his voice, felt his breath, touched his firm and gentle hand. She no longer saw him live; she could no longer realize that the air, the lights and shadows, all the life of the world, harmonized itself with his life!—Suppose that door never should open again—that he never should return to me!—No, that could not be. He would surely cross that threshold again in a few minutes, and once more she would receive him into her eyes and into her very soul. But alas! in a few days, would he not thus disappear again, as he had disappeared now? And first the field, then the mountain, then other fields and mountains and rivers, then the strait and the ocean, the infinite space that neither tears nor cries can cross, would they not come between her and that brow, those eyes, those lips? The image of the far-off brutal city black with coal and bristling with arms, filled the peaceful island; the crash of hammers, the grinding of wheels, the puffing of engines, the immense groaning of iron, drowned the melody of the springtime. And with each of these simple things—with the grass, the sands, the brooks, the seaweed, that soft feather floating downward, perhaps from the breast of a songbird—was contrasted the vision of streets overflowing with the human torrent, houses with thousands of deformed eyes, full of fevers that are enemies to sleep, theaters filled with the restlessness or the stupor of men who yield one hour to relaxation from the ferocious battle for lucre. And still, as in a vision, she saw again her own face and her name on walls contaminated by the leprosy of posters, on boards carried by stupid bearers, on gigantic bridges of factories, on the doors of public vehicles, here, there, and everywhere.

"Look! Look at this! A branch of flowering almond! There is an almond tree in bloom in the monastery garden, in the second cloister, near the sacred pine! And you could detect the odor!"

Stelio ran toward her, joyous as a child, followed by the Capuchin, who bore a bouquet of fragrant thyme.

171

"Look! Take it. See what a wonderful thing it is!"

She took the branch, trembling, and her eyes were bright with tears.

"And you knew it was blooming!" said Stelio.

He perceived the glittering silvery drops in her eyes, which made them look like the petals of a flower. And at that instant, of all her adored person, he loved most blindly the delicate lines that went from the corners of her eyes to her temples, the tiny veins that made her eyelids look like violets, the sweet curve of her cheek, the tapering chin, and all that never would bloom again, all the shadows of that impassioned face.

"Ah, Father," said she, with a bright glance, repressing her sadness, "will not Christ's Poor Man weep again in heaven for this broken branch?"

The friar smiled with playful indulgence.

"When this good gentleman saw our tree," he replied, "he gave me no time to speak, but had the branch in his hand in a moment, and I could only say Amen. But the almond tree is rich."

He was placid and affable, with a crown of hair still nearly black, with a refined, olive-skinned face, and great tawny eyes, as clear as a topaz.

"Here is some savory thyme," he added, offering the herbs to La Foscarina.

They could hear a choir of youthful voices singing a Response.

"Those are our novices; we have fifteen with us."

He accompanied the visitors to the meadow behind the convent. Standing on a bank, at the foot of a blasted cypress, the good monk pointed to the fertile isles, praised their abundance, mentioned their varieties of fruit, lauded the more delightful according to the seasons, and directed their attention toward the boats sailing toward the Rialto with their new harvest.

"Praise to Thee, O Lord, for our Mother Earth!" said the woman with the flowering branch.

The Franciscan was susceptible to the beauty of that feminine voice, and was silent.

Lofty cypresses encircled the pious field; four of them showed the marks of lightning strokes. Their tops were motionless, and were the only sharp outlines in the level of the meadows, and waters that blended with the horizon. Not the slightest breeze now stirred the infinite mirror. A profound enchantment like an

172

ecstasy filled the lovely place with rapture. The melody of the winged creatures still continued to float from invisible regions, but it, too, seemed to begin to flag and soften in this silent sanctuary.

"At this hour, on the hills of Umbria," said he that had despoiled the flowering almond of the cloister, "every olive-tree has at its base, like a covering that is shed, a heap of its cut branches; and the tree seems more beautiful because the heap of branches hides its rugged roots. Saint Francis passes in the air, and with his finger he heals the pain of the wounds made by the pruning-knife."

The Capuchin made the sign of the cross, and took his leave.

"Praise be to Jesus Christ!"

The visitors watched him as he moved away under the deep shadows cast by the cypresses.

"He has found peace," said La Foscarina. "Does it not seem so to you, Stelio? There is great peace in his face and his voice. Look at his gait, too."

Alternately a ray of light and a bar of shadow fell across his tonsure and his tunic.

"He gave me a piece of the sacred pine," said Stelio. "I will send it to Sofia, who is devoted to the seraphic saint. Here it is. It has no resinous odor now. Smell it!"

For Sofia's sake she kissed the relic. The lips of the good sister would touch the spot where she had pressed her own.

"Yes—send it."

Silently they strolled along, their heads bent, in the footsteps of the man of peace, approaching the landing between the rows of cypress trees.

"Do you not sometimes wish to see her again?" asked La Foscarina, with a touch of shyness.

"Yes, very much," was Stelio's soft-spoken answer.

"And your mother?"

"Yes, my heart yearns for her—for that mother who looks for me each day."

"And would you not like to go back there?"

"Yes, I shall return, perhaps."

"When?"

"I do not know yet. But I do wish to see once more my mother and Sofia. I long to see them very much, Foscarina."

"And why do you not go to them, then? What holds you here?"

He took the hand that hung idly at her side, and they continued to walk thus. As the oblique rays of the sun lighted the right cheek of each, they saw their united shadows preceding them on the grass.

"When you were speaking of the hills of Umbria just now," said La Foscarina, "perhaps you were thinking of the hills of your own part of the country. That figure of the pruned olive tree was not new to me. I remember you speaking to me once before of the pruning of trees. In no other form of his labor can the farmer gain a deeper sense of the mute life that is in a tree. When he stands before a pear, an apple, or a peach tree with the pruning-knife and shears that may increase their fertility and strength, but which could nevertheless as easily cause their death, the spirit of divination surges within him, from the wisdom he has acquired from his long communings with the earth and the sky. The tree is at its most delicate moment, when its senses are awakened, and the sap is flowing to the buds that swell and swell, and are just ready to open. And man, with his pitiless knife, must regulate the mysterious movement of the sap. The tree is there intact, ignorant of Hesiod and of Virgil, in labor with its flowering and its fruit; and every branch in the air is as full of life as is the arm of the man that wields the knife. Which is the branch that must be cut off? Will the sap heal the cut? You told me about your orchard once—I remember it. You said that all the cuts should be turned toward the north, so then the sun should not see them."

She spoke as she had spoken in that far-off evening in November, when the young man had arrived at her house, breathless from the tempest of wind, after he had borne the hero in his arms.

He smiled, and let himself be led by that dear hand. He inhaled the fragrance of that flowery branch in which was a suggestion of bitterness.

"It is true," he said. "And Laimo would prepare the ointment of Saint Fiacre in the mortar, and Sofia would bring him the strong linen to bandage the larger wounds, after they had been cleansed."

In fancy he could see the kneeling peasant, pounding cow-dung, clay, and barley-husks in a stone mortar, according to an ancient recipe.

"In ten days," he continued, "the whole hill, seen from the seas, will be like a great pink cloud. Sofia wrote to remind me of it. Has she ever reappeared to you?"

"She is with us now."

174

"She is now standing at the window, looking out at the purpling sea; and our mother, leaning on the window-ledge with her, says to her: 'Who knows whether Stelio may not be on that sail boat which I see waiting at the mouth of the river for the wind? He promised me he would return unexpectedly by sea, in a small boat.'—And then her heart aches."

"Ah, why do you disappoint her?"

"Yes, Fosca, you are right. But I can live far-away from her for months and months, yet feel that my life is full. Then—an hour comes when nothing in the world appears to me so sweet as her dear eyes and there is a part of myself that remains inconsolable. I have heard the sailors of the Tyrrhenean Sea call the Adriatic the Gulf of Venice. To-night I remember that my house is on the Gulf, and that seems to bring it nearer to me."

They had reached the gondola once more, but turned to look back at the isle of prayer, where grew the tall cypresses with their imploring arms.

"Over yonder is the canal of the Tre Porti that leads to the open sea," said the homesick one, fancying that he could see himself standing on the deck of the little brig, in sight of his tamarisks and myrtles.

They reëmbarked, and floated away, silent for a long time. The aerial melody still fell softly on the archipelago.

"Now that the plan of your work is finished," said La Foscarina, beginning again her gentle persuasion, though her heart trembled in her breast, "you will need peace and quiet for your labor upon it. Have you not always worked best at your home? In no other place will you be able to soothe the restless anxiety that possesses you. I know it well."

"That is true," he replied. "When the yearning for glory seizes us, we believe that the conquest of art must be like the siege of a fortification, and that trumpets and shouts accompany the courageous assault; while in reality the only work that is of real value is that which has been developed in austere silence—work performed with slow, indomitable perseverance, in hard, pure solitude. Nothing is of any value save the complete abandonment of soul and body to the Idea which we desire to establish among men as a permanent and dominating force."

"Ah, you know it, too!"

The woman's eyes were filled with tears again, at the sound of those inexorable words, in which was expressed the depth of virile passion, the heroic necessity of mental domination, the firm determination to surpass himself and to force his destiny without flinching.

"Yes, you know it well!"

And she was thrilled, as one that beholds a noble spectacle; and, contemplating that embodied force of will, all else appeared vain to her. The tears she had felt in her eyes when he had brought her the flowering branch now seemed mean and weakly effeminate in comparison with those that in this moment welled up and were alone worthy to be kissed away by her friend.

"Ah, well, then—go back to your sea, to your own countryside, to your own home. Light your lamp once more with the oil of your own olives."

Stelio's lips were closely compressed, and a deep frown wrinkled his brow.

"The dear sister will come to your side again to lay a blade of grass on the difficult page."

He bent his brow, which was clouded with a thought.

"You will rest in talking with Sofia by the window; and perhaps you will see again the flocks of sheep on their way from the plain to the mountains."

The sunlight was approaching the gigantic acropolis of the Dolomites. The phalanx of clouds was disordered as if in battle, pierced by innumerable darts of light, and steeped in a marvelous blood-like crimson.

Slowly, after a long silence, Stelio spoke:

"And if she should ask me about the fate of the virgin who reads the lament of Antigone?"

La Foscarina started.

"And suppose she asks me about the love of the brother who searches through the tombs?"

The woman felt a dread of this phantom.

"And suppose the page on which she lays the blade of grass were the page wherein that trembling soul tells of its secret and terrible battle against the horrible evil?"

In her sudden terror, the woman could find no words. Both relapsed into silence, looking long at the sharp peaks of the distant mountains, which glowed as if just emerging from primordial fire. The spectacle of this eternally desolate grandeur awakened in them a sense of mysterious fatality and a certain confused terror which they could neither conquer nor comprehend.

"And you?" said Stelio suddenly, after a long silence.

176

La Foscarina made no reply.

The bells of San Marco sounded the signal for the Angelus, and their tremendous clamor swelled in ever-widening waves over the still crimson lagoon which they were leaving to the memories of shadows and death. From San Giorgio Maggiore and San Giorgio dei Greci, from San Giorgio degli Schiavoni and San Giovanni in Bragora, from San Moisé, from the Salute, the Redentore, and, from one place to another, throughout the whole domain of the Evangelists, even to the distant towers of the Madonna dell' Orto, of San Giobbe and Sant' Andrea, the bronze voices answered, mingling in one great chorus floating over the silent stones and waters, a veritable dome of sound, invisible, yet the vibrations of which seemed to communicate with the scintillation of the first stars. And the reverberation above the heads of the two in the gondola was so great that they seemed to feel it in the roots of their hair and in the cool shiver of their flesh.

"Oh, is that you, Daniele?"

Stelio had recognized at the door of his own house, on the Fondamenta Samedo, the figure of Daniele Glauro.

"Ah, Stelio, I have been waiting for you!" cried Daniele breathlessly, striving to make himself heard above the pealing of bells. "Richard Wagner is dead!"

CHAPTER XV
THE LAST FAREWELL
All the world seemed to have diminished in value.

The nomad woman had armed herself anew with courage, and planned the route of her next professional tour. From the thought of the hero lying in his coffin, a lofty inspiration came to all noble hearts. La Foscarina knew how to receive it and to convert it to the thoughts and actions of daily life.

It happened that her beloved surprised her at the time she was packing her familiar books, the little cherished treasures from which she never parted—things that for her possessed the power of imparting dreams or consolation.

"What are you doing?" Stelio asked.

"I am making ready to leave the country."

She saw a change pass over his face, but she did not waver.

"And where are you going?"

"A long distance from here—I shall cross the Atlantic."

177

Stelio became slightly paler. But suddenly he was seized with doubt; he thought she was not speaking the truth; that she wished only to prove him; that her decision was not absolutely fixed, and that she expected to be persuaded to remain. The unlooked-for disillusion on the banks of Murano had left its mark on his heart.

"Have you really decided on this, then, so suddenly?"

She was simple, sure of herself, and prompt in her reply.

"My decision is not exactly sudden. My idleness has lasted too long, and I have the responsibility of all my company on my shoulders. While I am waiting for the Theater of Apollo to be opened, and for The Victory of Man to be finished, I shall go once more to bid farewell to the Barbarians. I must work for your beautiful enterprise. We shall need a great deal of gold to restore the treasures of Mycenæ. And all that is connected with your work must appear with unrivaled magnificence. I do not wish Cassandra's mask to be of some base metal. But, above all, I wish to satisfy your desire that for the first three days the populace shall have free admission to the theater, and after that on one day of every week. My faith aids me to leave you. Time flies. It is necessary that each person should be in his own place, ready and full of strength, when the great day comes. I shall not fail you. I hope that you will be satisfied with your friend. I am going away to work, and certainly the task will be more difficult than I ever have found it before. But you, my poor boy, what a burden you have to bear! What an effort we demand from you! What great things we expect from you! Ah, you know it!"

She had begun courageously, in a tone that was almost blithe, trying to seem what above all she must be—a good and faithful instrument at the service of a powerful genius, a strong and willing companion. But a wave of repressed emotion would rise in her throat and stop her speech. Her pauses grew longer, and her hand wandered uncertainly among her books and treasures.

"May everything be ever propitious to your work! That is the only thing that really matters—all else is nothing. Let us lift our hearts!"

She shook her head, with its two wild wings, and held out both hands to her beloved. He, pale and grave, clasped them close. In her dear eyes, that were like sparkling springs of water, he saw a flash of the same beauty that had dazzled him one evening in the room where the fire had roared, and he had listened to the development of the two great melodies.

"I love you and I have faith in you," he said; "I will not fail you and you will not fail me. Something springs from us that shall be stronger than life itself."

"A great melancholy," she answered.

Before her, on a table, lay the familiar book, with pages turned down and margins full of scribbled notes; here and there a petal, a flower, a blade of grass lay

178

between the leaves—signs of the sorrow that had asked and obtained from them the consolation of relief or of forgetfulness. Before her were strewn all the little cherished objects dear to her, strange, varied; nearly all were things of no value: a doll's foot, a silver heart, an ivory compass, a watch without a dial, a small iron lantern, a single earring, a flint, a key, a seal, and other trifles; but all were consecrated by some memory, animated by some superstitious belief, touched by the finger of love or of death, relics that could speak only to one of war and of truce, of hope and of sadness. Among these objects were figures to which artists had entrusted their secret confession, signs and enigmas, profound allegories, hiding truths that, like the sun, could not be gazed at by mortal eyes.

The young man put his arm around his friend's waist, and silently they went to the window. They saw the far-distant sky, the trees, the towers, the end of the lagoon over which Twilight was bending her face, while the Euganean hills were as quiet and blue as if they were the wings of earth folded in the peacefulness of eventide.

They turned toward each other, looking into the depths of each other's eyes. Then they embraced, as if to seal a silent compact.

Yes, all the world seemed to have diminished in value.

Stelio Effrena had asked of the widow of Richard Wagner that the two young Italian men that had carried the unconscious hero from the vessel to the shore that night in November, with four of their friends, might have granted to them the honor of bearing the coffin from the death-chamber to the boat and from the boat to the hearse. This request was granted.

It was the sixteenth of February, at one o'clock in the afternoon. Stelio Effrena, Daniele Glauro, Francesco de Lizo, Baldassare Stampa, Fabio Molza, and Antimo della Bella waited in the hall of the palace. The latter had come from Rome, bringing with him the artisans engaged in the building of the Theater of Apollo, that they might bear at the funeral ceremony bunches of laurel gathered on the Janiculum.

They waited in silence, without even looking at one another, each overcome by the throbbing of his own heart. Nothing was heard save a faint dropping of water on the steps before the great door, where, on the candelabra at the doorposts appeared the two words: DOMUS PACIS.

The boatman, who had been dear to the hero, came to call them. In that rough yet faithful face, the eyes showed that the lids were burned by weeping.

Stelio Effrena advanced first, followed by his companions. After ascending the stairs, they entered a low-studded, darkened room, filled with the melancholy odor of flowers and fluids. They paused there a few minutes. A door opened. They passed through the doorway one by one into the next room. Each turned pale as he entered.

179

The body was there, enclosed in its crystal coffin, and beside it stood the woman with the face of snowy pallor. The second coffin, of polished metal, stood shining on the floor.

The six bearers ranged themselves about the coffin, awaiting a sign. The silence was profound, and no one moved; but an impetuous sadness shook each soul like a tempest of wind.

Each gazed on the elect of Life and of Death. An infinite smile illumined the face of the hero lying there—infinite and distant as the glint of a glacier, as the sparkle of the sea, as the halo of the star. Their eyes could not bear to look long at it, but their hearts, with an awe-struck fear that made them religious, felt as if they had the revelation of a divine secret.

The woman with the snow-white face made a slight movement, yet preserved the same attitude, rigid as a statue.

Then the six friends approached the body, extended their arms, summoned up their strength. Stelio Effrena took his place at the head and Daniele Glauro took his at the feet, as on that day in November. The young men lifted their burden with one movement, at a low-spoken word from the leader. The eyes of each were dazzled, as if a sudden ray of sunlight had pierced the crystal. Baldassare Stampa broke into sobs. The same knot was in each throat. The coffin swayed, then it was lowered into its metal covering, which enveloped it like a suit of armor.

The six friends remained overcome with grief. They hesitated to put the cover in its place, fascinated by that infinite smile. Stelio Effrena heard a light rustling, and looked up. He saw the white face bending over the body, a superhuman apparition of love and grief. That instant was like eternity. The woman disappeared.

When the coffin was closed, they lifted their burden a second time—heavier now. Out of the room and down the stairs they bore it slowly. Rapt in a kind of sublime anguish, they could see their fraternal faces reflected in the polished metal.

The funeral barge awaited them at the entrance. The pall was laid over the coffin. The six friends waited, with heads uncovered, for the family to descend. They came, all together. The widow passed them, veiled. But the splendor of her face would remain in their memories forever.

The procession was short; the funeral barge went first, followed by the widow with her relatives; then came the young men. The sky was cloudy above the broad road of stone and water. The deep silence was worthy of Him who transformed the forces of the universe for man's worship into infinite song.

A flock of doves, flying from the marbles of the Scalsi, winged their way with a flash of plumage above the bier and across the canal, circling the cupola of San Simeone.

At the quay a silent gathering of faithful friends was waiting. The large wreaths perfumed the air. The water rippled softly under the prows of the boats. The six companions lifted the coffin from the boat and bore it on their shoulders to the railway and placed it in the proper compartment. No one spoke.

Then the two artisans from Rome came forward, with the clusters of laurel gathered on the Janiculum. They were tall, powerful men, chosen among the strongest and finest, and seemed cast in the mold of the ancient Roman race. They were calm and serious, with all the wild freedom of the Agro in their eyes. Their bold outlines, narrow foreheads, short curling hair, solid jaws and bull-necks, recalled the profiles of ancient consuls. Their bearing, free from any servile obsequiousness, showed them to be worthy of their function.

The six young men, rendered equal in their fervor, took the branches of laurel and strewed them over the hero's coffin.

Noble were those Latin laurels, cut on the hill where, in a time long past, the eagles descended bearing prophecies; where, in more recent though still fabulous times, a river of blood has been shed for the beauty of Italy by the legions of the Liberator. The branches were straight, dark, and strong; the leaves were firm, deeply veined, with sharp edges, green as the bronze of fountains, rich with triumphal aroma.

And they journeyed toward the Bavarian hill still sleeping beneath its frost and ice, while their trunks were already budding anew in the light of Rome, to the murmur of invisible waters.

Settignano di Desiderio:
February 13, 1900.

181

Made in United States
North Haven, CT
12 October 2021

10266449R20106